THE TURTLE CATCHER

THE

Turtle Catcher

Nicole Helget

Houghton Mifflin Harcourt

BOSTON   NEW YORK   2009

For information about permission to reproduce selections from this book,
write to Permissions, Houghton Mifflin Harcourt Publishing Company,
215 Park Avenue South, New York, New York 10003.

www.hmhbooks.com

Library of Congress Cataloging-in-Publication Data
Helget, Nicole Lea, date.
  The turtle catcher / Nicole Helget.
    p. cm.
  ISBN 978-0-618-75312-3
  1. German Americans — Minnesota — Fiction. 2. Young women — Fiction.
3. Abnormalities, Human — Fiction. 4. Brothers and sisters — Fiction. 5. Men
with mental disabilities — Fiction. 6. Murder — Fiction. 7. Farm life — Minnesota — Fiction. 8. Domestic fiction. 9. Psychological fiction. I. Title.
  PS3608.E39T87 2009
  813'.6—dc22   2008047273

Book design by Melissa Lotfy

Printed in the United States of America

DOC 10 9 8 7 6 5 4 3 2 1

TO NATE

We explode. We explode. We explode.
We make the loveliest colors.

A HUMPED CREATURE lopes the shore and shallows of Spider Lake. The neighbors say that Lester Sutter morphed into a turtle man, that his lungs broadened to hold volumes of air, his skin dried to leather, his back hardened to plates. The jaws of his hairless head snap at man and beast alike. He pulls his fresh catch below the surface and waits for it to drown, in the slow, patient way of a turtle.

PART *I*

I

New Germany, Minnesota, 1920

I N   T H E   T I M E just after the big war, when banks weren't to be trusted and when snapper turtle stew, a cheap meal for the big families common in those days, bubbled on stovetops in farm kitchens, the three Richter brothers led Lester Sutter to the edge of Spider Lake to watch him drown through the sights of their rifles. They drove him in with the barrels of their guns and stood guard among the cattails as the water filled his boots and soaked his overalls. The rocks they'd stuffed and then stitched into his pockets sank him. Lester Sutter had earned this. Even if he wasn't quite right in the mind, thought the brothers, he should have known better than to violate their sister.

Only an hour before, Herman Richter, the middle brother, had ordered Liesel, the Richters' only sister, to stay in the house. He directed his other brothers to hide in the grove and wait for Lester Sutter to come. He always came, Herman knew. Lester would linger at the edge of the grove until Liesel came out with the supper slops. He would slink around the oak trees. Sometimes he sat at the foot of a tree trunk and watched Liesel from afar. Some-

3

times he trailed back and forth, just a few feet behind her, as she bustled about the yard. When she'd whip around to face him and plant her hands on her hips, he'd turn around too, show her his back, and pretend to be studying some far-off cloud or tree. She usually smiled and returned to her work without scolding him. Liesel had always been far too permissive. Sometimes Lester approached her, and they talked. Of what, Herman had no idea. Lester Sutter was dense as pipe smoke. At times, Liesel put Lester to work hoeing in her garden or carrying heavy water pails from the well to the house. Though Liesel had insisted she didn't mind Lester's company, Herman did. He told her to stay away from Lester. But she hadn't listened. And Lester got too close.

Now here he was, splashing at the water's edge, taking a few steps forward and then backing toward the shore, croaking like some amphibious animal and making this deed harder than it needed to be.

"Get in the water, Lester," Herman Richter yelled. His eyes were pale blue and his ears bright red. He spoke in English but with a slight German accent. The Richters' papa, a German immigrant, spoke German but had learned English well and had insisted his children do the same.

Lester Sutter turned to face the brothers on the shore. He worked out the meaning of the words and mouthed them with his thin and cracked lips. Then he imitated Herman Richter: "Get in ta water."

Herman fumed. He directed the tip of his gun back and forth between Lester's chest and the middle of the lake. "Get in," he said.

"Get in," repeated Lester. He giggled and glanced from one brother's face to the next.

"I will shoot you!" screamed Herman. His brothers looked at him. One told him to take it easy. "I have shot better men than this," Herman yelled. "I will not hesitate to shoot this dog too."

4

But really, Herman hoped he wouldn't have to. He hated guns and killing and blood. Why couldn't Lester see that Herman was giving him a chance to do the dignified thing and die on his own terms?

Sweat ran from Lester's head into his eyes. As a boy, he had pulled out all of his eyelashes, and now none grew. The rims were perpetually red and irritated, but the whites of his eyes were always clear and not a red vein crossed them, not even when the sweat nipped at his eyeballs like the bites of hay mites. Lester knew what a gun could do. His own pa hunted with one, and Lester didn't want to risk the blast of smoke and bullet by disobeying the men. He didn't want to feel that blow of hot metal invade his head or heart or anywhere. The day was cloudy. Heat a man could reach out and hold was trapped between the earth and sky. The sun throbbed against the backs of the clouds, waiting for its chance to press through and ignite the day.

Lester Sutter, standing now knee-deep in Spider Lake and wringing his hands, wasn't an educated man. He suffered from the sort of weakness that came from years of hard blows from his pa's fists. He didn't understand why he was here, why these brothers, his neighbors, whom he'd always thought were friendly, were pointing guns at him. At first, he'd thought maybe they were playing a game. But now he was scared and wanted to see Liesel.

The youngest gun-toter, Otto Richter, no more than a boy really, a boy who had fished and hunted turtles with Lester Sutter many a time, saw that he was confused. So Otto looked up from his rifle, unsquinted his aiming eyes, and yelled over the long steel barrel to his old friend, "He said to get in the water, Lester."

Lester waved to Otto, then pointed to himself and said, "It's me. Lester."

"I know," said Otto.

The boy was shushed by Herman and told to get his gun back up. Otto rested the thick wood of it against his bony shoulder. His long bangs hung nearly into his eyes.

"Do not talk to him," said Herman. He took short steps on the shoreline toward Lester, closing the distance between them to fewer than a few steps. He pointed the gun from Lester to the middle of the lake again. "Get in, Lester," he said. "We don't have all day."

Lester understood finally and backed up. Dark fingers of lake water curled around his thighs and bade them come in.

In this place and just after the war, punishment of criminals was mostly left to individuals. The German immigrants here no longer trusted the government. The people here had learned to keep matters among themselves and to keep the law and lawmakers out of their business. The people here had learned their lesson. Last time they had invited politics, politicians, laws, and lawmakers into their town, good farmers had lost their land, the doors of schools and businesses had been chained and locked, a town had been divided as definitively as if some grand hand had broken it like bread; neighbors had destroyed neighbors, boys had defied fathers, and a European war had found a battlefield right here in their little town of New Germany.

No, Herman Richter decided, he would not turn the power of judgment over to strangers with titles and suits again. And so this is how Lester Sutter found himself in the waiting waters of Spider Lake. The brothers had decided he had committed a crime against one of theirs, and they intended to right it as well as it could be righted.

Lester moved to run only once. He pumped his legs high, in and out of the lake, and darted to the side. Herman Richter thought to let Lester wear himself out, as water is an unforgiving place to run and soon does a body in. But Lester kept up a good lick for quite a while, splashing to the right and then off to the left again, and then, almost before Herman had registered it, Lester got near shore. He fell for it. He placed his hand on the sandy ground to steady himself. Herman muttered, "Damn," and sprang toward Lester. And though it probably wasn't necessary, he swung the butt of his gun against Lester's temple and opened up a long red wound. Lester raised his hand to it. The blood came from between his fingers. Herman looked away. Lester, heaving and wet, cowered and sat there in the shallows where a little batch of minnows braved the rippling water rings to swim up to Lester and see what was what. He dipped his blooded hand into the water, and the little fish scatted. Herman saw them too. He thought a second about getting them for fish bait. He was glad for the minnows, a normal thing. He composed himself, told Lester to stand up and raise his arms into the air. Lester did and backed farther into the water.

Otto wanted to yell *Stop* but didn't want to disappoint his brothers or appear a coward. Instead he held tight to his gun and swallowed what felt like fire in his throat. He swatted a bug trilling near his ear. A company of cicadas had gathered in the sky and hovered like vapor. When one or another flew too close to the lake and weighted its legs on the tiniest fleck of water, the minnows nosed up and pecked the insect to pieces. The minnow schools fared well this time of year, lucky as they were about the carelessness of cicadas.

Lester backed farther and farther until the rim of the water reached his thighs. He kept his arms raised, lost his footing, tripped, and fell backward. He struggled and stood, only to be shooed deeper into the depths. His pockets, weighted with rocks, pulled him into the heavy embrace of the lake weeds. When the rim reached his lips, he let go a couple whimpers. He begged the brothers with bulging eyes.

Herman stepped to the water's edge and shouted, "Don't make me shoot you, Lester. Damn it. All the way. A shot in the head will hurt more."

"Just do it, Lester," said Otto. "It's a peaceful way."

Though Lester had never learned to swim, he had always been comfortable in the water. He had been coming to this very lake for all the years of his life. He'd pulled snakes and crawfish and snappers from her shallows and lugged them home to his sister for cooking. He'd many times waded into Spider Lake to his waist or chest when hunting dinner or requiring a cooling from the summer sun. Sometimes after seeing Liesel, he'd come to this lake for a different sort of cooling. Today, though, was the first time he'd been pushed out so far into the deep. He had never even considered that the lake dropped deeper than his own chest. How deep did it go? Did it go down far as the blackness of a well? If he yelled his own name, would it echo on and finally be lost somewhere far away?

That first watery step beyond the height of his heart set his lungs to cawing for air in a way they'd never had to before. Even as his head still bobbed above the water, leaving his nose and mouth free to breathe, Lester Sutter couldn't seem to suck air fast enough. He gasped and wheezed, but the effort didn't satisfy his urge for oxygen. The brothers on the shore yelled at him. Deeper. Get deeper. And he did. With each step, the cool lake pressed harder and harder against Lester's trunk. Like twine, the water wrapped around his chest and forced air out of his lungs. He gasped again to refill the empty space. But no matter how quickly or deeply he panted, his lungs would not fill up, would not be satisfied.

"Keep going, Lester. Get all the way in, you sick bastard. Get the hell in or I will blow off your damn head."

The lakebed loved Lester's boots and tugged at their rubber. He wrestled his feet out and gave the boots up to the muddy suck. His bare feet tiptoed as long as they could. Spiky tendrils of coontail weeds yanked at his overalls, and broad green palms of pondweed slapped at his arms, his neck, and then his face. He fluttered his arms through the water and was raised high enough to take a breath. He submerged again, flapped his arms, surfaced, and gasped another mouthful of water and air.

Lester's body felt heavy to him. When had his arms petrified

8

and his legs stiffened to lead? When had his head become weighty as iron? He understood then why the brothers had filled his pockets with stones of different shapes and sizes, why one brother had held his hands behind his back and why another had stitched shut his pockets with needle and twine used for burlap. Now the weight of those rocks drew him down into the lake. He tried to reach into his pockets to lessen the load and keep his nose and mouth above water at the same time. He tugged at the crude seams but couldn't force them to separate. And though Lester wasn't right in the human mind, he had enough animal survival in him to reach for his overall clasps and yank at their metal to relieve himself of the denim. But the clasps had always been complicated. And this final struggle was the one to do him in. In the throes of his battle, he sank to the bottom of Spider Lake. The lake opened up her arms and welcomed the new inhabitant.

2

LESTER SUTTER DIDN'T require a bullet. Herman Richter felt relief. The brothers leaned the rifles against their legs and waited for Lester's head to stop breaking the surface and gasping for air. The heat closed around Herman like praying hands. He took off his shirt.

Herman, who stood more than six feet tall and was lanky and skittish as a horse, paced the shore looking wide and near for signs that the deed was being witnessed. Once, he thought he saw someone move among the cattails, but it was only the daylight playing tricks with the reflecting water, making roving eyes where there were none. Herman was jumpy since he'd returned from the war against Germany, less his left arm, which he'd lost in a muddy crater of No Man's Land. He'd lain there bleeding to death under gunfire and explosions. An American medic crawled to him, used his thumbs to lift Herman's lids, and considered his chances. The medic said, "Sorry," and moved on. Herman had wandered between consciousness and unconsciousness for hours until the battle ended and a pair of German soldiers picked him up. Their surgeon amputated his arm and picked out most of the metal from his body. But gray shrapnel still poked up in jagged pocks just beneath the skin on his buttocks and legs, and he was still plagued half to death by the walking, talking, and accusing ghosts of all the American boys who'd died because Herman had made a mistake and all the German boys he'd shot or bayoneted. The guilt of killing his own kind haunted him. The Richter boys' papa, who'd told Herman not to come home unless he switched sides and came home wearing a German uniform, died of influenza while Herman fought in Europe. This haunted him too. Now he wanted to live a life that would've made his papa proud, a life in which he'd finally marry Betty, the good German girl his papa had so approved of; nurture the Richter farm back to health and prosperity; father a whole passel of children; and resurrect the pride of the family. He'd resolved to farm for the rest of his life, the way his papa had wanted.

Since Herman had returned from Europe, rectitude bit at him like the peskiest swarm of midges, another type of insect that proliferated in the standing water of Minnesota and bore down upon its people in coming and going waves. His brothers and Liesel couldn't understand how important it was to do what was right, every day, every moment. They had no idea how not doing the right thing would come back and get a man. They didn't know how a tactical error or moment of weakness or sympathy could kill good men. Herman had seen it. He saw it still. When his lids fell over his eyes, explosions lit up, wounded men screamed, blood ran black and congealed into jelly, flies swarmed, rats scratched, fires scorched skin and hair, and his heart thumped until he opened his eyes again. Herman's family didn't know that a man could not hesitate to rid the world of evil. This purging had to be done swiftly and with a courageous heart.

When, at last, Spider Lake stopped frothing and the insect rumpus quieted, Benjamin, the oldest Richter brother, sat down among the lake reeds and cattails and whittled a crude turtle toy out of a cottonwood stick for Otto. Benjamin was somewhat shorter than Herman but more muscular by a sight. He had a terrible time with his hair, caught all species of insects in it, and was watching the cicadas closely to keep them from landing in there. Some were big as baby bats. When he caught himself worrying about his hair rather than about the man dying in the lake or his sister suffering at home, Benjamin felt ashamed. He closed his eyes. Benjamin had big, brown, kind eyes, the color and shine of a bronze penny. Right now, he was fighting to keep them dry. *What the hell am I doing here?* he wondered.

Though Benjamin might have been the oldest of this bunch, he wasn't the bravest. He couldn't look long at the scene in the lake and tried not to picture the man choking on mud at the bottom of it. Drowning was peaceful, he'd been told. Perhaps Lester Sutter was simply falling asleep. Benjamin turned toward Otto. "It's just like going to sleep," he assured his little brother.

Benjamin knew better, though. Benjamin's capacity for feeling was more stout than most, and it was true that at this very moment, his own lungs would not fill. Try as he might, he could not get a full breath. He sneezed. Otto pulled out a handkerchief and placed it on Benjamin's knee. Benjamin took it and sneezed into it. He blew his nose. Benjamin had thought maybe a scare or warning would be enough for the Sutter boy, but there was no convincing his younger but more stubborn brother Herman, and frankly, Benjamin didn't have the gumption to challenge him anyway. There was no winning an argument against Herman, even when you were in the right and Herman was in the wrong. Herman had a quick and forceful way. Benjamin felt that there had been some sort of misunderstanding between Lester and Liesel. He was sure of it. He thought that if they could just give Liesel a while to calm down, maybe they could talk to her and find out what happened. But Herman could not be deterred. At the very least, Benjamin would have liked to keep Otto at home in the care of Liesel while grown men took care of Lester, but Liesel wasn't talking and had seemed to need some time alone. Benjamin tried to concentrate on getting this deed done and getting back to the regular ways. He thought about Sonnen, his wife, his dear and good wife. He thought about how she deserved her own home, away from his family. He could give her that. But he couldn't abandon his brothers and sister. They all needed him. Oh God, how he wished he could lay his head on Sonnen's lap right now. She would rub his head and kiss his ear. She would smell like bread, as always. She would have dough under her nails. She would have flour across her cheek, and her red, untamed hair would hang down her breasts.

Benjamin sighed. It was so hot. He carved plates into the turtle toy's back. He tried to remember lighter times, when the universe didn't seem so complicated. He felt like crying. He handed the toy to Otto.

Otto Richter sat next to Benjamin on the bank. He preferred Benjamin to Herman. Herman had come home from the war crazy, as far as Otto could tell. Otto was afraid of him. Otto's favorite brother, Luther, was dead. His mother was dead. His papa was dead. He placed his rifle across his knees, picked slivers from the turtle toy's shell, and rubbed his yellow eyes. Otto had been born on a full-moon night, and the whites of his eyes seemed to be marked with its glow. He tried to keep his mind off Lester Sutter, the man who had been a friend to him and to his sister. In his head, he practiced spelling the words Liesel had given him to memorize. She presented Otto and Lester with ten new words every week and tested them on Sunday nights. Otto wondered how she seemed to know everything when she'd hardly stepped off the farm place. He didn't understand why exactly he was at the lake, but he knew that Lester Sutter had done something bad to Liesel and that his older brothers had decided that the punishment for the crime was to do away with him. Otto couldn't stand the thought of anyone hurting his sister, the one who had fed him, cuddled him, bathed him, protected him, taught him, and raised him from the hour he had entered the world until this very moment. Otto loved her more than anyone else. He would do anything for her. But hurting Lester didn't seem altogether right.

3

A WHITE FIRE BURST behind Lester's eyes. Water, water, black, dirty water rushed into his mouth, down his neck, and into his chest. His arms and hands gave up swimming and worked instead to claw at his face and ribs, as if some sort of outside protest could convince the lungs to work, to breathe underwater, to strain pure air from liquid. The muscles of his throat trembled and jerked until the menace went down, sending his stomach into spasms. His arms and legs seized. The water came back up, and Lester purged, but inevitably gulped again. In, out, in, out. Soon he fell into a regular rhythm of sucking in and expelling water. His fingers and toes curled into small stubs. His arms and legs stiffened and fattened hard as wood. He curled his head toward his legs. He made up his mind to give his body over to the new existence and waited for the blackness to devour him.

The man at the bottom of Spider Lake, below the weeds and black bullheads, breathed water and sludge into his chest and opened his eyes wide to a shard of sunlight breaking through the clouds and through the murky water. Lester Sutter leaned back, listened to the light, and let his lungs fill.

To Lester, the sunlight seemed clean as the chalk the school-teacher had given him many years ago when she'd come to the farm, walked right up to the pigsty, and asked his pa why he didn't send the children to school. Lester's pa looked up to answer as he held steady a sow between his powerful thighs and cut the curling tail from the pig's behind. He said for the teacher to mind her own business and mind her place among men. When the sow quit screaming, he added, "Children of mine earn their keep."

"A full school is a benefit to the entire township, Mr. Sutter," the teacher said. "Surely you could spare this little one a few hours a day for reading and writing at the New Germany Turner school. You want your son to know how to read, correct?"

She nodded toward Lester, who stood in the shadow of his pa. Lester's hands were full of the sow tails his pa had sliced and tossed into the manure. Lester used them for bullhead bait.

"Seems you don't know too much for being an educated woman," Lester's pa said. "That one's not right in the head." He tapped Lester's head with the trimming knife. "He's best left diggin' in the shit and catchin' fish. That's thinkin' enough for his kind."

"All children can learn, Mr. Sutter," said the teacher.

"No child of mine will be sittin' in a German school learnin' to be a German." Lester's pa put the knife in his overalls pocket. He loosened his grip on the sow, slapped its thigh. "Now, git," he said to the teacher.

Lester wiped a loose spittle of drool from the corner of his mouth with the back of his tail-stuffed hand.

The schoolteacher thanked Lester's pa for his time, nodded her head, and turned to leave. But before she did, she pulled a stick of chalk from her apron pocket and held it out toward Lester. He wouldn't drop the pig tails.

"Here then," she said, "open up."

She slipped a stick of chalk into his mouth.

"This isn't for eating, dear," she said. "It's for writing." She walked away.

Lester had scratched the chalk with his teeth and tasted how easily it flaked away. He dropped the tails into his pocket and handled the stick of chalk. He never used it but kept the chalk all his life under a hollowed-out turtle shell in the corner of the granary, where he slept in the warm months.

The odd metamorphosis that links life to death was just beginning. Pleasant things came to him in random series. The flaky chalk, hollowed turtle shells for hiding treasures, the big orange sun on late fall days, clean straw for sleeping in, a flannel shirt in winter, fresh bread every Sunday, his little sister's yellow hair, Liesel Richter's voice. The tang of her lemonade on hot days. The curl of her thin but strong arm through his. Her wide, tanned face. Her loamy brown eyes. Her mouth. Her hand.

The blood in his vessels raced from the heart to all his parts. What little oxygen the blood had quickly bubbled and popped into something useless. The iron in his blood seemed to congeal, spreading a hostile stiffness throughout his body.

All day the clouds had come up from the south and gathered in great masses over New Germany. Their undersides, heavy with rain, hung fat as boulders. When at last the rain came, the surface of Spider Lake roused into a spectacular dance of drops leaping and tapping. The Richter boys waited together until the sky dumped a hard downpour onto Spider Lake.

"Cold rain," said Otto. He leaned his head back and let the rain wash over his face. He opened his lips to it.

"It is," said Benjamin. He too lifted his face toward the rain. He was thankful for it. Tears could come and not be noticed by Herman. Benjamin sighed. "We had better get you home," he said.

The Richter brothers didn't linger on the edge of Spider Lake.

They were satisfied that what had needed to get done had been finished completely. When Otto stopped and turned back to look on Spider Lake, his older brothers told him, "Come on."

"Well," Otto said. "I guess we took care of him." He thought to impress Herman. He didn't know why.

"This is nothing to talk about ever again," Herman said. "Do you understand me?"

"I was just saying," replied Otto.

"No," said Herman. "Not ever again. You walk away from here and forget about this. We did what needed to be done." He placed his gun under his stump, then jabbed a finger at Otto. "This is it. Papa would have done the same, and Mother would have said to keep quiet. So not another word from any of you. Not to Liesel especially."

Benjamin and Otto nodded their heads yes. And while all may've been eager to agree and forget, each man tucked this day and his last image of Lester Sutter into the oldest, hardiest lobe of his brain, the part where memories don't die but fester, the part of the brain that allows experiences to seep into daydreams and night dreams, into afternoon cold sweats and nocturnal terrors.

"Now let's get home," said Herman. The rain urged them back to the farm. Each brother stepped quick.

"A man like that," said Herman. He spoke to but looked at neither of his brothers. "It is a mercy what we did to him. A mercy. An act of God." He swung his gun over his shoulder the way soldiers are taught. "People like that do not belong with other people."

Sometimes a thing can be so black that it burns and turns bright. Sometimes in the pitch of darkness, white will emerge. Whether it was that single sun ray penetrating Lester Sutter's dark grave or whether the light that wrapped up the drowned man and filled his chest with air burned from the black, black water itself doesn't matter. What matters is that after the three brothers left, after the rain stopped, after more than thirty minutes had passed since one gasp of breath had crossed Lester's cracked lips, and after millions and millions of pounds of water had pressed down and tried to crush his life with its weight, Lester Sutter opened his blue eyes in that black place, expanded his lungs, and found himself alive.

4

ARLIER THAT DAY, Lester Sutter had walked down the Richter driveway with a burlap sack swinging at his side, a stroll as regular as any other day's had been. It had not occurred to him then that these steps were to be the last of a mortal kind for him.

Liesel had hoped that this day might mark a new beginning in her life, her own life. She wanted to be married and have a house too. Her opportunities to make that happen were tightly bound by her condition. Lester was her closest and best chance at a life away from her older brothers, away from their women. And she needed to make her move soon, today. When Liesel saw him, she set down her washing and walked to greet him. This was going to be the day she set her own future. If she'd learned anything from the past few years, it was that life could be very short.

It was true that Lester was much older than she. She didn't know by how much exactly, ten, maybe even fifteen, years, but somehow his innocence made him seem younger, made him seem closer to her own nineteen years.

"What did you bring for me today, Lester?" she asked.

"Uh," he said. "Just one."

"Looks big, though," said Liesel.

"He prit'near ate my thumb off."

"Mind if I watch you butcher him?"

Lester shook his head no.

"Have you been reading those books I gave you?"

Lester focused on his boots. He kicked his foot so that the loose sole slapped against the ground. "Some."

"How do you spell *turtle*?" she asked.

Lester coughed and quickened the pace of his kicking.

"Come on now, Lester," she said. "Let me hear."

"I don't know. I don't know." He slapped his palm against his temple and then began picking at his brow. She hated when he did this. Liesel pulled down his arm and held on to his fisted hand. Maybe she was pushing him too fast. Sometimes he'd resort to a piercing scream in times of frustration. She didn't want that. But Liesel felt an intense desire to get things done and get her own life started. Benjamin had Sonnen now. Herman would soon marry Betty. Even little Otto seemed not to need her as much.

"Okay," she said. "It's all right. It doesn't matter."

Behind the silo, the flies buzzed and moved when Lester and Liesel spread the long grass with their steps. Sometimes a stray dog would come along and pick up the turtle heads for a chew toy, but mostly the heads just collected on the ground and eventually dried out and turned to ash under the summer sun. Liesel kicked an old head aside and leaned against the brick. In the shadows, the world was cool.

"Come here, Lester," said Liesel. "Come over here."

Lester hoisted the bag up to his chest and clutched it tight.

"Oh, put that down now and come here. Did you get shy on me?"

He twisted the top of the bag and set it softly in the grass. He took short steps to Liesel. He rubbed his nose with his knuckle.

Liesel pulled his hand away from his face. "Kiss me a little, Lester."

He put his mouth on her neck. She put her hands on each side of his face and slowed him.

"Yes," she said. "That's better. Go slowly."

He pumped his body against hers. Liesel unclasped his overalls, and Lester stood waiting for Liesel to stroke him the way she had a few times before. This time, though, she opened her own blouse and held the weight of one breast with her hand and looked Lester in the eye.

"Do you want me to touch you?" she asked. He watched her hand move over her own skin.

"I like you touching me," he mumbled. He rubbed his nose with his knuckle again.

"I know you do," she said. "But I want to feel good like you do."

"Yeah," he said. He stood there, rocking back and forth.

"Come here," she said. She pulled Lester's head to her breast. She rubbed him under his chin, and he opened his mouth.

"That's right," she said. "Now I feel good too."

She took him in her hand and pulsed back and forth. She dropped her hand just before Lester let himself go. To Liesel, everything in that moment felt just right. In that nameless place where women knit together their first impulses, their innate impatience, and their intuition, that little whisper that says *yes* or *no,* Liesel felt right.

"Doesn't this feel nice?" she asked. "You want it to feel nice for me too, don't you, Lester?"

The sky shivered with mating cicadas, electrified to be alive after a seventeen-year incubation under the black soil.

She pulled her skirt high for him. She tugged him close again and tried to keep his attention with her eyes.

Then she guided his hand between her legs.

With her other hand, she covered her ugliness, a drooping

measure of skin that had been there since her birth, a thing that she knew no woman was supposed to have, a thing she had willed away a million times but that couldn't be willed away. She covered the thing that kept her from any hope of marriage, of children, of a normal life.

She pushed herself against him. She'd never felt so full. Lester's breath came hard and heated against her neck. She imagined them together in a small house, a house her brothers could slap together in a week. She'd cook and clean and tutor the township children when time allowed. And Otto could live with Lester and her, like their son. She and Sonnen and Betty could be sisters. Lester could farm with her brothers. He could butcher chickens and slop hogs as well as anyone. He could show Otto how to catch turtles. The hard work of the farm and the sense of her brothers would lift Lester's wits.

And then she thought to uncover herself completely. She thought, *He won't know. He's so simple. He won't know.* She thought the moment so sweet. And she did remove her hand, and the skin hung limp against Lester's wrist. He looked down. He pulled his hand from Liesel. He pointed.

"Oh, don't," she said. "Please don't."

Lester averted his eyes. He giggled and rocked in the way scared and confused loose-minded folks do. He stared at her shame. "A turtle tail," he mumbled to the ground. And then rising up his neck and reddening his ears, the scream began coming from within him, Liesel could see. She watched his jaws work the way they did before he let loose the high howling. Liesel searched her brain for a quick way to fix the mess she had made. But fear and rage clawed to the forefront of her mind and untied her tongue, and the girl who managed all her brothers, managed the house, managed everything with a normally quiet and calm manner, cracked.

"Help," she whispered, so quiet it was as though she were simply testing the word. Lester looked at her. She watched his lips thin when he widened his mouth and then fatten when he closed it. The scream was still coming. She said it again, louder. "Help." She watched Lester take a deep breath. Before he could exhale, she launched into a yell. "Help me! Help me!" Lester let go his own rattled voice.

He grabbed the waist of his overalls, darted past Liesel, and scuttled down the driveway and toward the grove in a sideways trot, holding his pants up with one hand and his burlap bag with the other. He wailed the whole way and looked like a thieving dog beat away from the hen house. She yelled above him and brought her brothers running from the corners of the farm. She ripped her skirt and ran toward them in a panic, tattling lies.

That most resilient human desire, physical urge, heightens all other senses when it isn't relieved. Feelings are sharpened. Actions that follow, precise. So were Lester's fear and confusion as he picked his path back home through the grove that seemed to have grown human eyes, across the field that seemed to have grown fingers, and across the very air between the Richters' farm and his own, the air that spoke to him and told him to hide.

At that physical rejection, Liesel felt her senses sparked to heights as well. She hardly recognized her own voice as she poured forth tales of an attack to her brothers. Otto wrapped his arms around her middle. Benjamin pulled out a handkerchief and handed it to her. Liesel fashioned tears. And they felt real. She felt as though she really *had* been hurt and that it *had* been Lester's fault. She believed herself. Herman flexed and unflexed his fingers, demanded details, which Liesel created and gave to him. She showed him her torn skirt. And even when the hysteria subsided, when she wanted to stop, when her heart scolded her for lying, her most basic survival impulses obliged her to keep talking, to protect herself.

After supper, she obeyed when Herman said to go on outside while he discussed with Benjamin the business of what was to be done. She sat in the grass beneath the kitchen window. She listened to Herman plan revenge. Liesel knew what the plotting would mean for Lester Sutter, but shame, anger, and panic still growled in her. She tried to think of a better way. She hoped Lester was smart enough to hide from her brothers, the way he knew to hide when his pa was drinking, but she knew he wouldn't. Wrought with a combination of idiocy and loyalty, Lester was more likely to stay and suffer the consequences. She knew that if Lester Sutter's life was going to be saved, she was the only one who could save it.

And so Liesel began the battle. Whose life was more important? Hers or his? And though she was quiet enough to hear, no answer came.

She didn't move when the screen door slammed and gravel crunched beneath three pairs of boots. After a while, she stood up, went to the kitchen, took a paring knife from the counter, and walked through the rain to the place where Lester Sutter butchered the snappers she bought from him every month, the place where she brought him lemonade or fresh bread, the place where she listened to his rambling and practiced flirting, where she sometimes palmed him up and down until he shuddered and wept in her skirts, ashamed and confused and apologizing for the mess he'd left in her hand. She carried the paring knife to the place she had romanced a retarded man known countywide for being a simpleton and for his skills trapping snappers.

Liesel knelt in the long grass; tossed aside a turtle head, its eyes gone to the birds; and pulled her skirt to her waist, pushing the rest of her wrappings sideways. She aimed the knife to where the strange organ that belonged only on men grew small but sure. She'd never understood why it grew there. In every other way, she was a woman.

Her mother had, long ago, tied a string around the organ to deaden the thing and make it fall away, but the string couldn't thwart the persistence of the growth and had only caused an infection and made her ill. Liesel aimed her knife to the skin and vein that her mother had kept hidden from her papa, from her brothers, from the family, from everyone in the county and in the world. Nobody but Liesel and her mother and God and now Lester Sutter knew what had mutated between her thin waist and thick thighs. And this secret kept her from any friend, any school, any life outside the Richter farm. She'd crept into her mind and stayed there. She'd tended to books when her brothers went to socials, she'd prayed at home when her brothers went to church, she'd hid in the house when neighbors came calling. She had only one real friend outside her brothers, and that was Lester. And after her bloody months started and breasts tendered to the slightest touch, she looked longingly at Lester Sutter. She made rose water and touched it behind her ears. She left buttons of her dress undone. She smeared candle wax across her lips. She stroked Lester, and he yielded to her hands.

Many memories saturated Liesel where she knelt. A snapper head hummed with activity: beetles crawled in and out of its eyes, maggots vibrated in its jaws; the sun had drawn all moisture from its leathery skin. Deep through the sockets, the creature's brain was alive with movement. Liesel focused past the empty portholes and into the well of the turtle's mind. In the most desperate moment of her life, she called out for her long-dead mother.

"Mama! Mama! Where are you?" Liesel listened but there was nothing. "Damn you, Mama."

Liesel Richter pulled taut the growth from between her hips and cut the thing from her body once and for all. She tossed it aside, fell back into the weeds, watched a cicada break from the soil and take flight, then lifted her eyes to the high, sighing sun.

DURING THE DAY, *it burrows into black mud, soothes its body — hot from the Minnesota sun — and sleeps light in reptilian slumber. At times, it opens marble eyes and reflects in a convex contortion all the reeds, stones, fields, and squirrels and deer around it. Tree trunks are rounder. Horizons longer. The sun alight with shooting lances of flame. The creature stretches forth its neck and tests the too-hot air with open jaws. The black tongue withers in the heat, the fine sinews of its muscle contracting against the roasting atmosphere. The creature closes its mouth and pulls its bald head back into the cool mud.*

PART *II*

5

Bavaria, 1897

NEAR THE END OF 1897 in a Bavarian village in south Germany, Magdalena Schultz, Maggie to all who knew her and just sixteen at the time, woke Frieda, her older sister. In the bed they shared, Maggie crawled over Frieda, threw her head just past the edge of the mattress, and vomited into the chamber pot.

Frieda wiggled out from beneath her sister and sat up. "How long's this been going on?" she asked.

"I don't know," replied Maggie. "A week or two."

"Papa will kill you."

Maggie rested her head along the rim of the pot.

"Whose is it?" asked Frieda. "Does he know?"

"No," said Maggie. She wiped her mouth with the corner of the blanket.

"You'll have to tell him," Frieda said. She lay back down on her pillow and rubbed her nose with the back of her hand. "You'll have to get married before Papa finds out."

Maggie cleared her throat, then sighed. Her large, smooth face was pale. "It's impossible," she whispered. "He's Jewish."

Frieda pushed the blankets back, swung her legs to the floor, and pulled on a tattered robe. She was taller and more angular than her sister. "God, Maggie. What have you done? Tell the Jew he'd better get you out of here, take you to America."

"His parents would disown him. He'd get nothing."

Though Frieda felt pity for Maggie, she also saw a way to get herself out of Germany, the country from which every decent, eligible man had emigrated, most to America to seek their fortune. Recent land laws made it impossible for younger sons to inherit a father's acres in Germany, and girls with wiles more insidious than Frieda's grabbed up all the available land-inheriting firstborns. Getting pregnant as a way to secure marriage was a common practice. But Frieda had no interest in motherhood, couldn't stomach the way babies cried and messed themselves all day, and she had determined not to subject herself to it, not even for a husband. So, while she saw her sister's problem as an act of idiocy, she also saw an opportunity.

"Trust me now, Maggie," she said. "Listen to your big sister. You have to tell him we need money. We need money to get to America. Tell him you need two tickets. One for you and one for me. Tell him it's the only way to save his inheritance and save his son."

It took only a couple of weeks for Maggie's lover to pilfer the funds needed for her trip, plus a bit more to get her established, and exchange it for American dollars. He taught Maggie what each bill represented, then stuffed them all in an envelope and kissed her forehead. He told her that it was all his fault, that he loved her and loved the baby. He told her he'd never forget her and for the rest of his life would see her face wherever he looked. A half a year before, the lover had spotted Maggie carrying an egg basket to the store near where he bought his paintbrushes. Her hair hung loose, a strange fashion for a girl of her age. Surely she was much too old to have her hair hanging to her bottom.

While he watched her move, the inspiration for a grand painting came to his mind: Mary Magdalene, the penitent prostitute, staring heavenward. The Catholic churches in this region couldn't get paintings of their beloved saints and sinners on the walls fast enough. He'd have no problem selling it. He approached the girl, and she agreed to be his model, and before the week was through, before the painting completed, they were lovers. He gave her a trinket, a brown cameo, a family heirloom pinched from his grandmother's jewelry box, and said he would always imagine Maggie wearing it. He finished that painting several weeks after he said goodbye to Maggie but kept it for himself behind a blanket in a dark closet and never picked up his brushes and paint again. He went to work with his father in the bank.

Frieda and Maggie's father didn't say so much as good riddance to them but observed aloud to their mother how strange it was that these girls had come to have so much money in such a short time.

"If money's going to be earned by whoring, then it may as well be earned here in Germany where the whole family could benefit," he said. "Surely I can set aside a stall in the barn and charge these useless daughters a modest rent. Perhaps I can solicit local customers tired of slapping the thighs of their wives time and again." He didn't wait for a response, only slammed the door and walked outside, toward his empty, rundown barn.

The man hadn't always been such a brute and a bully. Years and years ago, before the daughters were born, before the Franco-Prussian War called him away from his young wife, he had been renowned for the beautiful horses he bred. It was his breeding and caretaking skills that took him and the horses to the front-lines of the war, where he was charged with caring for the Prussian cavalry's horses until the steadily creeping railroads rendered the animals nearly obsolete. Then he was laden with a rifle and sent to fight, simultaneously demoted and humiliated. He was a proud man and never forgot the disgrace. He came home from the war angry, paranoid, and violent. He came back to his wife empty-handed but virile in seed and hate. He was never repaid for the animals the cavalry had conscripted into its army, and as a long economic depression settled in 1873, he became convinced that it was the Jews that kept him from his horses, wealth, pride. He couldn't read, but any fool could make out the gist of the newspaper cartoons: Jews sitting on piles of gold, Jews propagating by the millions, Jews riding on the backs of common laborers. He even blamed the Jewish midwife for the five daughters he had produced. After the birth of Magdalena, the youngest, he never touched his wife again. He was sure that his wife had been witched by the Jew to prevent him from having sons.

The mother ignored the girls' father, though she suspected the same thing he did of her two youngest children, Frieda and Maggie. She couldn't blame her daughters; she herself had mulled over the possibility of throwing up her hands and skirt to alleviate the poverty of the Schultz family. She had five daughters, not one of them married although the three oldest were certainly of marrying age. Those three weren't pretty or particularly smart or even very useful around the kitchen. They ate like animals. It was a complete mystery to her how the girls could be so fat when the sad garden produced only blighted potatoes, woody beans, and cabbage heads ravaged by worms. The few chickens and geese she raised were all skinny as twigs, or limping, or they already tasted old before they grew their adult feathers. Just this morning, not two hours after breakfast, she had pulled a cold chicken wing from the dimpled hand of her oldest. And then there was the business of her brother, who lived in a shack on their little farm. He was as frail and emotional as a woman and sometimes dressed the part, donning a sunbonnet and apron. True, he didn't eat much. But he was another source of shame for the girls' mother. Still, what could a body do? He was family, after all.

She had heard of women who earned money by sneaking into the army camps after dark, where the soldiers would pay for women, even older ones. The woman would name a price, peel back the blanket of the bunk, and straddle the man. The mere sound of the shaking bed was enough to arouse other men into finding a few coins and holding them in their palms until the woman finished with the bed before and peeled back the blanket of the next. The mother had heard that enough money could be made in one night to buy oil, cloth, and shoes for an entire family. Perhaps this was how her daughters came to have so much money.

She felt some relief at the girls' departure. Two fewer bodies to feed and bed was a welcome reprieve, certainly. But in Frieda, she'd seen her last hope. That girl, at least, was trim and motivated and intelligent. Frieda'd take good care of Maggie, she supposed. So she told the girls to be good, and she pressed into Frieda's hand a scrap of paper with the names of two aunts living in a place called New Germany, located in the middle of America, where everyone spoke German. The mother watched on the doorstep as the girls walked to the train station carrying a small parcel apiece. Maggie leaned on her sister and cried quietly. She clenched in her hand a brown and white cameo from the father of her unborn son.

"This was a good thing he did," said Frieda. "This is the right thing for everyone."

"I don't want to leave," said Maggie. "I love him."

"For God's sake," said Frieda. "He's Jewish. And Papa would kill you both. You get on that boat, you save three lives."

"What will I say to people?" asked Maggie.

Frieda patted her hand. "I'll take care of everything. For now, you say your husband is dead and that you are going to America to live with your sister. That's truth enough, isn't it?"

"I guess." Maggie rubbed her fingers over the fine features of the face on the cameo. Frieda grabbed Maggie's hand and demanded to see. She passed her eyes over the small ivory face of the charm.

"You know," Frieda said, "we could sell this for money."

"Never." She pulled her hand away from Frieda and wrapped up the cameo in a handkerchief.

"Maggie," said Frieda.

"What?"

"Is it true what they say about the Jewish boys?"

"What's that?"

"You know."

"I don't."

Frieda pulled Maggie close and looked around to make sure no one was near enough to hear. "That their man part is long and curved to pleasure a woman and drive her mad with desire."

Maggie exhaled into her sister's sleeve. "I'll never tell."

6

THE WIND OFF the North Sea blew in cold and irate, lifting the sea's surface into mad, toothed waves and throwing them heavily against the ships in the Bremen port. The waves smashed against the docks, which weathered the pummeling a mite better than the people standing in wait. Seawater pelted every man, woman, and child eager to be loaded onto the SS *Hamburgia,* a ship America-bound. Maggie's bones ached from much terrible shivering. Her jaw was sore from clenching her teeth. Her fingers were paralyzed from the death grip she had on Frieda's arm. She hated the cold and wondered if cold and shivering could cause her baby harm. She wondered if the baby could die. She wondered if that would be best. She wondered what the weather was like in America. Sunny and hot, she hoped.

Seagulls, birds the girls had never seen before, called and walked among the people as if they were part of the crowd. Frieda kicked at several of them until they took off, only to land within an arm's length again. She tugged Maggie toward a stack of crates, told her to sit, and tucked her own shawl around her sister.

"I am going to get the tickets," she said. "Do not move." Frieda jumped and tried to see above the heads of hundreds of people. Maggie watched her until she disappeared into the horde of them, mothers holding babies, children clutching the hands of smaller children, men nearly toppling under the weight of bags. Dock men rushed back and forth moving crates from the dock to the SS *Hamburgia,* each time sending the gulls flying and the mice scurrying.

Maggie untied her boots, slipped her feet out of them, and exposed her feet to the air. Her stockings were thin and worn completely through on both big toes and heels. Her toes felt warmer now that they weren't cramped. She leaned her head against the crate and closed her eyes. The smell of wheat beer seeped from it. Maggie wished she could pry one open and take a bottle for herself. She cried again as she'd been crying all week.

Frieda bought the tickets and returned to where Maggie was sitting and found her crying.

"Come on now," she said. "It is not that bad."

"It is too," said Maggie. She sniffled and had a hard time talking. "It is very bad."

"Look around," said Frieda. "We are having an adventure."

"I hate adventures."

Frieda knelt and helped Maggie put her boots back on.

"Toughen up," said Frieda.

They climbed the ramp to the ship and were directed toward the ladder leading between the decks. Down they went, into the belly of the ship. Between the floor and ceiling, there were two levels of cots, going all around the shell of the ship. Down the center ran two rows of labeled cargo: alfalfa seed, beer, porcelain china, watches, cloth, dolls, wigs, cheese, and even a crate of trumpets. Everything rattled against everything else as the ship rocked and rasped.

All of the cots in midship were taken, so the girls walked toward the hull, where they claimed a bottom bunk and lay down to rest. When it came time to set sail, Frieda leaped up and climbed the ladder to wave goodbye to Germany forever. Maggie stayed below to protect their cot. She stretched out and was glad that, if nothing else, the place was warm.

A little mother with two babies on her lap sat on the floor nearby. She arranged and rearranged her bags for better comfort. The babies whimpered and cried each time she moved.

"We have room here," Maggie said. She threw Frieda's bag on the floor and then rolled toward the wall.

"Are you sure?"

"Yes. Yes," Maggie said. "Come on."

The mother picked up her children and laid them next to Maggie. The babies squirmed briefly but then settled in. The mother lay down on the outside edge of the cot.

"Thank you so much."

"Of course," said Maggie.

The children's bodies emanated heat. Maggie snuggled close and put her nose in the little girl's hair. It smelled like alfalfa.

"Where is your husband?" Maggie asked the woman. She immediately regretted asking the question. She hoped the woman wouldn't reciprocate. Maggie believed that everyone could read her pregnancy on her face somehow.

"He is in America. He has a job in Chicago in the stockyards. He has made much money for us in only six months."

"My name's Maggie."

"Enta," said the woman. "And these are Helmut and Gladys. Thank you again for sharing your cot."

"Really, it is no trouble."

"I am so happy to be leaving this country," said Enta. She leaned up on her elbow. "The whole place is going to hell with the Jews taking over all the jobs and running the economy. An honest person cannot make a living here anymore."

Maggie felt cold again. "Oh," she said. "I do not know much about politics and such things. Your children are very beautiful."

Enta looked at them and smiled. "That they are."

Above, on deck, Frieda wrestled her way through the crowd to the ship's railing facing the Bremen port. Around her stood men and women waving vigorously to loved ones at the port or to no one at all, only at their last sighting of beloved Germany. One of the seamen wandered among the crowds offering a booklet titled "The American: A Guide in the United States of America" to anyone who would take it. Frieda took one from the man and leafed through it. It was written in English on one side and German on the other. All manner of information was contained in it, about the history of America, its economy, the nature of its citizens. Of American women, the pamphlet read:

> The American ladies in general are very pretty, fascinating, attractive, sociable, and refined. Even in the humblest circumstances they try to acquire a good education and often show great talent for music and the fine arts. They beautify their homes, developing good taste. They are also fond of display and fine dress and always appear tidy, making themselves attractive. Yet they possess great willpower and self-denial and are not apt to succumb in calamity. Bouts of hysteria, womanly fits, nagging, complaining, scoffing at her husband's ideas, and melancholia find no place in the American lady's disposition. American ladies take it upon themselves to lead their husbands and children to religion, and, above all, represent to their family the values learned in the church and Bible. Many hold responsible positions in public life, as teachers, clerks, etc., where they have proven their efficiency.

Frieda didn't give one damn about wifehood, motherhood, or religion, but she knew she'd probably have to succumb to all three. She seriously considered the last line of this pamphlet. Perhaps she'd involve herself in public service in Minnesota. America truly seemed the place for such opportunity.

The Germany Frieda was leaving behind had little tolerance for women moving beyond the domestic life. Men, it seemed to her, clung to the sentiment that women who pursued things greater than child-rearing were perverted. When she'd expressed opinions in her village, she'd been labeled *bull-girl*. When news of that got back to Mother, Mother'd confined Frieda to the farm, the same way she'd confined her brother there so many years before to prevent him from further embarrassing the family with his strange ways.

Frieda was thinking of Uncle Boris when she left the deck and returned to mid-deck. She found the cot full, so she lay across the bottom and used her bag for a pillow.

Frieda's kinship with her uncle Boris, or Beatrice, depending on what sort of day he was having and whether he fancied slacks or an apron, had begun in his little cottage, where Frieda could escape the tirades of Papa, the silent, self-imposed martyrdom of Mother, and the oppressive stench of her three older fat sisters. Their rolling bellies seemed to bowl over every spare inch of the already-cramped house. Maggie, the little imp, was usually up and out of the house and off to town before noon. Frieda never really wondered why or where she'd go. No matter. Now it was apparent that she'd been off in a dalliance with her Jewish boyfriend, getting herself impregnated.

Boris's cottage stank of mold and cheese. He owned one chair, which moved between a place in front of the fire and a place under the one window. The only things Boris required were books and ink and paper. Papa called him queer and useless, but Frieda found in her uncle a vessel to a higher plane of thinking. On his best days, he'd grab her arm before she stepped foot in the door, pull her inside, and plant her harshly in the chair.

"I have it now!" he'd say. "Brilliant! Brilliant!"

Frieda knew not to say a word. It was bad to interrupt the surge.

Sometimes Boris would pace with his hands covering his ears, as though trapping a great thought there. Frieda'd wait.

"Listen. Have you ever considered *why* men war?"

"Yes, of course."

"No! No, you have not!"

Frieda listened.

"I suppose you believe men war for money, or religion, or pride, or land."

"Well, that is correct, is it not?"

"No! Men *war* because they have no predators to threaten them collectively. Look to the insects. Men are like insects in number and industry. Ants do not war one another. They work together to survive! If men were like ants, there would be no war."

Many times, Boris's rantings were silly. But they always made Frieda think. And she was never bored. More than anything, Frieda hated to be bored. In the little cottage, Boris put Frieda to work embroidering birds or fish on bedding, putting buttons on his shirts, or darning his socks. Once, he pulled five brass buttons out of his pocket and dropped them into her palm like gold pieces. "These are for you from the Queen of England to do with as you please." Since she knew her sisters would rip them right off of anything she wore, Frieda stitched them to the hem of Boris's apron. He wept like a woman at the gesture. When she asked why a grown man wore an apron, he stopped crying and said, "I can piss sitting down as well as you can. If I want to wear an apron, I will wear an apron."

Frieda hadn't meant to hurt his feelings. "I have leg hair as men do," she said.

"There you have it," Boris said.

• • •

Frieda tapped her sister's boot. "Won't you miss Uncle Boris?" she asked.

"God, no," said Maggie. She sat up on her elbows and crinkled her nose at Frieda. "That brute." She lay back down. For her part, Maggie would not miss Boris at all. Their uncle frightened her with his strange tales of creatures and dwarfs roaming the forests of Germany. When the girls were small, he would take them on walks to the peat bogs and threaten to leave them as a sacrifice to Nerthus if they were bad.

"Here is where Nerthus emerges from the fog on a chariot led by white cows. Nerthus will sometimes appear as a handsome man and sometimes as a handsome woman, covered by a great curtain to hide tremendous beauty."

"What does Nerthus want?" Maggie had asked.

"A sacrifice, you simpleton!" Boris had said. "This bog is filled with people who dared come to the chariot and lift the curtain."

"Why can't anyone look beneath the curtain?" Frieda had asked.

"Because Nerthus is the body of perfection. Mortals cannot possibly manage such knowledge."

"I do not believe you," Maggie had said.

"I suppose you don't believe in dwarfs then either," Boris had said.

"Of course not." But Maggie did believe in all manner of witches and *Narren*.

"Stupid girl," Boris had said. "The race of dwarfs is all around."

"That's enough," Frieda had said. "You are scaring our little Maggie."

Frieda wiggled her toes in her boots to bring the cold things back to life. "At least he was interesting," said Frieda. "Uncle Boris, I mean."

"Wolves with snapping teeth are interesting too," whispered Maggie. "Will you miss them as well?"

Frieda smiled. That was a clever retort by her little sister. Perhaps Maggie was smarter than she'd thought. Maggie spoke so little and so quietly that it was hard to tell if anything at all was rumbling around between her ears. Frieda slapped at Maggie's boot again. "Your feet smell," she whispered, but Maggie was already breathing heavy in sleep.

They slept this way for fifty days at sea. During those days, Frieda worked on the memories of Germany she wanted to keep: the creamy texture of the Honey River, the cool moss beneath heavy trees, the music, the poetry, and especially Boris. Mother, Papa, and the other sisters? Ugh. To hell with them.

Maggie spent most of the trip sick and shaking her head at the men Frieda found for her. There was a man nearly dead of old age, a dockhand with black teeth, a Frenchman who spoke no German or English, three drunkards, a schoolboy traveling with his mother, and one know-it-all who followed her around like a pesky fly, insisting that she eat lemon peel to prevent scurvy.

"Leave me alone," Maggie told Frieda one afternoon near the end of their journey. She climbed into the cot and over Enta and the kids. She was at the point where she really regretted having offered to share the cot with them. Enta talked nonstop. The kids messed themselves constantly and cried over their diaper rash the entire trip.

"You all settled on a Jewish man then?" Frieda asked.

Enta jumped up and nearly smacked her head on the bunk above. "Jewish man?" said Enta. "Are you crazy? You cannot marry a Jew. The children will have tails."

"Enta," said Frieda, "shut up."

Maggie was glad for her sister.

After the boat trip, the girls boarded a train to Chicago. They followed Enta and her children onto it, and as soon as Enta chose one car, the girls chose another. From Chicago, Frieda and Maggie boarded another train to Minneapolis, Minnesota, and then south to a town called Mankato, where they hitched a carriage ride to New Germany, which looked much like the villages of their old country. The streets were dirt, but straight and ungullied, and the windows on the buildings were spotless, most with flower boxes below them filled with wild red roses. The town even smelled like home. The hops and grains from the brewery sweetened the air, and from the butcher shop drifted the scent of seasoned sausage, a woody and gruff aroma. Frieda and Magdalena were relieved to stretch their legs in what was to be their new home. The girls looked around and eyed the nicest building in town, a tall, tan, and sharply peaked structure with dark wood accents and *Deutsche Chronik* painted on a wooden plank hanging above the doorway.

"A newspaper," said Frieda. "The *Deutsche Chronik*. Maybe I can get a job there."

"This may be America, Frieda, but no one's going to hire a woman for such a job here either."

"Have faith, Maggie."

The girls dragged their bags and walked to the building. They knocked on the door, and a tall handsome man in a white shirt and glasses greeted them in English, then in German. Frieda pulled the piece of paper with the names of relatives on it from her pocket and presented it to the man. He assured the girls that the town was small and showed them the quickest walking route to a series of tidy farms in the direction of their great-aunt's place. Frieda pressed him for more information about the town and the newspaper, in particular. The man revealed himself to be the editor of it. While Maggie sat in the corner and rested, exhausted from the long journey, the editor and Frieda spoke of news and politics. Later, he offered to get them a ride to their great-aunt's with a friend of his, but Magdalena and Frieda declined, saying the exercise would do them good. They began the mile walk to the first farm place on a road that was well worn but patched with new gravel where cavities had emerged after the thaw.

"Oh, I think we'll like it here," said Frieda. She inhaled deeply.

"You have your eye on him already," said Maggie. She didn't look at her sister but looked instead at the little gardens, the wheat fields, and the glistening lake beyond.

"No, no," said Frieda. "We need money. I will get a job there."

"I have money," said Maggie. "Enough for a while, anyway." She reached into her pocket and fingered the cameo.

Frieda stopped, bent, and picked a rock out of the ankle of her boot. "I have to get a job." She threw the rock toward a growth of cattails, and up sprang three brown wood ducks. "A good job. I'll be damned if I am going to sew or cook or do laundry."

Maggie raised her eyebrows at her sister. "How did you get so particular, or bold, for that matter?"

"And we must get you a husband first, of course." Frieda stuck her elbow in Maggie's side. "But he was handsome, was he not?"

The girls met their mother's aunt, a round and proper woman who had hardly even heard their whole story before she took them in her enormous arms and squeezed the pair. She took their bags, piled them on top of one of her sons, and told him to carry them into the loft. She set her daughters to work fixing beds and clearing space for Frieda and Maggie to stay. She offered them cake and coffee. The great-aunt inquired about the girl's mother, their sisters, and Uncle Boris. The girls filled the great-aunt with ridiculous statements of how happy their mother was, how fruitful the harvests had been, how local boys nearly banged down the door with marriage proposals for their sisters, and the great health of Uncle Boris. The great-aunt nodded her head and smiled, but across her brow ran the lines of disbelief. Clearly, she knew better. But what could be done with relatives half a world away? She settled the girls into her upstairs loft alongside her two little girls. Frieda asked her great-aunt about the man from the newspaper. She told Frieda that no, Archie Richter wasn't mar-

46

ried, and yes, he was kind. Frieda knew she ought to be looking first and fast for a husband for her pregnant sister, but she found herself wanting that newspaper man for herself, despite what she had told Maggie. Maggie collapsed onto the bed and slept for three days straight.

Frieda, quick as a pinprick, worked her charms on Archie. Her great-aunt had baked a pan of rhubarb cake, and before it could even cool off on the counter, Frieda wrapped it in a dishcloth and set off for town. When she opened the door of the newspaper, a bell rang her arrival.

"Hallo?" she called.

"Yes," replied Archie from the back room. "I'll be right there." He emerged from the back, wiping his inky hands on a long white apron.

"I am Frieda," she said.

"Yes, I remember."

"I brought you cake, and I have come for a job."

Archie smiled. "My. You get right to the point," he said. He motioned to a table and bade Frieda sit down. She did. And over cake and Archie's strong coffee, the two talked of the old country, which was how Archie referred to it. She told him the way it really was, the oldest story in the history of any organized nation: the rich get richer, the poor get sent to war, the rich get more powerful and more imposing, the poor get poorer and more numerous. The poor talk of revolt, sometimes do it, and sometimes move.

Archie had a much more nostalgic idea of Germany, a place that he had never even seen. He, like Frieda, had a great love of the language and the writers and thinkers of the country. He told her that the longer she lived in the United States, the more she too would grow to appreciate and love her old Germany.

They couldn't agree, it seemed, on how many children a married pair ought to have. As many as possible, said Archie, a semi-devout Catholic. Zero, said Frieda, a Catholic too, but not the practicing kind. Archie supposed that things like that worked themselves out in the marriage bed.

Archie hired Frieda on at the newspaper, and a month after that, he married her in St. Leopold's Catholic church, where Magdalena stood as an attendant. Magdalena could hardly believe her sister's luck.

At the barn dance after, Frieda's new husband introduced Magdalena, just beginning to show the weight of her baby, to Wilhelm Richter, a local farmer and cousin to Archie. Wilhelm admired Magdalena's quiet manner. He thought highly of the modest way she tried to keep her body from touching his while they danced. They waltzed as though someone had stuck a barrel between them. *Yes,* he thought, *this is the type of wife for me.* Before the night was out, Richter raised his stein and promised the stars above that he would marry Magdalena Schultz.

"He's a dirty farmer," complained Maggie to her sister. "He smells like the barn. Worst of all, he reminds me of Papa."

"Maggie," said Frieda. She grabbed Magdalena's elbow and spit advice through tight lips. "You are not in a position to prefer the smell of your Jewish banker over the smell of this barn dweller. You're going to have a baby. You're going to have that baby either with no one, fathered by a Jew who's too far away to matter, or with a live man who owns a farm, owns land, and, despite your thick waist and dense skull, thinks you're someone he's taken a shine to."

"He was an artist," whispered Magdalena. "His father is a banker."

"What?" said Frieda. She leaned closer to her sister.

"Nothing," said Magdalena. "Is there no one else? Someone less brutish?"

"You could saddle up with old Sutter." Frieda pointed to a pig farmer with a thumb hooked in one coverall, drinking something out of a brown bottle. "He's already driven one wife to her deathbed and I hear he's looking for a big-boned replacement. He's got at least seven little ones to look after. And the middle one isn't right in the head, if you know what I mean. I heard he took a knife after one of his sisters. You can manage that, can you?"

Magdalena wondered how Frieda had become privy to all the town gossip so quickly, but she believed her nevertheless. She said yes to Wilhelm Richter's proposal, which came just a week after her sister's wedding. She insisted upon a quick ceremony, which Wilhelm misunderstood as enthusiasm. On the morning of the ceremony, she poked her cameo through the neckline of the same dress Frieda had worn on her wedding day, though the darts had to be loosened. She stood in St. Leopold's in front of the same priest to repeat the same vows. That night Wilhelm lit a lantern in the bedroom and savored many minutes removing her wedding dress, corset, and stockings and rubbing his coarse hands over her curves. She couldn't help but compare the touch of this man to the gentle caresses of her artist. Wilhelm climbed on top of her, and she cried out in the way a virgin wife was expected to, thanks to the reminder Frieda had murmured that very day. Wilhelm kept up a good rhythm for several minutes, which Magdalena counted away on the licks of the lantern flame next to the bed. When he finished, she petted his head and admitted to herself that it wasn't so bad if she just looked into the fire and imagined the boy she left behind.

Soon enough in their marriage, it was she who climbed on top of Wilhelm, eyes feral with flame, and rocked herself back to Germany and to the small bank office of her love where she had conceived the child that now grew bigger and bigger each day until the bump of it almost entirely blocked out the face of the man beneath her.

When Frieda pulled a wiry, red boy from Magdalena several months after the wedding, she handed him to Wilhelm before she let Magdalena see. Wilhelm looked down at the boy's clenched fist and smiled. Frieda nodded to her sister. Magdalena pulled the lantern closer and said, "Give me that boy," and Wilhelm did. Magdalena presented her breast to him and he latched on hard and fast. She closed her eyes and willed the milk to come in, and it did. The baby kneaded at her breast. It was all she could do not to cry for herself.

"I'd like to be alone now," she said. Frieda suggested that Wilhelm might want to hold his boy again, but Magdalena told them to get out of her bedroom and leave her be, leave her be. Frieda led Wilhelm out and lit the stove for a pot of coffee.

"Women become this way after babies sometimes," Frieda explained. "It'll pass."

He nodded and admitted he didn't know much of these matters. He took the schnapps down from the cabinet. "Let's celebrate my son," he said to Frieda.

"Yes," said Frieda. "He's big for being early."

Wilhelm and Frieda sat together in the kitchen drinking coffee and liquor, listening to the muffled sobs of Magdalena. When she emerged from her room seven days later, she declared the boy's name was Benjamin, though both Wilhelm and Frieda had assumed the child's name would be Wilhelm, like his father.

"No," said Maggie. "This boy's name is Benjamin." And then, seeing a tightened expression creep over Wilhelm's lips and a glare of warning from Frieda's eyes, Maggie softened some and said, "Perhaps next time we shall use Wilhelm, on a son that favors his father more than his mother." She passed the baby to Wilhelm. "See how he has my face and even my fingers? See?"

Wilhelm took the boy, and he saw.

In the next few years, another son and then another was born, and still his own name was not to be used. By the time Magdalena grew large with the fourth child, in 1902, Wilhelm had decided and insisted that this one bear his name.

"It may be a girl," said Magdalena.

"Liesel, then," said Wilhelm. "After my mother."

7

ONLY MAGDALENA KNEW anything was amiss with her baby. The baby Liesel had all the parts of a girl, but an extra tag of skin, no bigger than a pinch at first, extended from there too.

On the night of Liesel's birth, Magdalena had reached between her own legs, gripped the bloody head of the baby, pushed, and lifted the child to her own bare belly. Magdalena took the ready shears and cut the cord. She patted the baby on its back until a small cry soared. And no matter how much Magdalena may have lamented her life or, rather, the one she wished she had, this first cry from this baby on this night brought to her such a pang of love that her neck hurt. *Oh, baby,* she thought. *I am so happy to have you.* Then she rubbed, cleaned, and studied the child. After having already delivered three boys, Magdalena could plainly see that this child was no boy. There were the girl parts, for certain. But why so swollen? Was this how baby girls were supposed to look? As a child, she and her sisters had referred to boys' parts as *beef* and girls' parts as *bread.* Simple, but functional. She looked closer at the baby. Here was the girl's cleft. That looked normal to

Magdalena. But at the top of it lay a little . . . what? She didn't know. Magdalena covered the baby's bottom. She counted the fingers, counted the toes. She cleared out the little nose and ears, all the while thinking she'd made a mistake and everything would look normal in a minute or two. She set the baby aside and washed herself and tidied the bed. Wilhelm knocked at the door, and Magdalena told him she was not ready and to go away.

Wilhelm opened the door just a crack. "Is it a girl this time?" he whispered.

"Yes," said Magdalena, "a girl. Now go back to bed."

"I love you, Maggie."

"Go to bed, Wilhelm."

He closed the door.

When she was sure Wilhelm was gone, Magdalena went to the kitchen for an extra lantern and more water. She returned to the baby and unwrapped the nappy. She put the lanterns all around the child and with clean cloths washed the baby. *What's this?* she wondered again. *My God, what have I done?* She blanched with panic and nausea. She covered the child's body with a blanket, then unwrapped it and looked again. She picked up the baby and held it to her chest. She walked to the window and looked across the yard to the lake. The whole night felt foul. She held the head of the tiny beast with one hand and the neck with the other. She considered the conundrum. *Babies die all the time.* No one would question her. She gave a slight twist. The child cried out and then nestled its face in Magdalena's breast, rooting to be fed. Magdalena brought the child to her breast, and the child suckled eagerly. Milk came and the baby swallowed. The decision to feed the child annulled the need for any other decisions that night.

In the morning, Wilhelm crept into the bedroom and looked down at his wife and new daughter.

"She is perfect," he said.

"More perfect than the rest," Maggie responded. Another

strange quip from his wife, thought Wilhelm. He kissed her fore-head and that of his daughter. He told Maggie he'd tend to the boys for the day so she could rest, but she'd not have it. She was up and cooking before the boys woke.

As Liesel grew, Magdalena sometimes wondered if she had done the right thing. As Liesel grew, so did the odd protrusion. On Magdalena's darkest days, she thought about dropping Liesel into the old well to be done with the business altogether. She thought about slicing Liesel's neck, about leaving her lost in the rolling plains or the jagged bluffs of some remote part of the countryside where the long grasses would surely reach up and grab hold of the girl and pull her back into the black dirt where a creature like Liesel belonged. Magdalena considered holding her hand over the small pink mouth and nose of the child until not one iota of oxygen could get to the girl's lungs, despite the eyes that would beg, the little arms that would flail, the paper-thin nails that would scratch. How long would such a death take? A minute? Maybe two?

What to do with a child that was *mostly* girl? What could pos-sibly become of her? What kind of life could she possibly have? What possible good? The child was a constant reminder of Mag-dalena's own sins, her own monsters. She knew how these things worked. Back home, a woman had given birth to a baby with a birthmark on its face. Why? Because the mother had let her hus-band suck on her in unsavory places while the baby grew. Had Magdalena not given herself to a Jew, this wouldn't have hap-pened. Had she not gotten pregnant, this would not have hap-pened. Had she not lied all these years, this would not have happened. Had she not favored Benjamin over the other chil-dren, this would not have happened. This child was a constant reminder of a future that was as useless as a slow rain after hail. A waste of human flesh, human blood, human feeling and mind. What, she asked God, is a child such as Liesel meant to do? Why did you punish the child for the mother's sins? The child was a secret that must be kept but could never be kept. A scandal, a humiliation always just a flicker away from kindling.

Eventually, she accepted Liesel as a penance for her own sins. She accepted Liesel as a sign that demons hovered above the Richter family with torches, ready to burn the entire lot of them, and she learned to go about her life knowing that to be true.

The only thing Magdalena could do to help her daughter was toughen her, to prepare her for the explosion that was to come.

When the baby Liesel would cry, the mother Magdalena would stand over the crib and stare silently at the crying child for ten or fifteen minutes before picking her up. When the toddler Liesel would fall down and scrape an elbow or knee, the mother Magdalena would mix salt water and instruct the child to rinse the wounds herself. And so the pattern of Liesel's life was set in this way. Comfort always came late. And it always came with pain. But in all of this, Liesel felt the love of it. Magdalena did love Liesel. She loved her very, very hard.

8

WILHELM RICHTER'S Monday mornings began with coffee and the reading of the *Deutsche Chronik*. While Magdalena milked the cows and brought in the milk, prepared breakfast and dressed the children, he read all the German, American, and world news it offered, reading many stories aloud to the children and to his wife. He didn't scan or skip one word. He read and absorbed all of it. On one morning, he read a particularly interesting article in the German business section.

"A man from your village has been promoted to vice president of German Bank," said Wilhelm to Magdalena.

"Oh," she said. She brushed Liesel's hair out of her eyes.

"Benjamin Wechsler. Do you know him?"

Magdalena brushed the ends of Liesel's hair with new ferocity. "No," said Magdalena. "Never heard of him."

"That is a big accomplishment and a big responsibility," Wilhelm went on, but Magdalena couldn't hear him over the hammering in her head.

• • •

While the boys, especially Benjamin, took up all of Magdalena's attention, Liesel was a light and a joy for her papa. One morning while the Richter family ate their breakfast together, the little girl's first steps were toddled from the leg of the kitchen table into her papa's waiting arms. He swooped her up and hugged her tight.

"She walks!" he cried to Magdalena. Benjamin and Herman clapped for their sister's achievement.

"All children do," Magdalena replied.

"None so well as this one," he said, and kissed the girl's forehead.

"Benjamin walked at ten months," Magdalena said.

Luther hopped off his chair and stomped his feet to show that he, too, could walk. "See?" he said to the family. "I walk better."

"So he did," said Wilhelm to Magdalena. "Come on, boys. Time to do the chores." He put Liesel down, stood, and roughed up Benjamin's hair.

"Needs a haircut," Wilhelm said. "He has goat hair."

"Feel mine," said Luther. "I have goat hair too."

Wilhelm lifted Luther. "No, my boy. You have the best hair. Soft as milkweed seed."

"I have the best hair," said Luther to his brothers.

"Benjamin's hair is like mine," said Magdalena. "He has the hair of the Germans of the south. My mother's is the same."

"Whose hair do I have?" asked Herman.

Wilhelm pinched a strand of Herman's hair in his fingers. "A horse's, I would say." Herman wiped his papa's hand away.

"Do not," he said. "My hair is like a king's."

"Enough hair talk," said Wilhelm. "The straw needs binding and stacking. Up, boys."

"Benjamin has to help me today," said Magdalena. "He stays in the house with me."

"So be it," said Wilhelm. "Luther. Herman. Come along."

This is the way Magdalena preferred it. She insisted on having Benjamin near her always. For one, he was her oldest, her favorite. Also, she couldn't stand to be alone with Liesel. The child scared her. And sometimes, she honestly didn't trust herself to be alone with Liesel. Magdalena had intense, contradictory feelings for the girl: repulsion, love, hate, guilt, shame, affection. Mostly fear. Fear for herself, fear for Liesel. She felt fear for Benjamin too. What if Wilhelm one day looked at Benjamin and discovered his secret? It seemed so obvious to her. The boy looked every bit his father, except for his stoutness, which obviously came from her. How could Wilhelm look at Benjamin and not see that the boy wasn't his? And so to be safe, or at least safer, Magdalena kept these two close to her side, where she could protect and hide them.

Before she touched the breakfast dishes, she lifted Benjamin onto the table. She went to her sewing box and pulled out her shears.

"Hold still, son," she said. She gripped and lifted curl after curl and snipped the boy's hair. When she was done, she swept up. Liesel sat quietly in the corner, watching. Magdalena walked to her, knelt, and twisted Liesel's hair around her finger.

"Pitty," said Liesel.

"Yes," said Magdalena, "pretty."

Liesel's hair was curly yet, baby hair. Magdalena swiftly picked her up and set her on the table. What came over the mother next was hard to describe. It was an intense desire to do the girl harm but also an intense love for her, not unlike a feeling she once had when she was small and found her little dog had been kicked by a horse and lay bleeding and half paralyzed in the pasture. Then, she had gone to her father in tears, and he had followed her to the dog. He bent and without a word of warning snapped the dog's neck.

Magdalena took a deep breath, slid the blade of the shears above Liesel's ear, and squeezed the blades together, slowly. A beautiful strand, acorn brown, floated into Liesel's lap. Liesel, just over one year old but already aware of her complicated place in her mother's heart, looked at the hair and then lifted her eyes to her mother. She said nothing.

"Mama," said Benjamin. "What are you doing to Liesel's hair?"

"Never mind, son. Go play."

"Do not cut *her* hair. Girls have long hair."

"Benjamin," said Magdalena, "I said never mind."

Benjamin wedged his way between his mother and his sister. "At least let me hold her hand," he said, "so she is not afraid."

"That is a fine idea," said Magdalena.

Magdalena took another breath, smiled at her child, and cut the girl's hair short as Benjamin's.

When Wilhelm came in from the morning chores and saw his girl, he charged at Magdalena and demanded to know what she had done. Magdalena presented reason after reason: her hair was in her eyes, the girl had been scratching and maybe had lice, and, most telling, girls who are too pretty attract too much attention.

"Maggie," said Wilhelm. "God. The girl has never been farther than the grove. She is only a baby. Attention from whom?"

"Wicked people."

"Who could harm a baby?"

"This place is full of wickedness."

"Woman," he said. But that was all. He could think of nothing else. Something that Wilhelm referred to as "a state" sometimes came over his Maggie. At these times, it was best to leave her alone.

That afternoon, Wilhelm prepared the wagon and team and announced that all the boys were going with him to town. Magdalena, who would normally fuss at Benjamin's going anywhere, was quiet. The boys hopped up and down in the back of the wagon like happy coons. Liesel waved to them from the porch of the house.

"Bye-bye," called the boys. "Bye-bye, Liesel."

Liesel waved bye-bye.

In New Germany, Wilhelm led the boys into the general store. He said hello to Dr. Mathiowetz and his little daughter, Betty, who was licking a big lollipop. He prompted the boys to say hello and they did. All but Herman, who even at his young age was thunderstruck by the lovely little girl with the black hair and very red lips.

"Good day to you, Richter," said Dr. Mathiowetz. "Bring those children in for checkups one of these days."

"Will do," said Wilhelm, even though he knew he wouldn't. Magdalena had a strict sense of privacy. She wanted no one but herself tending to herself, her husband, and her brood.

Wilhelm perused the row of ribbon reels, the whites, yellows, blues, flowered, striped, and spotted, and finally settled on a bright red color, the color of the girl's lollipop. He stretched out his arms to show the merchant how much he wanted.

"Mighty fancy for a farmer," joked the merchant. He cut and folded the ribbon, pinned it, and wrapped it in paper.

"You are a funny man," said Wilhelm. "This is for my daughter."

"Why do you not ever bring her in?" asked the merchant. "She must be, what? A year now?"

"Yes," said Wilhelm, "only a year."

"You should bring the whole family to church one of these Sundays," said the merchant, a strict German Catholic.

"Perhaps sometime I will," said Wilhelm, a not-so-strict one.

"As fine a child as your boys, I suspect," said the merchant. Benjamin and Herman politely smiled. Luther wanted to know what he was getting. Wilhelm thumped him on the head. The boy sulked to the corner of the store where a large barrel sat, full of floating pickles. He nibbled on five different pickles and threw them back into the brine before Herman marched over with Benjamin following and kicked Luther in the behind.

"Boys!" Wilhelm called.

Benjamin and Herman stopped fast. Luther belted both his brothers on their arms and then slipped beneath a table of lanterns to hide. The table shook and the lanterns clanked against one another. Wilhelm walked over. Herman pointed to where Luther hid. Wilhelm bent and pulled out Luther by the arm. "So you want something too?"

He bought each boy a pickle and paid for the ones Luther had ruined. When Wilhelm returned home, he cut the ribbon into two strands and tied one around Liesel's waist and one around her head.

"Pitty," said Liesel.

"Very pretty," said Wilhelm.

Late that night, after her husband and children slumbered in dreams, Magdalena Richter woke. She lit a lantern and took the one mirror she had, a small brass hand mirror, and set it against the mantel. She loosened her own hair, and it fell in beautiful waves to the bottom of her back. She pulled the lantern close to her face and peered closely. Gray strands were just coming through along her hairline, but otherwise, the brown color that covered Benjamin's, Herman's, and Liesel's heads was the same as her own. Over and over again, she pulled a brush through her hair and remembered how her lover had stroked it, had brought it to his nose and smelled it. Magdalena Schultz had not been the prettiest of girls, but her hair was a treasure and she had cared for it vainly: washing it, plaiting it, and allowing it to dry, then loosening the braids and letting the waves reflect light and emanate the good smells of homemade soap. Her older sisters had called her a flirt and had said that pretty hair could not hide an ugly face. Magdalena hadn't cared. She knew how lovely it was to have her hair be the only thing between her cheek and the chest of her lover. She saw how beautiful she was in his eyes when she stood before him with only her hair covering her naked chest. Her lover had said she looked like Botticelli's Venus. For the first time in a long while, Magdalena indulged herself with tears. She'd grown

60

so hard here in this place with Wilhelm and the children. She hated the farm. She hated Minnesota and the cold. She hated all these complications she had brought on herself. She hated Wilhelm, but loved him too, as people who grow into each other often do. And her children. What a messy group of ragtags they were. Herman and Luther would be fine, she was sure, but she knew that she was the only thing between Benjamin and Liesel and catastrophe. She was the only one who could protect them, hide them, keep them safe from harm. But she felt that she herself was haunted by demons. Even as she stood in front of the mirror, the devils taunted her. Their black shadows danced all around and whispered to her. Her face glowed by the light of the lantern. The tears magnified her eyes and blurred her vision.

In the mirror, she could clearly see someone standing at the window behind her. The moon's light reflected off a white, bald head. She wouldn't turn around.

"You are not real," she said. Her breath fogged the glass, and the image disappeared.

Magdalena drew the shears from the sewing box and started above her ear. When she'd finished, Magdalena swept up her hair and walked out into the night. Once outside, she waited and listened on the porch. Nothing but the usual night creatures — crickets, bats, and owls — moved. No sign of the man who'd been in the window. The man who she wanted so badly to be her lover. She knew he hadn't really been there and never would be. Briefly, she worried that she couldn't trust her mind.

Magdalena walked to her garden and sprinkled her hair around the periphery of it. Human hair could keep the deer and rabbits out of her vegetables. Perhaps it kept other devils away too. Why not? It was as good a charm as any other form of prayer or spell.

The night air cooled Magdalena's neck. She shook her head and wondered how to keep her hair out of her face now that it was too short for a bun. Magdalena decided not to mind. She felt purged and freed. Lighter, suddenly. And too refreshed to sleep. Magdalena went to the barn and lit a lamp. The heifer ready to birth stood in the corner huffing heavily, a sure sign that her time was near. Magdalena lay her hands on the heifer's middle, which trembled and constricted beneath the soft fur.

"Relax, girl."

Other than keep her calm, there wasn't much she could do for the animal in this time but wait. Magdalena decided that as long as she was already awake, she'd milk the cows early, and by the time the sun was up, the milking was done and the heifer had delivered. Magdalena felt strangely playful. The little calf wobbled on stick legs a few minutes after birth. She remembered the first steps of her own children and thought such things might be miracles. She rarely thought of the causes of good things. Magdalena had an odd sense of religion. She believed fully in evil and in its manifestations on Earth. She believed in devils and trolls and bad people. She believed that if a person did something bad, he or she would pay for it here in this life and after. Her own mother had prayed and prayed and went to Mass each morning, but Magdalena never saw any good come of it. It seemed to her that bad things were far more common than good. Magdalena sat on a bale and scratched behind the calf's ear. The calf's mother sniffed the bloody sac from which the calf had emerged. Magdalena speculated about what kinds of things wandered in the cow's brain. Did she love her calf? Did she know when it was hungry or in pain? Did the mother cow know how this calf would be fattened and then fed to Magdalena's own children? Was this cow just a complacent witness to her calf's misery? The cow licked the sac and then chewed a corner. Simple beast.

Magdalena carried the calf across the yard, up the porch, and into the house. She sneaked into Liesel's room and put the calf near her bed. Then Magdalena touched Liesel's cheek with the back of her hand. When the calf bellowed, Liesel woke and sat up. The calf's head was just at the height of Liesel's bed. She reached out to pet it.

"Mine," she said.

"No," said Magdalena. "This calf belongs to his mother. But you can pet him."

Liesel ran her hand up and down the nose of the calf. She stuck her fingers in the nostrils and pulled on the ear. The calf sneezed. Liesel laughed and tried to pinch the long lashes of the calf.

"Gentle, now," said Magdalena. She put her own hand on Liesel's and showed her to pet gently along the cheek.

The boys named the calf Clarence the Calf and took turns feeding him from the big calf bottle and riding him around the yard. Luther held on to his tail while the animal bucked and sliced the air with his hooves. Sometimes they placed Liesel on Clarence the Calf's back and led her around the yard. Every day, as soon as breakfast was done, the children raced outside to play with their pet. But one morning, when Clarence the Calf was only a few weeks old, Wilhelm forbade the children to take him out of the barn. He requested that Magdalena follow him to the calf and told Benjamin to keep an eye on Liesel.

"What are you going to do, Papa?" asked Luther.

"I have to help your calf grow big," said Wilhelm.

"He's already growing big," said Luther. "Are you going to kill him?"

"Ha," laughed Wilhelm. "No. I am not going to kill him."

Wilhelm tied the calf to a post. Magdalena held the calf's head in her apron. Wilhelm pulled a long string from his pocket and told Magdalena to hold him tight. Wilhelm wedged his way between the calf's back legs and pulled down on the calf's scrotum. The calf jerked and bawled while Wilhelm wrapped and wrapped the string around the upper skin.

Magdalena leaned over to watch closely.

"It doesn't hurt much," said Wilhelm. "He's mostly afraid of having his head covered."

Magdalena nodded and tightened her grip on the calf, which kicked heartily at Wilhelm and wrestled his head back and forth.

"A few weeks of this at most." Wilhelm finished with a strong knot. "Take him to his mother. Nursing will bring him comfort."

What was especially difficult for Magdalena to determine was the exact extent of Liesel's problem. Magdalena spent the first year of Liesel's life being horrified, being afraid, and being protective of her. But when Liesel was almost two, Magdalena set out to toilet train the child and resolved to fix Liesel's problem. Over the course of the child's short life so far, Magdalena had discovered that Liesel urinated the same way she did. The odd growth seemed to have no function at all. She thought, then, to remove it before the child could attach any memory to it or to the act of removing it. Magdalena knew she couldn't cut it; such an act would surely hurt Liesel, and the blood would alarm Wilhelm. And so, as she had seen Wilhelm do with the calf, she wrapped twine around the growth and hoped it would disintegrate and fall off. She simply stood Liesel before her, wound and wound the string, and tied it off with a tight knot. No touching, she told Liesel. After she'd done it, she felt the smallest hope. Hope was such a rare phenomenon to her. She hardly knew what to call it. At first Liesel was none the worse for the procedure. Some days later, though, the child could scarcely be encouraged to get out of bed and her brow glowed wet with sweat and fever. Magdalena diligently removed Liesel's undergarments and was horrified to see what a painful mess she'd made of her child. The growth and the area all around it was tomato red and the string had cut into Liesel's skin, leaving an open wound. What was worse was that the string had loosened and yielded. Magdalena pulled the embedded string from Liesel's skin and cleaned her gently with soap and water.

Magdalena dared not hope again. She completely severed communication with her sister and grew more and more distant from Wilhelm, though he hardly had time to notice. In the next years, his wealth grew. He bought more and more land on credit from the New Germany bank before the bank stopped extending credit. The Norwegians and Swedes of New Germany noticed that Mr. Schneider, the bank president, stopped extending credit to them first and only later, much later, to the German people of the area. Germans were loyal to their own. Some neighbors, Norwegians mostly, who had spent big on cow herds and the new machinery that seemed to come out every new planting season, couldn't make their land payments, and the New Germany bank foreclosed on the farms and then sold them cheap to the highest bidder. Wilhelm sat on enough money to buy the entire section. He bought up a parcel here and a parcel there until every one of his neighbors in the section had lost some portion of his tillable land to Wilhelm Richter. The men walked outside in the early mornings to relieve themselves on the spring dew, and at one time or another, each had seen Wilhelm running a horse and plow across what used to be his land.

Only once did Magdalena presume to question him about his finances. Along with buying land, Wilhelm received German bank notes for hundreds of American dollars every month. Letters from Wilhelm's German family came too. Wilhelm never shared them with his wife, and when she asked him about the money and letters, his answer was the first and only slap he ever delivered his wife. How could she not see that everything he did, he did for her and for the children? How could she not see that he was ensuring their future? The future of their children? She was the woman, the wife, the mother, who tended to the children, the cows, the garden, and the house. He was the man, who tended to the crops, the money, the business, and the big decisions.

It was simple. Though he left her alone mostly, he loved Magdalena. But he couldn't abide being told his business by a woman. No good man would stand for it.

As if to make his point again, he pushed her past the table and to the bed. They conceived their last child that day. He didn't understand then, in the bed, after he had finished, that this copulation would set to spinning the fate that would take his wife from him. He didn't understand then, as he looked at her lying in the middle of the bed with her skirt hitched past her waist, what her words meant. "What good's a woman anyway," she had said. A final baby took hold that day in Maggie's womb, and as he developed, she withered.

9

MAGDALENA RICHTER, stacked chest-high with the weight of her last child, passed the final few weeks of her pregnancy sweating her shape into a patchwork quilt and eating loaves and loaves of bread. At night, the mice crawled up from beneath the floorboards, nosing their way toward the tiny crumbs Magdalena wasn't able to pinch between her fat fingers. Just a few weeks before, she'd sequestered herself in the bedroom. She'd gathered a bread loaf and a jam jar in her hands, trod to the bedroom, and butted the door closed to her husband, three sons, and her daughter, Liesel, all eyes hopeful for supper. She dropped onto the bed, tore bread blocks from the loaf, and plunged them into jam. "What good's a woman anyway?" she asked herself. Before long, she heard Liesel, trained to work as hard as any of the boys, pull the fry pan from the cupboard and order her father and brothers outside to wash up. The smell of venison soon wafted under the door, and Magdalena pulled a pillow over her nose to bar the scent.

Nine-year-old Liesel did her mother's work. She lugged water from the well, washed dishes, milked cows, hoed potatoes, and beat dirt out of her father's and brothers' clothing using soap mixed and molded herself because her mother retched at the scent.

Though Magdalena had tried to keep Liesel at a distance, that rejection only inclined Liesel to be more pleasant, more helpful toward her. What Liesel wanted, more than all, was to climb into that great lap of her mother's, tap at the round belly, and listen to what thrashed inside. Each night, Liesel prepared a washbasin with heated water and sand and gravel from Spider Lake to massage the strain out of Magdalena's swollen feet. The girl took small, warm stones and rubbed them against the heel of her mother's sole until Magdalena moaned and said, "Be grateful you will never suffer with such a burden." Liesel blinked at the statement. Her mother was sometimes apt to say strange things.

So while her mother lay in her room incubating the baby, Liesel saw her brothers off to school in the mornings. It was the end of May now, nearly time for them to stay home for the summer. Liesel loved those days, but until then, she resolved to be as helpful as she could to them and to her mother by fixing them breakfast and making sure their socks and boots were clean. She often followed them down the driveway on their way to the New Germany Turner school. She did this mainly to be sure that Luther actually made it to the end of the driveway. If someone wasn't watching, he would dart to the grove and rally with the neighbor boys, the Sutter brothers, for a day at the lake fishing or fighting. Sometimes he did this whether she was watching or not, but she never told on him. He simply didn't seem to understand what a privilege it was to go to school. Herman did. Herman brought books home from school for her. He shared with her everything he learned. It was Herman who had taught her to read. Liesel'd been reading so long, she had no memory of not reading. Often she wondered what would happen if she simply kept walking, kept going all the way to the schoolhouse. At the end of the driveway, she could see the other country kids skipping down the road with their books in hand. She saw many, many girls but none up close, and she always ran back to the house so that they could not see her up close either.

Herman Richter and Betty Mathiowetz met officially at the New Germany Turner school, though Herman remembered clearly the first time he'd seen her, years ago in the general store, when she'd had a red lollipop stuck in her mouth. At lunch break each day, Mrs. Lehrer sneaked to the outhouse for a smoke while the children ate their lunches and ran about. Several of the boys hung around the outhouse picking giant foxtails, watching the smoke waft out of the crescent-moon cutout on the door. After school, the boys would collect the smallest bits of paper and tobacco, light them, and smoke the remainders. Luther Richter led this group of rapscallions with his brother Herman close at heel. Herman had only meant to keep an eye on his wandering brother but found the smell of the smoke so intriguing that soon it was he searching high and low for tobacco bits to smoke. Each day, too, the boys scavenged for dead animals. They were ever a curiosity to boys.

Herman, at the height of his pubescence, found a dead robin and thought it an ideal present to leave for Betty. He sneaked into the cloakroom and stretched the bird across her boots. Mrs. Lehrer never allowed boots or shoes in the classroom in the rainy months, and Betty's boots were easy to identify. They were always new, always shiny. She was daughter to Dr. Mathiowetz, after all.

Herman watched from behind the door of the cloakroom. The girl looked at the bird, expecting it to lift its head and fly away. When it didn't, she bent to get a closer look, poked it with her finger, and figured it dead. To Herman's surprise, she picked up the bird by the wing and let the wing stretch out with the weight of the limp body. She turned around but saw no one. She picked up her lunch bucket, stuffed the bird in her apron pocket, and went outside. Herman followed her to the back of the school-house and spied.

"You may as well come out, Herman," she said. "I know you're there."

Herman didn't reveal himself.

"Suit yourself," she said. She set aside her lunch, laid the bird across a large rock, and searched the area for stones to hold down the wings.

"I suppose you thought you'd scare me with a little old dead bird." With the metal fork from her lunch bucket, Betty stabbed a prong into the neck of the bird and pulled down to separate the breast. She pushed aside breast muscle and bone, seeming indifferent to the blood collecting on the stone.

"My daddy's a doctor, you know," she said. "I've seen plenty."

Herman could control his twelve-year-old urges no more. "Can I help?" he asked. Betty didn't even turn to look at him.

"Sure," she said. He knelt on the ground beside her and listened as she pointed out heart, liver, lung, and kidney. Herman decided that he loved Betty.

The plenty that Betty had seen included a night like the one before, but she couldn't bring herself to tell Herman about it. Lester Sutter, the Richters' own neighbor, had rapped on the back door of the Mathiowetz house just after the sun had set. Betty and her father were sitting at the table playing a card game. The doctor opened the door. Betty stacked the cards and set the deck on the table.

"Come help her," said Lester.

"Well, Lester," said the doctor. "Come in, son. What are you doing here?"

Lester didn't come in. "She needs help." Lester rubbed his palm back and forth over his shorn head.

"All right, all right." Dr. Mathiowetz put his hand on Lester's shoulder. "Calm down. Who needs help?"

"Perny needs help," said Lester. "Come help her."

"Perny?" said the doctor. "Your sister needs help?"

"Faster, please," said Lester. He grabbed the doctor's hand and pulled him to the door.

The doctor turned to Betty. "Betty, get my bag. Tell your mother I'm going out for a while."

"I'm coming too," said Betty. She scooted out of her chair and stood.

"No," said the doctor. "You better stay here."

"I'm coming."

The doctor turned back to Lester.

"Lester, where's your pa at?"

Lester shrugged his shoulders. He pulled on the hem of the window curtain.

"All right, Betty," the doctor said. "Put your boots on and grab my bag." He turned back to Lester. "You can ride in my car. We'll drive." Betty expected Lester to be excited about driving in a car, but he didn't express the slightest acknowledgment of the privilege.

Before the doctor left the house, he loaded his small pistol and tucked it into his waistband. Betty had never seen her father do that before.

Betty remembered that in Chicago, her daddy had sneaked down the stairs of their nice home many times in the night to open the back door of their house for raggedy men carrying giant loads. These men always stank of mud and cigarette smoke. Her daddy would point them to the kitchen table, where they would drop the cargo and then stand in the shadows until her daddy licked his finger and pulled several bills from the money clip he kept in his vest pocket. In his vest pocket her daddy also kept his spectacles, and after the men left, he pulled them out, stretched one metal band over his right ear, the other over his left, and peeled back the blanket from the load on the table. Here would be the tight face of a body fresh from a ground-covered coffin. Always, the men her daddy sent away kept the trinkets and jewelry that had been buried with the dead. Betty didn't think much wrong with this, and neither did her daddy, she supposed. Many of the country's wealthiest people lived in Chicago, and Betty imagined that sometimes the takings were quite good. But while she may have been interested in the gold pins hanging on lace collars or satin lapels, the jeweled brooches tucked safely under the grim chins of rich women, the ruby rosaries tangled tightly in saintly hands, and the diamond cuff links cinching the wrists of politicians and packinghouse owners, her daddy was not. The fortune for him dwelled inside the cadavers, in the secrets their livers, hearts, and brains held. The biology, the science of it all, was the treasure. Dr. Mathiowetz honored these bodies and found them fascinating. He had no problem separating a person he had known in life from a body he now studied in death. His knowledge improved the health of the living. He couldn't see how anyone could find dishonor in that. This is how he learned of the relationship between hard drinking and livers. How the degeneration of one organ affected another. How a blood clot to the brain could paralyze a hand, a cheek, or an eye. How all things were connected.

In New Germany, Dr. Mathiowetz ran a well-respected practice, and he couldn't rely on a steady supply of cadavers. He used, instead, animals. And Lester Sutter had proved a worthy finder. His presence at their home wasn't unusual. But tonight, his posture seemed markedly different to Betty. If it was possible for a person like Lester to feel worry, this was what it looked like, she thought.

When they pulled up in front of the Sutter house, Dr. Mathiowetz whispered to Lester, "Keep an eye out, son. I want to know if you see your pa coming, okay?"

Lester agreed and hung in the background near the door of the farmhouse and watched as Betty's father looked over Pernilla Sutter, who lay in a heap on the floor. Betty bent and smoothed back the girl's hair. Betty didn't know Lester's sister but identified the same blond hair, small face, and sharp nose, though Pernilla was some years older than Lester. She was also large in the belly, but not anywhere else. Betty guessed she was having a baby.

"Who did this to her?" Betty asked her daddy.

"Never mind that, Betty. Bring the lantern close."

She pulled the lantern closer to the girl. A great gash cut across her forehead, revealing muscle and white membrane below. The ridge of her nose was swollen, and a purple bruise grew around the periphery of it.

"My word!" said Betty. She put a hand to her mouth.

"No," said her daddy. "You mustn't react that way when you see a wound. You'll frighten the patient. If you want to be a big enough girl to attend me, then you need to be composed. Understand?"

"Yes, Daddy."

She opened the black bag. The doctor grabbed a needle and thin sheep intestine and stitched Pernilla's forehead back together. Betty dabbed at the blood dripping around the wound. When Dr. Mathiowetz was finished, he opened a jar of smelling salts and ran the rim under the nose of Pernilla Sutter.

Pernilla moaned and fluttered her eyelids.

"Shhh," said the doctor. "Be calm now."

Pernilla reached her hand up toward her face and traced her fingers over her wounds.

"Oh," said Betty. "Don't touch."

"Who're you?" said Pernilla. "Get out of here." She tried to sit up but could only turn her head and cover her stomach with her arm. "Get out of here. You're not supposed to be here. Pa'll get you."

"You're safe, Pernilla," said the doctor.

"Lester!" Pernilla screamed. "Get these people out of here." Pernilla Sutter grasped hold of a table, hoisted herself up, and stumbled to a bedroom. She slammed the door behind her. Lester stood in the doorway and said, "Go," to the doctor and Betty. While Dr. Mathiowetz cranked up the car, little Sutter heads peeked out from all the windows of the house. Betty waved, but no one waved back. When the car finally jolted alive and took off, the Sutter children ventured from the house and down the porch steps. Even in the dark, Betty could see their black shapes creeping down the driveway.

On the ride home, Betty snuggled close to her daddy. He was always warm, and the closer she was, the better she could hear his leather gloves rub against the steering wheel. She loved that sound.

"Daddy," she said. "Why was that girl so mean when you were helping her?"

"It's complicated, child."

Betty hooked and unhooked the clasp on his doctor bag. "I didn't think it was very nice of her to yell at us that way," she said.

"You shouldn't judge a person in pain too harshly. Remember that. In the same way a hurt animal will lash out, a hurt human will too."

"Maybe, but it still wasn't very nice. Will she be all right, though? And her baby? She is having a baby, isn't she?"

"Yes, Betty. She'll be fine for now. And she's a strong girl. Her baby will probably be born in a couple more months."

"Does that girl have a husband, Daddy?"

"No, Betty. I don't think so."

"Then how'd she get a baby?"

"Close your eyes now. It's late."

She closed her eyes and leaned against her daddy's arm.

"What's wrong with Lester?" she asked. "Is he crazy?"

"No, I don't think so."

"Why does he talk so funny and slow then?"

74

"What Harald Sutter has done to those children is a tragedy and should be a crime, Betty."

"What's he do to them?"

"He beats them. He uses his fists and whatever else he can get his hands on and hits them."

"Like a spanking?"

"No. Not like a spanking. He's damaged Lester. Do you understand?"

"I think so. But why doesn't somebody stop him?"

Dr. Mathiowetz put an arm around his daughter and pulled her close to his side. "It's complicated, Betty. People have trouble discerning when it's important to intervene in the private lives of their neighbors and when it's not."

Betty allowed Herman Richter to carry her books home, even though it was out of the way for him. He was polite to her father, said, "Good day," and shook his hand like a man. Her father asked after his mother, brothers, and sister. Herman said they were well.

"I didn't know you even had a sister," said Betty.

"I do," said Herman. "Liesel."

"Why doesn't she come to school?" asked Betty.

"Mother says for her not to."

"That's dumb," said Betty. Betty thought girls ought to go to school too. Perhaps she should intervene.

"It is not dumb," said Herman. "Liesel's job is to help Mother at home and learn about running a home. That's school too."

Betty thought maybe Herman was right.

"Plus I teach her everything anyway," added Herman. "I taught her to read when she was just little."

Betty walked a little closer to him. She thought about all she'd learned at home from her daddy. He could probably teach her everything she needed to know. He was so smart. Maybe Liesel's mother was smart too.

10

WHEN THE BIRTHING PAINS bent Magdalena for that fifth and last time on a late summer night, she cried out, and Liesel woke.

The large eyes of a barn owl perched on the branch of a black walnut tree stared through the window of Liesel's bedroom. And though she was young, she was unafraid and stared back. Her parents were downstairs talking.

"Is something wrong?" said Wilhelm.

"Close that door!" hissed Magdalena.

Wilhelm opened it farther. "I'm getting Frieda," said Wilhelm.

"Devil take you if you do," said Magdalena. She wouldn't have her sister near her anymore. Frieda had attended at the births of Benjamin and Herman, as Maggie had refused to be seen in the great-with-child state by anyone else, even a doctor or a midwife. "She wasn't this modest in Germany," Frieda had said, laughing, to Wilhelm when Maggie's time to deliver Luther drew near. Wilhelm had laughed too and understood Frieda's comment as a silly joke, but Magdalena had determined not to trust her sister with anything ever again. She threw Frieda out of the house. Frieda, she decided, didn't know how to keep her mouth shut. And so she'd delivered Luther and Liesel herself and would now deliver this one without her sister's help, without anyone's help. Also, she feared what she might be birthing this time. Her children seemed to get progressively worse. Benjamin was fine. Herman was fine, if a little righteous. She often felt the urge to twist his ear. Luther was a glory to look at but had the head of a devil, as naughty a child as she'd ever seen. He was beyond her control entirely. She just had to be sure to keep matches and knives out of his reach lest he burn down the house or stab out the eye of Herman, whom Luther could not stop tormenting no matter how many spankings or belt whippings she delivered to him. Oh, Christ. And then Liesel. An honest-to-goodness child with the body of a beast. Who knew what would come next? Perhaps she'd lie in this bed and give birth to the Fallen Angel himself, red, scaled, and with a spiky tail. She'd not be one bit surprised.

"Wake Liesel and get to bed," Maggie said to Wilhelm.

Magdalena's panting twisted up the stairs to Liesel's room.

Liesel pushed the blanket from herself and stood in the dark. She kept her eyes on the owl and stepped backward toward the door. Then she padded down the hall and to the stairs. At the bottom, her father stood with a foot on the first stair, as if considering something grave. His hand was poised on the banister.

"I'm here, Papa."

"Your mother is calling for you."

"Yes. I heard. Go to bed, Papa."

"You're a good girl, Liesel."

"Yes, Papa. Good night."

"Good night then."

Father and daughter passed each other on the stairs. He reached out a palm and placed it on her head. "A good girl," he whispered. He continued up the stairs and opened the door to Luther's room, vacant in summer when Luther slept in the hay barn to escape the heat of the house. Wilhelm Richter crawled onto the soft mattress. He felt guilty about his dirty shirt and trousers and about not being useful to his wife and daughter during this time, but these things were best left to Magdalena, who'd cauterized the wounds of her sons, set the broken leg of her husband, and delivered herself twice. And this birth would be no different, though almost a decade had passed since the last child. Such were the ways of his wife. And sleep took him the way it takes a farming man. He slept sound, knowing that his seed was fertile, that his wife was strong, that all his sons rested hard, worn through by work and the hot sun of the day, and that throughout the years he'd multiplied his acres threefold. In the end, he'd have enough land to supply each of his sons with a farm and livelihood of his own.

In Magdalena's bedroom, Liesel crawled onto the bed between her mother's massive thighs. Blood, urine, and defecation soiled the sheet, but Liesel did not cringe. She looked at her mother's naked body and saw what there was to see. Liesel was confused.

"Mother?"

"Liesel," she said. "We don't have time for that now. You have to cut me."

Liesel took her papa's hunting knife from her mother's hand.

"Be quick or it'll die in me."

"All right, Mother. I can see the feet."

Magdalena bent as far forward as she could and helped Liesel guide the tip of the knife to soft tissue. With a groan on the swell of the next contraction, she whispered to Liesel, "Now."

Liesel took the knife and slit the skin from below the baby's foot to her mother's bottom, the way that she had learned to separate the wing from a fryer chicken. It was a clean cut, Liesel saw as her mother arched her neck, hit the pillow, and bit on her bottom lip. She saw her mother's eyes fill and red stars appear where capillaries broke from the strain and pain and power of her body. She could not see how her mother's heart pumped, how the arteries were overwhelmed with the pure volume of blood she forced through them. All through the body, little explosions took place. A burst in the leg, one in her chest, dozens in her face, and two near her brain. With each push, Magdalena grabbed the hair on her own head and yanked. Sweaty strands of brown hair clung to the pillow and around Magdalena's hand.

Liesel kept her eyes on the task at hand. She had many questions but knew it was not the time to ask and wasn't sure if a time for such questions even existed. A great weight settled on her shoulders in those minutes. Tears came, and she whimpered. Magdalena focused on her daughter for a brief moment, enough time to say, "No, Liesel. Never cry for yourself. You've been dealt a lonely lot, but never cry. Resign yourself to being alone and being strong."

"No crying," repeated Liesel.

Magdalena's mind cracked with thoughts and eruptions. In a moment, she was fifteen years in the past, watching her younger self lean back to welcome that first boy into her body. In another instant, she stood on the deck of a boat, then heard herself marry Wilhelm Richter, then gave birth to Benjamin, to Herman, and to Luther. On the birth of Liesel, her mind lingered. Another contraction brought her back to the toil of delivering the fifth, and a thought of gratitude toward Liesel sputtered in Magdalena's brain even though she would never articulate this sentiment to her daughter. She had raised Liesel not to need such words.

Liesel leaned forward and peered over the ocean of her mother to see her face. Magdalena's mouth hung open, leaked blood and bile down her cheek to her chin. Her eyes stared at the ceiling.

"Mama?"

Her mother gurgled and waved a hand. "Get it out."

Liesel pressed her fingers around the small, slippery feet and pulled. She tugged against the suction of her mother's stubborn womb. And onto the filthy sheet she pulled a little boy, her brother.

"Mother, I've got him."

Liesel used her hands to massage life into the baby. The baby squawked and pinkened some, though his body had a yellow glow.

A whisper: "Cut the cord, Liesel."

"Yes, I'll cut it."

She put the baby aside, near her mother's foot, and knifed through the purple cord connecting her brother to the inside of her mother. Magdalena took a full breath, the kind of breath the dying take before the last. Liesel wiped the baby and wrapped him in a towel. She crawled off the bed and leaned over it to place the boy on her mother's belly.

"Here he is."

"Another boy," Magdalena said. Broken vessels reddened her eyes. "Four sons and you." She handed the newborn back to Liesel and then palmed Liesel's cheek. "Bury me with my cameo."

Liesel nodded. She had seen her mother holding it, cleaning it, and then wrapping it back inside a white handkerchief, but she had never seen her mother wear it. Not once.

"Yes," Liesel said.

Magdalena, on a wave of pain and relief, was taken back again to another time, to her favorite time. She heard her lover of years before declare his love. She remembered how he said those words over and over. She remembered tangling her fingers in his hair. That time seemed so close to this time. When was that? Last year? Yesterday? She turned to her daughter. Time was disappearing. Liesel was in this time. She must tell her some things before the time was gone.

"You've been a good child to me, Liesel. I'll watch over you from wherever I am." It was the best she could do.

Liesel stood alongside her mother until she died. When the last breath was expelled and the chest no longer rose but was still and quiet, Liesel touched the back of her hand to her mother's cool, wet forehead. She yanked her hand back. Liesel reached out to touch the forehead again and this time let the warmth of her own hand heat the skin on her mother's brow. Then she set the baby in the cradle and cleaned her mother. Liesel looked at her mother and studied what a woman was supposed to be. And here, at this time and place, after almost ten years of life, Liesel finally understood many things about herself and about her mother's distance and strange sentiments toward her. She understood why her mother had told her to resign herself to loneliness. And while not even the mess of birth or the tragedy of death had made Liesel sick, this understanding about her own body wrangled in her stomach until a rotten waste climbed into her mouth. "Oh God," she said. She opened the window to get the death stench out, and she allowed herself a few minutes of feeling sick.

But then there was the work to do, and Liesel tended to it. She lit every lantern in the house but didn't wake her papa or brothers. She dressed her mother and pinned the cameo onto her dress. She kissed the forehead and whispered, "I love you," into the pale, dead ear. When finished, she rocked the baby, wide awake with yellow in the whites of his eyes, and then she fell asleep until dawn, when her father's wailing woke her.

II

LUTHER RICHTER FIDGETED in the straw of the hay barn in an unusually restless sleep on the night of his mother's death, his brother's birth, his sister's discovery. A nightmare had a hold of him. He dreamed a form emerged from the dark, scattering millions of mice as it descended upon him. He could not move. The form, languid as morning fog, hovered above him. Though at first barely air, it morphed into a ghost and then a woman who mounted him and began to move. She smelled of decaying flowers. In his dream, she lifted Luther's arm and pressed his hand between her breasts. He found no flutter of heart. And then he was free to move but did not want to unbind himself from her. In the space that links sleep and dream, Luther held her thighs and pushed himself deep. When he arched his back and released into her, she smiled and pulled at his chest. She stood, and she was so tall he could not see her face. Filth dripped down her legs and onto his belly. Then she bent and breathed decay into his face. Her tongue was thin as a snake's, her teeth sharp as a wolf's.

I will make you strong, the woman whispered. Her voice

sounded hollow, yet booming. *I will make rocks of your fists and boulders of your arms. Your back will be stiff as oak.*

At the sound of Luther's father's screaming, the owls in the hayloft stretched their wings, took flight, and left the barn through a large window facing the Richter house, where lanterns burned in almost every room. The sun climbed in the eastern sky, sending long shadows over the yard. Luther awoke.

"Hell's bells," he said. He looked around him, found his crumpled shirt, and pulled it over his arms. He climbed down from the loft and walked to the house, where he found his sister holding a newborn, Benjamin crying into his hands, Herman laying strands of bacon in a fry pan, and his father in the bedroom spilled over the blue, still body of his mother.

"What's this?" Luther asked.

"You'll need to get a stone for the marker," Liesel said to him.

"What's that?" Luther pointed to the bundle in her arms.

"Boy, best I can tell."

"Best you can tell?" said Luther. "If he is anything like me, there should be no confusion." He looked to his brothers for jovial reassurance but found none.

Benjamin lifted his head from his hands. "Is that any way to talk in front of our dead mother?" he said. He stood and walked to his mother's bedroom. He took Wilhelm's place at her side. The Richters weren't much for religion, but Benjamin put his palms together and prayed. Wilhelm walked past his children and out the door.

"I guess not," Luther said. "But why is she always speaking so strange?" Luther tilted his head toward Liesel. "Liesel," he said. "You are a strange girl."

She clutched the baby against her chest and stared into his tiny face.

"Yes," she said to no one in particular. "I know that now."

"See?" said Luther. "See what I mean?"

Herman turned down the flame on the stove and lifted the fry pan. "That's enough now," he said to his siblings. "Luther, shut your mouth for once. Come have some breakfast. It'll be a long day."

"Pa can have mine," said Liesel. The baby mewed and she stuck her finger into his mouth to quiet him. "He'll need milk from the store," she said.

"I'll eat hers," said Luther.

"Well, here it is then," said Herman. "I imagine Pa has no appetite either." He slid the bacon onto a tin plate for Luther.

After breakfast, Luther and Herman drove the wagon to town and stopped at their aunt Frieda's place to tell her the news. Frieda walked with the boys to the general store and collected what was needed to feed the newborn and said she'd be out later to help with the burial, though she never came. The boys stopped at the shop of the photographer and arranged to have him take the funeral photograph. They stopped at the undertaker's and bought a coffin. On the way home, Herman and Luther halted the horses along Spider Lake, and Luther hopped down from the wagon and ran to a boulder the size of a big dog.

"This is the one," he said to Herman.

"Leave that be. It's too big. We'll never get it in."

"No. It's perfect. See the nice flat face here for the engraving?" Luther patted the smooth side of it. "I'll get it. Just you watch."

Luther removed his shirt. The sun celebrated his chest. Herman spit onto the ground. Luther smiled. His brother was jealous. He walked to the boulder, bent, and wrapped his arms around it. Luther Richter sucked in air and felt a surge of energy course through him. He straightened his legs with little effort and stood there in the day's sun with the boulder resting securely against his body. He walked easy and tall to the wagon and dropped the rock in the back.

"Jesus Christ," said Herman. "You're going to wreck the coffin."

"Told you I'd get it."

"Get in," said Herman. "Giddap," he clucked to the horses before Luther was in.

Once home, Luther yelled, "Catch," to Herman and slung the rock from the wagon. Herman quickly stepped to the side, and the boulder landed in a grand humph of dust in the very place he'd been standing. Benjamin set to work chipping their mother's name into it. Herman and Luther carried the simple wood coffin into the kitchen. Luther grabbed his bat and walked out to the walnut trees. He picked up the green nuts, threw them into the air, and smashed them with the bat. For three days afterward, the sour smell of smashed walnuts clung to the air. Herman brought in the milk, which Liesel promptly poured into a bottle and stuck in the mouth of the baby. Wilhelm lay next to his wife's corpse in the bed where she'd died. After feeding the baby, Liesel stepped to the foot of the bed where her parents lay, touched the boot of her quietly crying father, told him the grave needed digging, and then tugged the baby's cradle up the stairs and placed it next to her own bed. There in her room, she peered through the window at her brothers below. Benjamin sat under the tree and pounded the chisel into the rock. Herman stood behind him, directing his work. Her papa broke a shovel into the black soil beneath the trees. Though sobbing, he threw giant, solid soil heaps aside.

Liesel took the baby from the cradle and laid him on the bed beside her. "Quiet now, baby," she said.

She unwrapped the blanket and lifted the baby dress. She unpinned the diaper and studied all the baby's parts. The umbilical cord curled against the boy's small belly, and below it, the boy's small penis lay. She picked up the tiny thing and looked beneath it to find what seemed to her a swollen bag.

Certainly she herself looked nothing like this. And certainly she looked nothing like what she'd seen between her mother's legs last night. "It's been a strange day, little baby."

She rewrapped the baby and placed him in the cradle. She

thought of all the names in the world to call him. She settled on Otto, the name of her papa's father, and tested it on the baby.

"Otto?" she said.

The boy's yellow eyes blinked back at her for just a moment before closing to sleep again. Before long, a black wagon pulled by a black horse rambled up to the house. The photographer hopped down from his seat and went to shake hands with Wilhelm. Wilhelm motioned him into the house. Herman called for Benjamin and Luther. They helped the photographer carry his instruments into the house. Liesel straightened her hair and went downstairs. She'd never had her photograph taken before and wondered what it would be like. Would it hurt? Would the photograph last forever? Who would see it?

The photographer under the black curtain wonders if he's ever tried to take so strange a funeral photo. He's been commissioned to take plenty of these final images and usually has no trouble with Norwegians and Germans, as both are stoic types. If the family were Irish, say, he would have prepared himself for a more expressive event. But this Richter family truly takes the cake. The coffin holding a fat woman rests on the floor. She's been stuffed into a dress much too small for her. The grieving husband sits on a stool in front of the coffin. He keeps asking, "But who will milk the cows?" He's still holding the shovel that dug her grave and refuses to give it up. Mud clumps lie at his feet. Three young men stand all around. The one with curly brown hair holds his head in his hands and won't look up. Blood has dried between the cracks of his fingers and on his wrists. He's been arguing with his tallest brother over a cameo. Apparently, the curly-haired one took it and won't put it back on the dead woman. The photographer raises his hand and asks, "Shall I come back later?" "No" is the answer from the tallest son. The tallest son, a jittery boy in a suit and tie who has the beginnings of whiskers darkening his lip, berates his curly-haired brother one more time, then turns his attention to his other brother, a bare-chested young man who wants to stand with one foot on the cover of his dead mother's box. That boy is strong and handsome. He has long blond hair and grins shamelessly. "Shoot the photograph. Shoot the photograph," he says as he poses in different positions. And a girl clings to a baby just hours old. She pays no attention to her brothers or her father. She stands with a straight back, making her look older than she must be. Her face is plain but pleasant to look at. She has large eyes and straight brown hair falling all the way to her waist. She hasn't been crying but looks so sad the photographer wishes he could gather her up and hold her. But she has a quality about her that warns him not to touch. He counts to three and squeezes the bulb.

12

New Germany, Minnesota, June 1914

B Y THE TIME Wilhelm Richter opens Liesel's bedroom door, Otto, nested in a cradle beside her bed, is already wide-eyed and reaching. He's been awake, but quiet, for hours. Wilhelm lifts the hefty boy.

"Shhh," he says. "Quiet. We mustn't wake your sister."

The boy mimics his father, puts a finger to his lips. After a year, his yellow eyes have softened to a buttery color. Wilhelm pulls a blanket up around Liesel's shoulders, then tiptoes out of the room.

Each morning he does this: brings little Otto to edge of the wood where they laid his wife last year in the grave he dug, where Luther hauled a large granite field rock, and where Benjamin spent days chipping her name and *Geschätzt Mutter* into the smoothest face of it. The peony bush that Liesel planted dangles, heavy with pink flowers large as melons. Wilhelm sets his son on the ground before the granite stone and tells him to say, *"Guten Morgen, Mutter."* On this day, Otto repeats, *"Gut ma."* And while the boy pulls dandelions and foxtails and shoves them into his mouth, Wilhelm talks to Magdalena. He has always been a great talker, and, since Magdalena never really was one for talking but more for listening, he finds comfort in speaking to her and keeping up that old routine. Today he will tell her about the new land he'll buy in Benjamin's name that afternoon, how cheaply the plot is going after the bank foreclosed on Sutter's west forty, how each son will have a farm of his own someday. He'll tell Maggie about his German investments. He'll tell her again that he's sorry for not telling her before. He'll say he shouldn't have been so hard and so secretive. But it's such a complicated matter. He hardly knew where to start. But he should have told her. He shouldn't have been rough with her. Husbands and wives ought not to treat each other in such a way. He'll tell Magdalena how strong the boys grow. How Benjamin shaves regularly, shows promise with figures. How he's been walking a nice girl, the marrying kind, home from school every day. How he comes home with rolls or cakes from the girl's family's bakery and that she's fattening him up. That Herman stands tall as himself and is far more stubborn but reads every German and English newspaper available, reads books, talks politics and religion, but doesn't show much interest in physical labor or farming. How he fancies himself a Teddy Roosevelt on horseback, shooting up anyone who dares challenge the great United States of America. How he too has a nice little girlfriend, Betty, a doctor's daughter, no less. How Luther has a strong batting average and an even stronger back. How handsome he is. How every girl from one end of town to the other wants him to carry her books. But good Lord, what a mouth on that boy! How little Otto is walking and getting into every nook and cranny of the house and keeping Liesel busy with his care. Wilhelm talks of her some. There's not much to say. Liesel's a good girl, he says. Takes proper care of the boys and me. She'll make some man a fine wife. That's what good a woman is, he says. When the time comes, I'll have to find a good match for her.

Someone industrious and hard-working. Someone not interested only in her name and the money and land that come with it. A good German boy from a solid family.

Most mornings, Magdalena is there, listening. Even in this new existence, she has affection for Wilhelm. But today, she is not there. Today, she sits miles away, more than an ocean away, on the window ledge of a German bank office where the man she loves, even in death, looks over papers and figures. Despite his family's best arranging efforts, despite his mother's handwringing and pleading, he's never married and has fathered no other children. Magdalena tries to touch this man, wishes to manage something as simple as steaming the glass of his spectacles, at which he might look around the room, might somehow see her sitting at the opened window today. Some days, this banker wonders if he feels her hand, and he places his own palm where hers seems to be. Times like these, he gets that old desire to paint again.

Some days, Wilhelm is sure he feels Magdalena's hand too. But it's never been her, only the wind or a flying bug or his vast imagination. He picks up his boy again and faces the field where the oats flicker green and in the distance the sun reflects gold off Spider Lake. He thinks that his dead wife must like this view and that all is right with the world.

13

ALL IS NOT RIGHT with the world.

On a day in late June of 1914, the royal driver turns onto a wrong avenue in Sarajevo, Bosnia. He is unfamiliar with the city. In the back seat of the open-air car, the Austrian archduke and duchess wave goodbyes to onlookers on the Sarajevo sidewalk.

A shot from the crowd springs a small bloody hole in the archduke's neck. *For heaven's sake,* the duchess cries and cups his chin in her palm. She looks into the crowd. For what, she doesn't know. Onlookers duck. It doesn't occur to her to duck. She looks at her husband again. *What has happened to you?* she asks. *It is nothing,* he says. *It is nothing.* A young Serb, standing only a few paces from the car, raises a pistol again and fires. The duchess falls forward, folds over her pregnant womb. *Sophie, dear,* her husband chokes. *Sophie, dear. Don't die.*

But both are dead before the driver reaches the hospital. It is 11:30 A.M. By noon, news of the assassinations taps over wires in Austro-Hungarian and German cities. Before the sun sets, the

Austro-Hungarian government calls upon its ally Germany. Serbia calls upon Russia.

Leaders of the world's nations, alerted to the death of Franz Ferdinand, the Austrian archduke, unroll maps over large desks. There is much to be gained and lost. In three different countries, three cousins — Kaiser Wilhelm II of Germany, Czar Nicholas II of Russia, and King George V of Britain — puff on cigars and drop ashes on the map borders.

Send a telegraph to my cousin, says the kaiser. *Tell him to stay out of Serbia.*

Send a telegraph to my cousin, says the czar. *Tell him to stay out of Serbia.*

King George rereads the stipulations of the Triple Entente, a treaty his father negotiated, and throws back the last finger of his scotch. He sends telegraphs to both his cousins: *For God's sake, stay out of Serbia.*

Each of the cousins instead calls upon alliances with other nations and brings down upon the world a war of trenches, of disease, of chemicals, of every means of death by warfare that the brightest of man's kind can conceive. For four years, battles will explode over the eastern half of the globe.

And for most of that time, America will watch. And she'll wait. Her citizens read newspapers and listen to radio programs and gather at the post offices and saloons for any news from the old country. In these years, America grows rich off munitions sales to Russia, Germany, and Britain. She grows rich off British war investments on Wall Street. President Woodrow Wilson says he's dedicated to neutrality, but the war feels very close to those with relatives in Europe. The German-Americans of New Germany pull their sons near, champion a pacifist stance.

In the coming months, Wilhelm Richter will watch over his oldest sons, Benjamin and Herman and Luther, as they harvest a bumper crop of oats from the new plot. He will stand before

Magdalena's grave and vow to her that their sons will never wear military uniforms, that war is a million miles away. He did not work this hard to lose sons to war.

At the *Deutsche Chronik,* the telegraph taps incessantly with new developments in the battles overseas. Archie and Frieda Richter turn their weekly newspaper into a daily and their front office into a sort of coffeehouse where the German residents of New Germany come each morning to talk of news from home. Many, many of them have nephews, brothers, and cousins in the army there. Archie and Wilhelm's own relatives have been sent to the frontlines to fight with the kaiser for Germany. The letters from the Richters of Germany pour into New Germany for the cousins, who feel helpless to do anything except to ensure that these sons of New Germany don't take up arms against their relatives. In the paper, Archie runs stories from the boys back in Germany. Frieda prints poems. In her mind, the poets of a place and time tell the truest tales. Wilhelm sips his coffee and pages through the paper.

Archie scans other local newspapers for stories he ought to pick up for the *Deutsche Chronik.* "The *Minneapolis Monitor* reports that Canada is taking American boys for its army," says Archie.

"They do not have enough Canadians to fight?" asks Wilhelm. He laughs at the idea.

"I believe they think it is going to be a long fight," says Archie.

"I don't think so," says Wilhelm. He takes a deep breath. "It will be over soon."

"I hope you're right," says Archie. "But I believe it will get a lot worse before it gets better."

"Perhaps," says Wilhelm. "But it's not our affair. America will stay out of it. She is friendly with Germany. And we did not start this, after all."

"We?" says Archie. "Careful, Wilhelm. Our loyalties will be challenged soon enough."

A few months later, Harald Sutter, neighbor to Wilhelm Richter, loads three of his boys in the wagon and drives toward Mankato. His son Lester waves to the Richter boys harvesting in the field.

"Stop that, you idiot," says Sutter. "What you have there is a pack of thieving, murdering Germans. Can't hardly speak English even."

Lester pulls his hand down and puts both his hands beneath his thighs. He sits on them to keep them still. Sutter shouts at Richter's sons, "Hop in, you cowards. Hop in if you have an ounce of courage in you."

Lester's hands become free. He claps and yells, "Hop in," then puts his hands in his pockets and fumbles with himself until he falls asleep to the clop of hooves. Four hours pass before Sutter stops at the train station where Canadian officers wait to recruit American boys into the army. When war called England, it called Canada too. And Canada's recruitment list spread beyond its own borders. For weeks, Canadian officers had been in Mankato coercing Minnesota boys to enlist. Some enlisted because they believed in the cause. Some for adventure. Some because they had nowhere else to go in life.

"Out," Sutter says to his boys. "Get your name on the list. Go see the world."

"But Pa," begins one of the boys.

"Can't afford to feed you forever," says Sutter.

Sutter hops down and pulls the boys from the wagon. He shoves the trio to the recruiter. The first two boys mumble their names, ages, and health status to an officer with a clipboard. They climb aboard the platform. Sutter pushes Lester toward the platform too.

"Hold up," says one of the officers. "You." He points to Lester. "What's your name?"

"His name's Lester," says Sutter.

"Name's Lester," says Lester. He nods his head but looks to the ground.

"How old are you, Lester?" asks the officer. He moves himself between the father and son.

"He's about twenty-five," says Sutter to the officer's back.

"Yep. About twenty-five or forty maybe," says Lester. He pouts his lips and stuffs his hands back in his pockets. He rocks back and forth.

"Quiet, boy," says Sutter. The officer studies Lester, who returns the gaze with an enormous grin, black holes where teeth should be and swollen red gums making him look clownish. The officer turns to face Sutter.

"He's too old, I'm afraid," he says to Sutter.

"Not too old to grab a gun and shoot the Huns," says Sutter. The officer holds Sutter's eyes until he looks away.

"Sir, take this boy home." The officer points to Sutter's other sons. "These two are fine, and the British Empire thanks you for volunteering them. You can rest assured that they'll be well —"

"Lester here's good too," Sutter says. "You take him."

"Too old," the officer says again, "*and* not right. Now I'll thank you to take him home."

"I'll thank you to take me home," Lester says.

The officer tips his hat and moves to the string of enlistees gathering at the station. Harald Sutter grabs Lester by the elbow and leads him back to the wagon. "You damn idiot," he says. "If your mama had cared what a damn idiot she'd spawned, she'd have taken you to the grave with her."

"Yep." Lester nods his head. "Mama got dead and bloody on the kitchen floor."

"Shut up, you stupid bastard, or that's the way you'll end up," says Sutter.

When Sutter gets the boy home, he delivers unto Lester a belt beating that raises red welts over his back and neck. When Sutter exhausts himself, he waves his arms and tells the boy to scat. Lester wanders down the gravel road, muttering "damn idiot" in the direction of his pa. "Damn idiot, damn idiot, damn idiot," getting louder the more distance he puts between them. Lester thinks to go find the boys he saw in the field earlier in the day, but it's gotten dark and he finds no one. So instead he crosses the harvested field and goes through the oak grove of the Richters' farm. There he rests beside a large granite stone and a peony bush, stuffs his hands into his pockets again, and listens to the distant lapping of waves until a girl leading a small boy by one hand and holding a bucket heaped full of potato peelings and bones with the other sends her shadow over Lester's legs.

"Go on, you," she yells. "You get away from there." Lester can't understand a word she says but recognizes the speech as the same as that of his German neighbors. "Go on," the girl says again, this time in English.

Two days later, he traps a snapping turtle in Spider Lake, guts it, and leaves the carcass and the shell in a burlap sack next to the large stone. He hides for several hours behind a tree in the grove and watches as she finds it, unties the string of the burlap sack, and peeks inside. Liesel cinches tight the top again and looks around. Lester tries to make himself as thin as possible behind the tree.

"It's for eatin," he shouts. Blackbirds take flight from the trees.

Liesel is startled. She looks up to where the voice came from and sees the turtle catcher hiding behind the tree. She takes a deep breath and smiles. Lester's so nervous, he wets himself and stuffs his fist into his mouth. When finally he gathers courage enough to peek out from behind the tree, he sees the girl walking away, swinging the bag at her side.

That night she throws the carcass in a pot with potatoes and onions and gives the shell and a stick for drumming on it to Otto.

"Good stew," Benjamin says.

"Tastes funny," says Luther.

"You're a fool," says Liesel. Even Otto stops chewing to look at his sister.

Wilhelm considers scolding her but too long a time passes before anything sensible to say comes to his mind. His brain these days is full of war thoughts, thoughts of land and legacy.

And though Liesel can't know why and can't see him, she knows that the turtle catcher sits at the edge of the grove, alongside the stone, and will stay there and wait until she comes, after the boys sleep deep and when the moon is hot.

14

As Liesel grew out of girlhood and lumbered into womanhood, a pair of knobby breasts knocking against her chest and coarse hair sprouting under her arms, she did so without a mother or friend. Of course, she had her brothers, but Benjamin was quiet, Herman was sullen, Luther a brute, and Otto just a boy. Her aunt Frieda rarely appeared. Liesel saw the schoolteacher, Mrs. Lehrer, once or twice when she came to chase Luther back to school after his long and recurrent absences. Both women were kind, but each made Liesel nervous and shy. She was afraid that other women would be able to sense, if not see, what set her apart from their kind. She'd witnessed among her brothers how boys could sniff out the coward among them and make him a fool, and she suspected that women had a similar sense.

She had learned all she knew about being a woman from what she remembered of her dead mother and from what little her instincts told her. She lived her days as ordinarily as she thought women did. She took care of Otto. She washed clothes. She milked cows. She tended the garden. She cooked. She mended clothes. She tried to be quiet and not attract attention.

Her mind, though, was on a different sort of journey. Since the birth of Otto, Liesel Richter had spent hours and hours in silence and in thought. On her occasional visits, Frieda slipped Wilhelm and the boys books of philosophy, religion, politics, and literature; when Wilhelm visited Archie and Frieda in their home or at the newspaper, she sent books home with him. She'd casually tuck them among baked goods or jars of preserves while the men talked of agriculture and politics. She'd not mention them again or ask for their return. These little gifts of literature were Frieda's way of caring for Magdalena's children after her sister died. Frieda knew some of the citizens of New Germany thought it would have been proper for her to take in those children, especially Liesel and the baby, but Frieda couldn't be tied down by such domestic responsibilities. She had submitted and birthed two children, two boys, for her husband. They were enough work for her and had finally gotten to ages where they didn't need her constant attention. She raised them more as students than as children, as minds to form rather than as babies to cuddle and hold. In Frieda's opinion, men's greatest fault was their need to be nurtured and coddled, and also in her opinion, it was their mothers who had created these ridiculous requirements. She vowed to raise clever men. She would love her sons in a different way than most mothers, and they'd be better for it. Her own life could go on and not be consumed by the needs of her sons the way so many women's lives got eaten up by their children. The life of pregnancy, birthing, and babies was not what she'd left Germany for. She had higher aspirations. And so, providing access to knowledge became how she parented her boys and helped her nephews and niece.

"What's this?" Liesel had asked the first time she pulled two thin books out of a basket filled with hard rolls, marmalade, and a *Schmierkuchen*.

"Your aunt sent them for the boys," said Wilhelm. "Do not worry yourself over them." He took a hard roll, broke it in two, and handed one half to Liesel. "She does not bake as well as your mother, but it is nice of her to remember us."

Liesel took the roll and smiled. She set the books aside for the day, but that night in her room, she opened each one carefully and put it to her nose. She sneezed. In his cot on the floor next to her bed, Otto stirred. She pulled the cover back up over him and climbed onto her bed again. She opened *The Jungle* by Upton Sinclair and listened to the cracking of the binding and stretch of the leather. Late into the night, she was still reading. The book was maddening. The author had made up a story to teach the readers lessons. Why go through all the trouble? Liesel wondered. Why not just give the facts and give them straight? She found herself flipping through the story to find the information. She promised herself that she would never hide truth in stories. She wouldn't tease Otto with fairy tales and nursery rhymes. She would simply teach him the certainties of the world.

When Herman woke to visit the outhouse, he saw candlelight coming from beneath his little sister's door. He opened it slowly and saw her lying on her side with the open book next to her.

"Liesel," he said. "What are you doing?"

"Nothing," she said.

"Give me that," said Herman. He walked into her room. Herman had been the one who'd taught Liesel to read. He'd escaped many farm chores by setting Liesel at the table and teaching her to read and write in both German and English. Tonight, he felt a short bit of pride at finding his sister like this.

"Quiet," she said, and pointed to Otto.

"Give me that," he said again. "I just want to see it."

"You can have it when I'm finished." She reached beneath her bed and pulled out the other book, *American Ideals and Other Essays, Social and Political,* by Theodore Roosevelt. She handed it to him. "You can have this one, but I want it back when you're done," she said.

Herman took it and shone his own lantern on the cover. "Get to bed," he said. He turned to leave her bedroom.

"Herman," Liesel said.

He turned around.

"We're never having canned meat again."

Herman nodded but had no idea what his sister was talking about. Like their mother, Liesel was sometimes apt to say strange things.

In the morning when Wilhelm went to wake Herman for the morning chores, the boy's bed was empty. Liesel poured her papa a cup of coffee and told him to look in the outhouse. And that's where Wilhelm found his son, squat over the hole, leaned against the wood wall, book open across his lap.

Wilhelm didn't mind Benjamin or Herman paging through the books so long as it didn't interfere with their farming chores. He couldn't see the harm in it, and he never minded when he found his girl, Liesel, sitting behind a door or slumped against a tree with a book on her knees, though he couldn't see the use of educating a girl.

Nowhere in all her books did Liesel Richter find an explanation for her condition. She skimmed *The Descent of Man* looking for any clue to the biological likelihood or function of a being such as herself. She skipped the chapters on insects, birds, and mammals. When she found no explanations, she read it again, more carefully this time, fearing that she had skipped an important part. Still she found nothing. On her own, with no one she could confide in or ask to help, she couldn't always make sense of the words. What didn't take any sort of genius to understand was the fact that her condition was abnormal. Liesel was abnormal and ashamed and afraid and alone. More than anything else, she was alone.

After the meal of turtle stew, the dishes, and feeding and bedding Otto, Liesel untied her apron and folded it over a chair. She took her shawl off its hook.

"Where are you going?" Luther said. He sat at the table rolling a cigarette.

"Just out for a walk. It's not your business."

"You sure have become a moody girl," said Luther. "Hasn't she, Herman? Isn't she a moody girl?" He put the cigarette to his lips and lit a match.

"Leave her alone," said Herman. "She has a right to get out of this house every once in a while."

"Woman's place is at home, I always say," said Luther. He inhaled deeply and exhaled.

"I'm just going walking." She opened the screen door. "And Otto's in bed, so you don't have to worry."

"Well, don't let the wild Indians catch and eat you," Luther said.

Herman walked to his brother and pulled the cigarette from his lips. He jammed it into the tabletop.

"I wish one'd find you in your bed and bash your head in," mumbled Herman.

Liesel let the screen door slam behind her and went out to visit her mother's grave, not so much out of sentimentality as out of the desire to escape the incessant bickering of Herman and Luther, as well as a magnetic curiosity about what or who might be there, waiting for her. It was exciting to think that someone in the world might seek her out. Though that night was black, the light from the moon made luminous the stone marker. Resting his humped back against the stone was the turtle catcher. He too was so pale that he seemed to glow. Liesel studied him before she approached. His head was nearly bald, not with old age but because it was shaved to the scalp. He had no mustache or beard. He wore jean overalls and a plain shirt beneath. One of his boots had the tongue hanging out. She decided not to bother about his appearance. She was strange and he was strange.

Liesel stepped forward, and when she was close enough, she stuck out her hand. She cleared her throat.

"I'm Liesel Richter," she said. Her voice was barely a whisper. Lester Sutter thought about her words and let them settle until he could filter through her accent and understand them completely. She misunderstood his long pause as his not hearing her.

"I'm Liesel Richter," she said again, louder.

Finally, her words registered with Lester. He stood and wrapped Liesel's hand in both of his own. He shook it up and down and giggled until she laughed too.

"You're Liesel Richter," he said. "I caught a turtle for you."

"Yes, you did," she said. "Thank you very much, Lester."

They sat there together for only a few minutes that night. Liesel quickly understood that Lester was simple but that he was very kind. She assumed the role of an older sibling or caretaker, the way she did with her brothers even though most of them were older than her by several years, as was Lester. She sat near him. She explained to Lester that her mother was buried here and that her mother had loved her very much when she was alive. Lester told Liesel that his mother was buried in the granary. Liesel asked Lester when his mother had died and he said a long time ago on the floor. She said, "It's hard not having a mother, isn't it?"

"For some," said Lester.

Liesel was quiet at this. She thought about it and determined it was true. Not having Mother was hard for her, and for Benjamin and Papa, but it really didn't seem that hard for Luther or Herman or even Otto, who had no memories of his mother and whose only image of her was from the photograph taken at her funeral.

So on this very first night together, Liesel learned that between bouts of nonsense, Lester Sutter somehow tapped into great truth and spoke it plainly.

"Well," she said. "I better get back in the house or my brothers will come looking for me."

"Like Pa has to find Perny and the dancing boys?"

Liesel wanted to laugh but didn't. Lester was being serious. Benjamin, Herman, and Luther all had stories of their dalliances with Pernilla Sutter.

"Then you understand," she said.

Lester used Magdalena's marker to help himself up and walked into the woods and was out of sight in seconds.

"Goodbye, Lester," Liesel called after him.

"Bye, Liesel," he said. "You're pretty."

As Liesel walked across the yard, Luther flung open the barn's loft door and shouted, "Whoo-hoo, Liesel's got a suitor." Liesel ignored him, tiptoed up the porch stairs, and gently opened the screen door. All was quiet in the Richter house. Wilhelm and the boys generally read quietly in their rooms each night. Luther had retired to his cot in the hay barn. Liesel knew, though, he often did not stay in there, that he took off toward the lake or toward town and didn't come back sometimes until dawn. She also knew that sometimes Pernilla Sutter stayed in the barn with him, that Luther organized card and gambling games in his loft, and that his foul morning mood was often the result of a hangover.

In her own room, Otto snored lightly on his nest next to her bed. Liesel reached under her bed and pulled out a book from Frieda, *A Young Lady's Guide to Womanhood*. In this book were all the things young women needed to know about their bodies and their feelings toward boys. Liesel's curiosity about such matters was practically taking over her brain these days, so she read this book cover to cover without skipping one word, even though her head throbbed from running her eyes over the pages. In her mind, there was something very unnatural about reading. Information was a thing to be shared, she believed. But why was reading the way to share it? Reading required quiet and solitude. And by the very act of creating a quiet and isolated place to read, people removed themselves from other people, other people's thoughts, and the possibility of sharing anything. Right? School, it seemed to her, must be the place to share information.

Every fall morning, she watched her brothers pack up and head off to the New Germany Turner school. They came back full of their tales and antics, and sometimes she wished she could go too. She wondered what other boys looked like close up. She wondered if they behaved like her brothers. She thought about what type of qualities she preferred in boys. If she could pick, she'd choose a boy who was quiet and sensitive like Benjamin, but smart like Herman. He'd have to be strong like Luther and sweet like Otto. But none of this could be possible for her. Could it? What kind of a man would want a deformed wife?

Lester Sutter was quiet and sensitive. He was smart in his own way. He was very strong and was sweet enough. He was also lonely, like she was. Maybe, she thought. Maybe this could work.

Liesel opened her book and read.

15

Each summer morning, Liesel pitched a collection of bones, fat, and lard beneath the tree where the cats sat cleaning themselves on too-sunny days. Then she took Otto's diapers and hung them from the branch to dry.

"You're too big for these," she said to him. She took her little brother by the hand and led him to the garden, where she spread a blanket on the grass. She picked her little brother up, and his dangling feet reached her knees. Up and down her thigh were bruises from the boy's kicking legs. She plopped him on the blanket.

"Stay put now," she said. She pulled three tiny wooden horses made by Benjamin from her apron pocket and tossed them between Otto's chubby legs.

The heaviest and reddest tomatoes submitted to Liesel's hand and released from their vines easily. She set them next to her little brother. She figured he'd soon fall asleep. He was a good napper.

"Keep away from those, Otto," she barked when he crawled toward the swollen globes. She'd been short with him all day. He looked up at her with wide eyes and put his dirty fingers in his mouth.

"Stop that," she yelled. "Germs." The boy pulled his fingers from his mouth, and tears sparkled in his eyes.

She picked up the smallest tomato and handed it to him. "Here you go," she said softly. "You can have this one." Otto took the tomato, but kept his eyes on Liesel.

"Go on," she said. "It's all right."

He bit into it, and strands of juice ran down both sides of his mouth onto the collar of the shirt she had made for him. There were few leftover shirts and pants from her older brothers for Otto. Luther had worn everything that ever touched his body to a point of unsalvageable disrepair or stained it too badly for it to be seen even by family only. Liesel didn't mind, though. She liked knitting sweaters and sewing clothing.

Liesel smiled at Otto. He soon lay on his side and fell asleep with the flies buzzing around and landing on his sticky hands and face. Liesel remembered to shoo them away each time she returned to the blanket to unload her vegetables.

She took up the hoe and dug out the bright green weeds growing between her tomatoes, then she moved to the potato plants. She loved the garden. She loved the scent of freshly turned dirt, pungent and human as sweat. Earthy potatoes emerged by the dozens, as if they were born and released to the world in groups thick as the minnows of Spider Lake. She put the biggest ones in a pile for eating and the smallest in another for next year's seed. Onions in rows straight as newspaper columns stood nearby. They looked so neat and orderly that Liesel hated to pull any of them for eating. Beets and carrots blossomed beyond them. She would gather up the ripest of all of these and stuff them into her apron. Then she'd set them in tidy heaps on the blanket all around Otto. She had harvested every one of these things herself. She'd carry them to the kitchen, wash and peel them, and cook them into stews and soups for Papa and her brothers.

All morning, a dreary ache had drummed in her belly, but the chores needed to be done, and Otto needed to be watched, so there was no time for resting. While she spread the eggshells around the garden plants, she knew she was being watched, and she knew by whom. She turned and found Lester Sutter standing near her mother's grave. Like always, he wore overalls and old boots. He held another burlap bag at his side. Lumps appeared here and then there on the brown sack, as the creature inside still moved. A turtle.

For the past year, Liesel had now and again found butchered turtles near her mother's grave. Sometimes Lester hid in the trees until she took the bag. A few times they had spoken. She spoke to him in English, and she spoke slowly so that he could grow accustomed to her accent. Once, she gave him a jar of tomato juice she had made, and she laughed when he opened it and emptied it in one long drink. Another time, she gave him a book with pictures of animals.

"Two tails," he'd said of an elephant.

"It's called an elephant," Liesel had said. "They live in Africa."

"Is that past Mankato?" he'd asked.

Now she put down her hoe and waved at Lester to come closer. He walked as though one of his legs were heavier than the other. She put her finger to her lips and pointed to Otto, asleep on the blanket. Lester put his fingers to his lips too.

"Boy's sleeping," he said.

"Yes," she said. "He's having a nap."

Lester lifted up the bag for Liesel to notice and pulled a knife from his pocket.

"Want me to butcher him?" he asked.

"Yes. That would be nice."

Lester stared at her feet for a long while.

"What?" she finally asked. He didn't look up to meet her eyes. Instead, he pointed at her bare calves with his knife.

"You're bloody," he said.

"What?" Liesel said. She looked at her legs. Reddish brown streaks ran down them toward her black boots. "What?" she said again. She turned her leg to the right and left to get a better view herself. "My God."

"Hurts," said Lester. He sucked on his bottom lip, then tucked the knife into his pocket and pulled the turtle by the neck from the bag. Liesel stepped back. She patted her hands over her stomach and thighs, though she knew she'd find no wounds.

"Blood hurts people," he said. He thrust the turtle toward her as if to bolster his point. The creature's legs stuck straight out, stiff.

"No," said Liesel, and she touched the soft underbelly of the turtle and pushed it back at Lester. She knelt and scrubbed at her legs with the hem of her skirt.

"Animals die when bloody," Lester said. He bent to get a closer look at her bloody leg. Then he said, louder: "But you're a human."

"What are you talking about?" She put up her hand to block his view.

"Maybe get a drink of whiskey," he said.

"Just be quiet, please," she said.

Lester stood up straight. The turtle wrestled against him, but Lester held it tight.

A strong wave of cramps passed through Liesel's belly, and she felt a warm flush between her legs. She knew what this blood meant. It had been right there on page 11 of *A Young Lady's Guide to Womanhood*. But how could it be?

Ever since the night of Otto's birth, Liesel had not been able to stand the sight or smell of human blood. She could stomach butchering animals of all sorts, but human blood was something else altogether. She felt faint and tasted iron in her mouth. She spit on the ground and laid her head on her knee. Lester spit then too. He garbled, "Whiskey, whiskey," into his chest. He stood over her and held the turtle still.

After a few minutes, Liesel stood. "Lester," she said. "Keep a watch on Otto, please. I'll be right back."

"I'll watch him good," said Lester. He dropped the turtle to the ground and quickly sat his bottom on top of the creature's shell. The turtle scratched at the dirt but couldn't move. He took his knife out and stretched the neck of the reptile.

"Not here," Liesel said. "You can't butcher it here." She looked around the farm and pointed to a place a few yards away, next to the barn, where she, her pa, and her brothers butchered chickens. "There," she said. "We'll butcher him there. But wait for me. I'll help."

She didn't wait for a response. She walked, her thighs apart and her skirt hitched high, to the outhouse behind the house. She sat on the wooden seat and let her stomach cramp and relax. She touched her fingers to the rawness and brought the bloody tips to her lips. This was a normal thing. She was not lonely with Lester. Maybe her mother had been wrong. Maybe she hadn't known about Lester, about how he was simple, about how they were friends, about how he wouldn't care if she wasn't exactly like other women. *This is a good thing,* Liesel thought. *I'm a woman now.*

16

A SNAPPING TURTLE is one of the oldest creatures on Earth. Memories two hundred million years old rumble and rest in his black eyes. The continents of the Earth are jammed together into one big landmass, one lapping ocean holding it; bumbling in the warmth are the world's first dinosaurs, thin-legged upright beasts, darting between plants, eating leaves from waxy bushes, drinking from freshwater pools; the world's earliest birds flutter their wings, taking flight in the new day.

In an explosion of earth and fire, the land breaks away from itself and water pours over the cracks. The turtle adapts and survives.

He waits for the next period of land animals to keep him company. New dinosaurs, bigger, louder, toothier, emerge. Mammals scurry, mice-like, in the black nights. Sometimes the turtle hides, waits, and snaps one between his powerful jaws. He chews slowly and swallows. He goes for a swim in a pocket of fresh water. Down there, he sees a drowned mammoth, its long trunk and fur swimming upright and reaching for the surface. The turtle cycles his fat legs and returns to the surface, pokes his nose above water, and crawls to a safe place in the reeds. The earth shakes again. There's fire, then blackness. All around him, the bodies of the dead lie and rot. The thick sky holds the stench in. The smell will soak into his own skin and follow him to the end of ages. It is the smell of extinction the turtle carries.

In the turtle's eye are humans crouched around a fire, sharpening spears. They build shelter. They make clothes, boats, buildings, roads, jewelry, words.

They make language, boundaries, religions, kings, and presidents. They make money and economy. Threats. They make war. They make poison gas and guns and tanks. All this the turtle has seen from conception to application.

A turtle is strong.

A turtle's age is marked by the rings around his shell's scutes. The scutes protect the turtle's bones. The shell protects the turtle's lungs, his heart.

A turtle uses oxygen efficiently. A turtle never does more than he has to. A turtle buries his body in mud at the bottom of ponds and lakes in November. He sleeps there all winter. His heart will beat only ten times in a minute. In March, he'll wake, swim to the surface, tap at the ice, and break free to breathe.

A turtle is patient.

A turtle hides from trouble.

A turtle will bite only if roused.

A turtle's heart is robust. A turtle's heart is good.

On another morning, Liesel Richter grabbed Otto by the hand and said to him, "Let's go." They met Lester Sutter at the edge of the grove and followed him through it to Spider Lake, where he tugged a rotted log onto the sandy shore and told them to sit down and be quiet. They did. Lester crouched near the water's rim and waited. When Otto got restless and pulled on Liesel's sleeve, she shushed him and slapped his hand.

Almost twenty minutes passed before Lester dashed into the

lake water, reached down, and pulled up an ancient-looking creature, flexing its jaws. Lester fell forward onto the shore and landed on top of the turtle, shell as big as a shovel. He grabbed the turtle's shell near its back legs, stood up, and lifted it high. Liesel and Otto clapped at the sight.

"Got him!" said Lester.

"Let's eat him!" said Otto. "Let's cook him!"

"Wait, wait," said Lester. "See how pretty." Lester plopped the turtle onto the shore. Otto ran to it. Liesel got up too and held Otto back.

"You can look," said Lester. "See how pretty."

Lester carried his catch to the Richters' farm, Liesel and Otto following close behind. She brought him her papa's ax. Lester set down the turtle, placed his boot on its shell, lifted the ax over his head, and brought it down in a smooth movement. The head of the turtle popped off and landed in the summer grass. Its jaws still snapped. Its legs still clawed at the ground. Otto jumped away from the parts, but then crept close to the turtle's head. He pinched it around the neck and lifted it up. He studied the face.

Lester pulled a knife from his overalls pocket. He flipped the turtle onto its shell and slipped the blade into the thinnest part, behind the front leg, and sawed through to the back leg. He did the same on the other side. Then he lifted the plastron from the outer shell and set it aside. And there, inside the cradle on the top shell, the carapace, lay muscle, organ, and bone. Lester knelt down and got to work separating the meat from the fat and innards. He stripped away the fine white meat and laid the chunks and slivers onto the plastron. When he was finished, he hacked the legs, tail, and what remained of the neck from the outer shell and handed it to Otto.

"Stinks bad," said the boy. He held the shell away from his body.

Lester plugged his nose.

"What do you say?" prompted Liesel to Otto.

"Thank you, Lester," Otto said.

"Yep," Lester said.

"I'll get a pot," said Liesel.

Liesel walked across the yard and into the house. She rummaged through her pots and pans cupboard until she found one big enough. She took it to Lester, and he dumped the meat in. It never looked like much at first. Rubbery and white. But when coaxed by Liesel's cooking, the turtle meat relaxed and became soft and tender, a bit more bitter than chicken and far more filling. Turtle meat was good stock for a big family's supper and was her papa's favorite meal.

17

WILHELM RICHTER'S PARENTS emigrated from Germany to America with their three sons when Wilhelm was just two years old. Wilhelm's earliest memory was of his father holding him tight as he was sick over the side of the big ship minutes after eating tapioca pudding. He remembered fearing that his father would drop him into the roaring ocean below and remembered the taste of salty water on his face. The Richters left behind Wilhelm's grandparents, four aunts, and two uncles, along with their families. Wilhelm's father had come to join his brother, who had settled in New Germany a few years before. While Wilhelm's uncle was interested in newspaper printing and built up the *Deutsche Chronik* building near the banks of the Minnesota River, Wilhelm's father was interested in farming and claimed a little section along Spider Lake. They both passed their passions on to their sons, who regarded one another as brothers rather than cousins and forged a path between the newspaper building in town and the Richter farm a few miles out.

The Minnesota River, a smoky white flooder of a river that brought steamboats and supplies to New Germany and took away the beer and grain produced there, cradled the town on the east. Spider Lake, a pool with a sludgy rim but deep waters and home to all species of reptile and fish, sat on the west of the small town. The German immigrants who first came to the place in the 1850s chose the area for the black farmland, the fresh water supply, the transportation, and the security and seclusion the river and lake seemed to provide. New Germany, Minnesota, had welcomed German settlers since its inception. The fertile farmland, groves, and waterways provided a sufficient foundation for German farmers, carpenters, and brewers of the Bavarian region who'd come to America looking for ways to improve their economic condition. And at first, Minnesota had been a tolerant place for thinking, and this attracted the philosophers and the teachers and the writers from intellectual German society who'd come to America looking for religious and political freedom. New Germany became a place where cultures combined and held tight to the things its pioneers had in common: German stoicism, German neatness, and German loyalty.

These immigrants built first the New Germany Turner school, a place where most of the immigrants' sons went to learn literature, arithmetic, and exercise. These immigrants believed in the important connection between a healthy mind and a healthy body, and all the children began their mornings with flexibility exercises and rigorous runs. The immigrants then built a brewery, a hospital, a bakery, a bank, and a baseball field, where they met each Sunday to stretch their legs and arms. Later, a Catholic church with a pair of jagged steeples speared into the sky, but it was built only to sate the ambitions of Father Anton, the son of the brewer, who wouldn't stop pestering the men at work or the women in their homes, preaching up a great storm about the need for a proper church. As quickly as the donations came in, the church walls went up. But the New Germany citizens' god was not the God of the Holy Mass. Their god was the god of land and hope in the future. Just as soon as the church was finished and Father Anton calmed, the Richter family established a German newspaper. *Deutsche Chronik* reported news from the old country as well as the new.

The waterways and fertile farmland attracted others, of course; Norwegian and Swedish farmers who settled along the periphery of the town and surrounded their German neighbors. At first, the Germans paid them little mind. It was only when the local Sioux, also known as the Dakota — starved, half-mad with frustration, and loaded to the shoulders with bows, arrows, knives, guns, and clubs — bore down upon the farmers and townspeople of the entire region in the Great Sioux Uprising of 1862 that the Germans made friends with their other white neighbors and united to fight the warriors and save their town and their lives. Norwegians, Swedes, and Germans took up arms and worked together to barricade the town against the Indian attacks. They hid their frightened women and children together inside the thick brick walls of St. Leopold's Catholic church. Catholics and Protestants, led by Father Anton, prayed together while the whooping, gunshots, and fires roared outside. German women tended to the wounds of Norwegian men. Swedish women wrapped up the children of Germans in their own shawls. When the battles were over and the dead on both sides collected and buried, the whites rounded up more than thirty random Dakota warriors, boys and old men alike, and hung them by their necks until they were dead, and then took another dozen or so braves and shot them on the fringe of Spider Lake, scalped them the way they thought Indians scalped, and suspended their hair from the Catholic church door. They tied rocks around the carcasses of the Dakota and threw the bodies into the depths of the lake, where fish, turtle, snail, and snake feasted on the flesh.

Before they put to rest each body, the settlers prayed an afterlife upon each dead Dakota man.

"Now you have got all the water and food and land you want, you murdering savages," they said to the dead eyes, bloody heads.

"God damn you, Owl Feather," they said and dumped the body. "God damn you, Spider Twig," they said and dumped the body. "God damn you, Two Dog."

And to the warrior who still breathed despite the terrible wound on his head, the warrior who just a few days before had slit open a pregnant German woman, pulled her child from her womb, and nailed the blue thing to a tree, the warrior whose own woman had lost her milk to dehydration and starvation and whose own infant son, toddler daughter, and young boy had starved to death the winter before, the warrior who tried to communicate with the men by gesturing and talking and grunting, the one whose skin clung to his collarbones and ribs, the one who cursed the men and the land and the lake before the men heaved him in, the one called Water Dweller, they said, "God damn you too. God damn you most of all."

The settlers hoped that would be the end of their Indian troubles.

All the settlers worked together to rebuild the town. The Norwegians and Swedes, a little more comfortable with their German neighbors now, moved a bit closer to the German town. They slapped their new German friends on the backs and built houses and farms nearer and nearer to the center of town. Everybody seemed at peace. But some said that the ghosts of those murdered in the battles and of the innocent ones hanged by the neck and butchered by the lake haunted the place. Maybe God did damn those Indian bodies. And maybe those Indian bodies brought damnation to each living thing that touched the shores of Spider Lake. Maybe. Maybe. But maybes get forgotten after a time. Maybes were forgotten here, in New Germany. The settlers kept coming.

After a long while, the Germans, though they'd appreciated the help in their time of need, wanted to be left alone again. Germans prefer to be among themselves, everybody knows. There's too much angst and stubbornness in them. And unless there's a celebration, the houses, churches, streets, schools, and towns can't be kept quiet or neat enough.

Most folks in New Germany spoke their native tongue at home, and when the schools popped up and opened, they learned English as their children brought it home from the schoolhouses. Most everyone was bilingual, at least. Soon enough, English became the language of business and church, and the citizens were expected to use it. But still, the Germans held on to their language, even as the years passed and the other nationalities assimilated.

Wilhelm's parents had been in New Germany for fewer than two years at the onset of the 1862 Sioux Uprising, when a group of braves seeking revenge against the white settlers for years of theft and manipulation by the white government pounded down the door of the Richters' farmhouse in the early-morning hours of a summer day. The Dakota knew the Richter house and farm well enough. Here was where they'd come the winter before to trade their blankets for eggs, sugar, and coffee. Along with all of that, Wilhelm's mother had given the men four jars of peaches and the innards from the chicken she'd been preparing for supper. But in times of war, past niceties are forgotten. The braves ran up the stairs and with their stone clubs bashed in the heads of Wilhelm's parents, Otto and Liesel, in the very bed where Wilhelm, just a small boy, slept between them. His father hadn't even had time to load the rifle he kept under the straw-ticking bed. Wilhelm opened his eyes to the warm spray of his father's blood dampening his face. The room was that shadowy blue shade the sky turns just before dawn. Young Wilhelm heard shuffling and then felt his mother throw her body over his own. She whispered to him to shush. That was the last sound from her lips. He then felt the thud of the club against his mother's skull. Blood seeped from her skull onto his own. His pillow and pajamas were soaked. He lay still, his eyes inches from the open, dead eyes of his mother. The braves left his parents' bedroom and busted into the bedroom of his brothers. They beat them to death before either fully awoke. The braves came back for Wilhelm, but instead of killing him, they pulled him out from under his mother, carried him down the stairs to the kitchen, and sat him at the head of the kitchen table. The Sioux men ransacked the house for food and tools, and before they left, they lit an oil lantern and fixed him a meal of cold side pork and bread. They left him there. It was three days before his uncle dared travel from New Germany. When he arrived at his brother's house, he found his nephew Wilhelm sitting in that chair, the blood of his parents dried and staining his face, and the meal in front of him untouched. The boy Wilhelm never cried.

Wilhelm's uncle didn't consult Father Anton before he dug the graves and wrapped up the bodies of his brother, sister-in-law, and nephews. There wasn't enough time, enough coffins, or enough forgiveness to think about anything holy. He buried them near the grove. He had Wilhelm say goodbye to his family and then took the boy to his own house and put him in the care of his wife. But it was Wilhelm's cousin Archie who watched over Wilhelm day and night. Archie who brought him sweets and smiled while he ate.

On the day of the mass hanging of the Dakota culprits, the uncle hoisted the boy Wilhelm to his shoulder and held Archie by the hand. Over the heads of dozens and dozens of neighbors and townspeople, Wilhelm saw the braves swing by their necks. A few yards away, a little girl with a gouged-out eye also sat atop a man. Wilhelm waved to her. She didn't wave back.

"Were the Indians bad to her?" Archie asked.

"Very bad," his father said.

"What did they do with her eye?" he asked.

"Quiet, boy," said his father.

A few days later the uncle set Wilhelm on his knee to watch a dozen more Dakota shot and scalped by white vigilantes on the rim of Spider Lake. Wilhelm closed and covered his eyes. It was enough blood. How he hated all the blood. He couldn't speak of it. He couldn't tell anyone what had happened in that house. He just closed his mouth and was silent. The aunt thought the stage would pass, that he'd been traumatized and would snap out of it soon and behave like a regular boy. But weeks, months, and then a year passed, and still not a word from little Wilhelm. Archie interpreted all his needs.

When it became clear to the family that Wilhelm would not speak, the aunt grew frustrated and wrote to her in-laws back in Germany, requesting that they take Wilhelm in. And so, with much cost to the family and a great to-do, the uncle journeyed back to Germany with Wilhelm.

Back in Germany, Wilhelm's grandmother pressed the boy to her big bosom and sobbed and sobbed over the loss of her son, daughter-in-law, and grandsons. After only a few weeks, it was clear to Wilhelm that his grandmother wasn't going to let him out of her sight ever again. He turned to his uncle and said his first words in more than a year: "I want to go back home." His grandmother cried and made him promise to write every week. Wilhelm said that he didn't know how to write yet. His grandmother pinched his ear and said, Don't sass me. Wilhelm grabbed his throbbing ear and was swiftly pulled into his grandmother's bosom again. Draw me pictures until you learn, she said. Wilhelm promised that he would.

And so his uncle repacked and towed him back to Minnesota. The uncle and his wife raised Wilhelm along with Archie and their other children. They worked hard to keep up the Richter house and farm. And when Wilhelm turned eighteen, he moved back into his childhood home and set to running the place himself. From his window in the very kitchen where the braves had left him alive, Wilhelm could see the lake where the other braves had been killed and thrown into the water. And he always felt they could see him.

On the edge of the grove, his brothers were buried in a single grave, and his parents were buried side by side. All four were memorialized with simple wooden crosses.

In the years after their deaths, Wilhelm formed fabulous fantasies about his parents. In his mind, they were forever in love and beautiful. He romanticized their accomplishments and their affection for each other. He would say things like "Those two. Always chasing one another like kids," "My father could grow apples on a wooden floor," and "I remember my mother baking a cake shaped like a ship once." Wilhelm tended toward an unnaturally optimistic look at the world. He worked day and night cleaning, painting, and reconstructing the house and outbuildings on the farm. Archie visited often but could not get Wilhelm to leave for even a short visit to town. Wilhelm seemed driven to make the place perfect. When Archie asked him why, Wilhelm said that he was preparing for his family.

Archie sometimes teased Wilhelm that he ought not to wait too long or he'd end up alone, like all those Norwegian bachelor farmers.

"There is always time," said Wilhelm. "There will even be time again for you."

Archie dug his hands into his pockets. "Perhaps," he said. Some years before, Archie had lost his wife to a strange growth in her womb. He couldn't bring himself to look upon any other woman yet.

"It is time for you to make a family as well," said Wilhelm. "Or the Richters of New Germany will be gone forever. For my part, I will fill this house with children."

"I believe you will," said Archie.

Some of the neighbors said the Richter house was haunted and that it ought to be burned to the ground. Some said the Sioux warriors had cursed that lake and the land around it. Some said their blood poisoned all who set foot in the water.

Wilhelm Richter prepared his farm and house for more than

twenty years before he thought it ready for a family. Every board was straight. Every nail was flush. Every shingle was flat. The hens laid dozens of eggs. The cows produced buckets and buckets of milk. New calves were born each spring. The acres rolled on. The crops stretched and took in the rain and sun. Everything was perfect. When Wilhelm set about finding a wife, it took him only one night to settle on the girl from Archie's wedding. The girl who looked so much like his own mother, with her long, thick brown hair and wide middle and that undefinable sense of motherhood. Although he was nearly forty, Wilhelm Richter married sixteen-year-old Magdalena, moved her into that same house, and some months later became a father to a boy, Benjamin. He became a father to another son, Herman, the next year. To Luther, a year after that. Two years after that, he fathered Liesel Magdalena Richter.

Profits forge the surest loyalties. Since the day he'd turned eighteen and returned to his family's farm, turning the sinewy earth into abundant fields, Wilhelm Richter had sent money to his family in Germany. They in turn invested it in munitions operations. As war crept near and the factories lurched to life, spitting out gun parts, bomb innards, and chemicals, money such as the family had never seen flowed in. In this way, Wilhelm Richter built a veritable fortune out of a few straggly acres, then invested more money in the operations and in more land.

Wilhelm Richter's fatal flaw might have been what was interpreted by his neighbors as flaunting. While other children played baseball with sticks and walnuts, Benjamin, Herman, and Luther swung bats made of pine and threw baseballs leather-bound and stitched with red. While other farmers used plows and planters inherited from their fathers, Wilhelm bought new. But the worst insult to the struggling neighbors came when they had to sell off their own land to pay their bills or they lost the land altogether to the bank, and Wilhelm Richter raced to the auction or the bank and couldn't seem to get his signature on the deeds fast enough. He often brought his boys. He thought it behooved them to learn of the farming business.

Benjamin was highly sensitive to these transactions. He could see the pain in the faces of their neighbors as the auctioneers rattled off prices for their properties. He thought it not right, but he respected his father and didn't feel in a position to object. His body, however, reacted to these uncomfortable moments with forceful fits of sneezing. Wilhelm Richter'd be signing up for loans and bidding on land with Benjamin behind him sneezing away as though there were a trophy to be won for it. All Benjamin wanted was a small place, a few acres, and a nice wife who would sit on the porch with him and bring him a drink of water and maybe a cookie once in a while.

Herman had no interest in farming. He found his papa's lifestyle boring and base. Messing around in the dirt or with animals did little good for Herman's brain. Since the beginning of time, men had been pulling things to eat from the ground, wiping the dirt off them, and stuffing those fruits in their mouths. What was so noble about that? Even animals could do it. Herman yearned for a life with more adventure and intellect. If he had to live on a farm for one minute past his eighteenth birthday, Herman thought he might turn murderous. He had a good idea for a book he wanted to write. He even had the title picked out: *The Weight of the World*. It would be about a man who was really smart but under the thumb of an overbearing, not-as-smart boss, and the man couldn't do anything about it because the boss had all the money and the man had none. And the man knew all the answers, but no matter how many times the man tried to share his knowledge with the boss, the boss wouldn't listen and kept plugging away, doing things the way he always had, as though he were a farm animal rather than a thinking man. Herman planned to use that comparison and had written it down on a piece of paper so that he'd remember it when the time came to write the book. On another piece of paper, Herman had written *social satire*.

Herman imagined it would be the greatest social satire of his time, maybe of all time. All he needed was the time to write it and sell it, and then he could relax and let the money come in. Herman thought he'd build orphanages and schools with the royalties.

Luther embodied the pride of his papa. He liked nothing better than tossing around bales or managing a plow near admiring girls or jealous boys. Everyone was jealous, especially his brothers. It was so hard. But when Luther was honest with himself, he had to admit that it was natural that his brothers were jealous. Why wouldn't they be? He didn't let it get to him though. It wasn't his fault he was strong and handsome and that all the girls wanted him. Every one of them. There wasn't even one who didn't. It was almost like a curse.

18

New Germany, Minnesota, October 1916

E VEN AS THE KAISER'S army marched all over Europe, even as Americans filed into the streets to champion the war, the German-Americans of New Germany, Minnesota, declared they would never enlist, they would not fight the kaiser's army. They would not have their sons wear American uniforms to kill German boys, the sons of their own families. If the world leaders wouldn't honor family bonds, they, at least, would. The Richter cousins of New Germany, Wilhelm and Archie, had forever kept up correspondence with their family in Germany and felt as near to them as they did to each other. Wilhelm, of course, had other interests in Germany as well. He kept these interests quiet. No one wants to be known as a war profiteer.

Archie stood in the door frame of his newspaper building and nodded toward the familiar wagon. He used his vest to wipe the glass of his spectacles.

"*Guten Tag,* Archie," said Wilhelm.

"Good afternoon, Wilhelm." Archie pointed to the advertisement of the Nonpartisan League meeting to be held at Archie's house. "Have you seen this? We could use a farming man like you to convince the others."

Wilhelm halted his horse team. "I have heard some rumblings of it."

"You come in and sit, see what we are about." Archie nodded toward Benjamin and Herman sitting in the wagon. "Bring the older boys."

"Oh," said Wilhelm, "they have no interest in politics." Wilhelm thought of his boy Herman, who most certainly did have an interest in politics but was too young and naive to fully understand.

"It is your responsibility to get them interested, Wilhelm, to guide their thinking. It is their future we are negotiating."

Wilhelm thought about this on his ride home. Perhaps other men would be able to sway Herman to correct thinking.

Even the stairs of Archie and Frieda's house were filled with New Germany neighbors, men who'd emigrated from Germany and were now farming land and raising families in Minnesota. "We must not support a war against Germany," said Archie Richter. He stood near the door and stopped his speech to welcome each new arrival, shaking his hand and finding space for him to sit. Frieda bustled back and forth from the kitchen with coffee and cake, stepping gracefully over the legs of the men listening with open ears to Archie. On days like this, she could hardly contain her pride in her husband. It wasn't so much that she cared what happened in Germany as it was that she reveled in the action and the intellect the war in Europe had stirred up in this country, this state, this town, and in her own home. Action was what she had left Germany for, and action and adventure were what she craved.

Archie stood tall. He smoothed his tie and wiped his hands on the front of his pants, an act that had become habit in the inky business of printing newspapers. He often used those stained hands to reinforce his positions, pointing now and again at a neighbor or his nephews Benjamin and Herman, who sat at Wilhelm's feet. In Herman he saw the look of a leader, the same quick wit, nose in the news, lowered eyebrows, and skeptical eyes. Herman was a bright one and just needed the right kind of direction.

Soon Archie turned the podium over to Arthur Townsley, leader of the Nonpartisan League, who had made a special trip from North Dakota to speak to New Germany's men about the Nonpartisan League and the pacification movement sweeping Minnesota. Townsley had a more citified look to him than Archie had. He wore a checkered suit and carried a cane for effect. He was trained as a lawyer and often had trouble relating to his constituents. But he was well known across three states and a political force the likes of which Archie admired. Archie translated the English words of Townsley for the older farmers who spoke only German. "Any man that supports the war is a traitor to his own kind and a murderer," said Townsley. Archie translated for the men who didn't understand, and all the men nodded in agreement.

Most of the old men in Archie's house had been born in Germany and as young men had fought in the German army against the French in the Franco-Prussian War. They had protected Germany then against invaders. They couldn't imagine turning sides now. They couldn't imagine doing anything to help any country, including America, bring down the Germans.

When war had first broken out in Europe, some had sent their boys to relatives in Germany so they could enlist and fight for their native country.

"And, too, the European warring nations need bread for their troops and civilians, and Minnesota grows the grain to feed them," Townsley continued. The farmers of New Germany, the farmers with land, had the means to fulfill this need. These war years were a fine time to buy more land and sell more grain. Wilhelm closed his eyes. He knew men were looking at him. He was the biggest farmer in the area.

"If you are fighting in Europe," translated Archie, "who will plant and harvest your crops? Your women?" He held his hands in front of his chest as if cradling large breasts. All the men laughed. Frieda did not. She never liked Archie's jokes about women. They reminded her too much of the ways of her father. But she figured Archie used them to appeal to the old Germans, most of whom had brought their old patriarchal ways with them from Germany. Nevertheless, she filled all the empty coffee cups except Archie's in silent protest. When he lifted his cup at her, she turned her back, pretending not to see him.

"All must admit," Townsley said, "war in Europe is good for business. And to help keep the money in the pockets of the men who work for it, we farmers must stay united." Again Archie translated, and all the men nodded. One rubbed his hand over his beard. Another patted his belly. One lit a pipe. Another crossed his arms over his chest and tucked his hands into his armpits. Each man did the thing he always did when deep in thought and hopeful.

Yes, thought Wilhelm. He placed a hand on each son's shoulder. *We must stay united.* Herman slumped under the weight.

After the meeting, Archie and Frieda cornered Wilhelm and the boys.

"My, my," said Archie. "These boys are giants."

Frieda handed a basket to Herman. "Books and bread," she said.

"Yes," said Wilhelm. Benjamin peeked under the towel on the basket, which released a baked scent. "They eat like giants too."

"Did you hear the news?" asked Archie. He was looking at Herman.

"Which is that?" said Wilhelm.

"August Mueller shipped his boy over to Germany to enlist in the army there." Archie tapped his spectacles on Herman's chest. "He's about your age, is he not?"

"Yes," said Herman. "We know him. Benjamin's got a soft spot for Sonnen Mueller."

Frieda smiled at Benjamin. "She's a nice girl, Ben. You make a good match."

"Mueller's boy?" said Wilhelm. "What about the girl he left behind? She is in the family way, no?"

"Whether it is loyalty to the old country or the fear of being a husband that causes us to protect Germany, it does not matter, does it?"

Archie slapped Wilhelm on the arm. Wilhelm supposed that it did not.

Frieda shook her nephews' hands and gave them stiff hugs. She reminded them to share the basket of goods with Liesel, and then excused herself.

New Germany, though small, promoted big ideas in the years leading up to the Great War. Archie and Frieda's paper, the *Deutsche Chronik*, advertised and organized meetings for the Nonpartisan League, a force dedicated to getting fair wages for workers, keeping children out of the workplace, keeping America out of the war in Europe, and getting good prices for crops. It was this last mission that attracted Wilhelm Richter to the league. Wilhelm believed that if the German farmers united, they could set their own grain prices and not wait on some business-suit bigwigs from Chicago to offer them a penny more or a penny less a bushel. Wilhelm planned to build a great legacy.

In February of 1917, Herman turned eighteen. He read each line of every newspaper he could get his hands on, soaking up every bit of war news. He studied the maps printed in the papers. He set up straw bales, placed Luther's empty beer bottles on top of them, and, from various distances, practiced his aim with a rifle. When Liesel asked him what he thought he was doing, he said he was "shooting the Huns."

That same month, the British intercepted a telegraph from Germany to Mexico. *Invade southern U.S.*, it said, *and we promise you the return of Texas and all lost lands.* Wilson sent troops to reinforce the Mexican-American border. He considered his liberal politics. He reviewed his booming economy. He reviewed the munitions and capability of his army and navy. He thought about the American work force. *Could it thrive without as many men?* he wondered. He considered America's large German population, large Irish population. Would they join the cause? Wilson considered his reputation and legacy. *How will history remember me?* he wondered.

Dear brother, Liesel thought. *You are the Hun.* But she loved Herman. He was prone to moody spells of long thought and then equally long jags of preaching what he knew. He'd taught her everything he'd learned in school. He liked to read and kept under his bed the poems of Walt Whitman and the plays of Shakespeare. When they were children, Herman and Liesel had passed the books from their aunt back and forth and discussed them. When Liesel knew Herman was reading in the barn, she wouldn't give him up to Wilhelm as he charged around the house and yard looking for the boy, ready to set him to work in the field. As Herman and Liesel got older, though, Herman pulled away from her, and she from him. They kept their own secrets. He grew brooding and suspicious. His dark brows fell low near his eyes, and a perpetual shadow of whiskers meaned his look. He was restless.

19

NOT EVEN WHEN Germany sank an Atlantic-crossing ship carrying American vacationers or when German spies blew up shipyards in New York harbors did the people of New Germany condemn their old country. They made excuses, said things like "The passengers of the *Lusitania* were duly warned" and "The shipyard was full of munitions for the British army." They cringed when Wilson called Germany the "mad dog of the world" but relaxed when he didn't declare war on Germany despite the demonstrators that flooded the streets toting signs reading Hell Is Too Good for the Hun and Death to the Germans.

Those of Swedish, Norwegian, and other ancestries could not understand their German neighbors' stance. Some complained to their elected officials at the capital, who took the complaints so seriously that they created the Commission of Public Safety, an organization dedicated to maintaining loyalty to the United States in this time of near war. The leaders in St. Paul declared the German language a treasonous tongue. They declared German-run schools illegal. They declared the Nonpartisan League illegal. They prohibited the private meetings of German citizens. The commission hoped that their declarations would be heard and heeded by Minnesota's German population. The commission wanted to be obeyed but didn't want to alienate these citizens altogether. Minnesota's German population was a desirable one, after all. They were organized and self-sufficient. They worked hard, were industrious. They built nice churches. They made good beer.

So, at first, the commission didn't do much about enforcing the new laws. But the reports about disloyalties committed by the German citizens of New Germany kept coming in. Their Norwegian and Swedish neighbors reported all suspicious, un-American activity to the commission.

Just before President Wilson passed the Espionage Act of 1917, an act that prohibited the distribution of any material that could interfere with the operation or success of the armed forces and any material that promoted the success of enemies, particularly Germany, a man called John Patterson took over the helm at the Commission of Public Safety in Minnesota. The day he took over, he'd been up all the previous night cataloging the pelts he'd earned on a recent African safari, and he was feeling tired. Patterson had a copy of the preliminary proposal for the Espionage Act, and requested that his secretary read a copy of the preliminary proposal for the act and provide him with a summary of it by the end of the workday. She did. What she wrote on a slip of paper was *Keep close eye on Germans of New Germany. They're probably conspiring with the enemy.*

Commissioner Patterson sat in a veritable flood of reports from concerned non-German citizens of New Germany regarding their German neighbors. Here were reports of polka music, German-language schools, a German newspaper, and an unnaturally high demand for cabbage. Commissioner Patterson sat back in his leather chair and had his secretary bring him a snifter of brandy and some zebra jerky. This was such a nice office, warm with the fire, heavy in mahogany, private, and soon there'd be a nice portrait of himself hanging above the mantel. He couldn't spend all his time down in New Germany. He had work to do here, at the capitol building. So, on the same slip of paper on which his secretary had summarized the proposed Espionage Act, Commissioner Patterson wrote *Watchdogs of Loyalty.* He circled it, and circled it again. *What good leaders do is delegate responsibility. Yes. That's the mark of a good leader.* He slugged back a massive swallow of brandy and closed his eyes. He imagined his lovely wife as she had been before the crippling arthritis had rendered her crooked, pained, and all but lost to him. He imagined the way she used to arrange flowers for the vase in the foyer, the way she'd tied her apron, the way she'd unpinned her hair. Patterson had been called many things — mooch, piker, pill, sap, double-crosser, cheat, good-for-nothing, coattail rider, pushover, and hot-air-filled buffoon — but no one could ever nor had ever called him a letch. His attentions were for his wife only, even as she withered past anything recognizably female or feminine.

After a brief snooze, Patterson opened his eyes and found himself smiling. He saw the pile of papers on his desk and remembered to get back to work. He tried to organize the reports of suspicious activity. Here were three complaints about a man named Richter: Three sons in a German school. Received forty-seven letters from Germany in the past few months. Patterson pulled out the plat books of southern Minnesota, found the place of Wilhelm Richter, and then drew his finger across the page to his nearest neighbor, Harald Sutter. Not German. Patterson scratched a star next to Sutter's name and decided to pay him a visit, see if he couldn't get him onboard to help protect the security of the United States.

During Patterson's meeting with Sutter, the commissioner decided he couldn't have been luckier. Here was a man whose loyalty to his country was steadfast. Here was a man who cared.

Here was a man who could be guided. Patterson flipped two hundred-dollar bills into Sutter's hand.

With Sutter keeping an eye on the Germans in southern Minnesota, Commissioner Patterson could focus on his work in his office in St. Paul. Sutter watched Wilhelm Richter very closely. In return, he got a few bills stuffed in his pocket and the hope that Richter's land or machinery would come up for sale. Sutter had little trouble rustling up others to join his Watchdogs. He had only to ask men who'd lost even a single acre to Richter. Every one of them knew a man in prison could not manage his land. And a man who could not manage his land would have to relinquish it. None of Wilhelm's sons was man enough to fight for it. The boys could be convinced to sell back the land to its rightful owners, the neighbors knew.

As U.S. involvement in the war seemed more likely, the commission issued a statement that strongly suggested every German boy over the age of eighteen enlist in the American army. The Watchdogs hung these issuances all over New Germany, even on the window of the *Deutsche Chronik* building, where it lasted all of five minutes before Wilhelm Richter approached the building, read it, and ripped it down for all to see.

"No boy of mine is going anywhere," he said.

Busy Watchdogs holding posters and glue stood all up and down New Germany's main street. Harald Sutter told his boy Cal to write that down. Write that down, what he just said. Write the whole thing down. And don't forget about the ripping-up-the-poster part. Write that down too.

In April of 1917, Wilson declared war on Germany. "The world must be made safe for democracy," he said.

The winter thaw broke through the Minnesota fields that week. Wilhelm woke his boys early to milk the cows, prep the machinery, and prepare his fields for planting. He saw the inkling of restlessness in Herman's eye that spring and planned ways to thwart it. Wilhelm sent him, more often than the other boys, out to the fields. He suggested to Herman that soon it would be time to set aside a few of their acres and build him a house and barn of his own. And though Herman never openly disagreed with his father and never disobeyed him, he felt in his blood a desire to fight. He respected his father's knowledge of farming and business, but not his indifference toward the country that had made him rich. He couldn't understand the contradiction, and he certainly couldn't respect it. When he told his father as much, Wilhelm said, "Herman, you have no idea. You really have no idea."

Commissioner Patterson hung the portrait of himself above his office mantel that week, or, rather, his secretary did while he considered whether it was straight or not. It was a fine likeness, though he thought perhaps he should have trimmed his mustache and that the painter had made his ears a little too large. He'd read the war declaration. He supposed he'd have to do something about all those Germans in New Germany. He'd have to make his mark somehow if he hoped to keep his post in politics, or keep his office anyway. It really was a fine office.

The Richters milked between sixteen and twenty cows, depending on how many were expecting, birthing, and nursing. Of all the chores on the farm, Herman hated taking care of the cows the most. He hated the smell. He hated tugging on their wrinkled teats. He thought it demeaning and disgusting. He didn't even like milk. So when his father sent him out to bed the calves after supper, Herman said he was tired and planned to head for bed.

What Wilhelm was tired of was Herman reading and rereading war propaganda and trying to get out of real work. Herman was so raw in his thinking and so easily influenced but so determined to be right, to do right, that it scared Wilhelm. He couldn't imagine a more dangerous state of mind.

"The calves need bedding," Wilhelm said. Herman didn't look

up from his paper. Benjamin sat by the fire, sanding the arm of a rocking chair he'd made for Liesel. She stood in the kitchen washing the supper dishes with Otto, who dried the tin plates as she handed them to him. Luther, like most nights, had gone down the road and walked to the boat landing, where local youths met and drank and mingled after supper, and he would be out until he was drunk enough to sleep. Bad dreams plagued him when he didn't have the liquor calming his brain, muscles, and mind.

"Tell Benjamin to do it," said Herman. He flipped another page of the *Minneapolis Monitor*.

"I told you," said Wilhelm. The scratching sound of Benjamin's sanding stopped until Herman stood, pushed back his chair, and stomped out through the kitchen. He slammed the screen door behind him. Wilhelm sighed.

Herman walked across the yard, stepped into the barn, grabbed a match, and lit a lantern. Lars Oleson and Cal Sutter, waiting outside, walked from behind a corner of the barn and blocked the doorway. Lester Sutter stood behind them.

"Richter," Lars said.

Herman jumped and turned. He was relieved to recognize these boys. He relaxed and smiled a bit.

"You scared me," he said. He turned up the lantern.

"I got my enlistment papers today," said Lars. "Where're yours?"

Herman stopped smiling. He didn't reply.

"I said, Where are yours?" said Lars.

"I won't be going," Herman said. His voice was straight and calm though his heart thudded as hard as hooves in his throat.

"You hear that, Cal?" Lars said to the other boy. "Richter says he's not going."

Cal grunted and stepped forward into the lantern light. He held a sickle.

"Your daddy not gonna let you fight in the big war?" teased Lars. "Or are you afraid to fight?"

"I'm not afraid to fight," said Herman. He eyed the sickle and wondered if Cal would actually use it on him. Then he looked at Lester and pursed his lips.

"What then?" asked Lars. "You plan on stealing our land while we go to war?"

"What?" said Herman. "Of course not."

"That's not what my pa says," said Lars. "My pa says your pa is a treasonous snake who plans on buying up this whole section while his neighbors go to Europe to fight for this country."

And then Herman said something he didn't believe: "Well, then your pa's wrong."

Cal dropped the sickle, pulled back his fist, and mashed it into Herman's mouth. Herman dropped to the ground, and his lip swelled immediately.

Lester rocked on his heels. "Ow, ow, ow," he said, over and over again. He pounded his own fist against his temple. Cal picked up the sickle and tossed it at Lester's feet. Lester stopped talking and rocking. He stuffed his hands in his pockets.

"Lester and me got two brothers fighting over there already," said Cal. He towered over Herman. "Brave enough to sign on with the Canadians, and you think you get to stay here and get what's ours. I'll be goddamned."

"Open your eyes, Herman," said Lars. "One way or another, you're gonna get what's coming to you." Cal and Lars walked out into the night. Lester ran behind them.

Herman stayed there with his arms over his knees thinking and thinking for hours about his father, this war, and his role in the family, the town, and the world. After he finally got up to pitch the manure out of the cow stalls and spread the feed, he decided to stay in the barn and curled up on a layer of clean straw. He stayed like that until the early-morning hours, when Luther wobbled in reeking of whiskey.

"What are you doing in here?" said Luther. "You plan to take my bed?"

"Where have you been?"

"Visiting Pernilla," said Luther.

"You can't call what you do with Pernilla 'visiting,'" said Herman. "It's shameful."

"Say what you want."

"You are going to drink yourself into the grave," said Herman.

"That doesn't sound so bad," said Luther. He walked past his brother to the ladder.

"I want to die doing what is right," Herman said.

Luther guffawed. "As you like, big brother," he said. "As you like." He climbed up the ladder.

"Don't you?" said Herman. "Don't you want to do something that's right?"

Luther paused on the ladder. "Go to war?" he said. "For what? I'm no glory hound."

"This war is not just about glory, Luther. It's about doing what's right."

"Ha!" said Luther. "And you get to determine what's right?" Luther began his climb again. "No, thanks. What's right for me is getting to bed." He didn't wait for a response, reached the loft, and collapsed on his coarse blanket. He pulled his pillow over his ear.

20

HERMAN THOUGHT EVERY DAY about how to tell his father he was enlisting in the American army. Wilhelm hoped every day that an end to the war would be announced. But instead, every morning Wilhelm read aloud from the *Deutsche Chronik,* which told of the horrors of burned-down churches and buildings, lost loved ones, and destroyed livelihoods among their German countrymen. Herman, in response, whipped out the *Minneapolis Monitor* at dinner and read aloud from the war reports, testifying to the bravery of the soldiers at Messines in early June of 1917.

"We'll have no part in it," said Wilhelm to his sons. "We'll do what we can to keep out of it."

"There's a draft," said Herman. "I may be sent whether you like it or not."

"Sending you to do what?" said Luther. "Pick up horseshit?"

"We can't go," said Benjamin.

"I said there's a draft," said Herman. "You must register. If you get notice, you have to go, you giant ass."

"The draft's for men," said Wilhelm. "Twenty-one years or more."

"It might be extended," said Herman.

"Sonnen's brother is there," said Benjamin. "You're the giant ass if you would shoot him."

"If I get a notice," said Luther, "I'm going to shoot off my pinkie toe and fake being Lester." He banged his fist against his head and dangled his tongue.

"That's because you're a selfish coward," said Herman. He threw down his fork.

"Selfish, maybe," said Luther. "Coward, no." He pulled Herman's plate toward him and ate from it. "Not my fault they don't want no nine-toed wacko holding a gun."

Wilhelm looked at all his children, from oldest to youngest. He wiped his mouth and stood. "You'll not be going," said Wilhelm. "None of you will be going."

After supper, Liesel washed the dishes while Herman read the newspaper again.

"I read a new poem last night," said Liesel. "I have it memorized."

"Mm-hmm," said Herman. He flipped a page of the newspaper and opened it flat. He leaned over to study a large map of Europe.

Liesel banged down a pot. Herman didn't even look up.

"It says the same things it said this morning," she said.

"There's many brave men dying over there, Liesel. There's some from New Germany who signed up with Canada to fight the Germans ages ago."

"Like Lester's brothers?" said Liesel.

"No! Not like *them*. Real soldiers. Like I would be."

Liesel sometimes felt the strongest urge to hit Herman or throw something hard at him. She always suppressed that desire, figuring it was a manifestation of all that was wrong with her. Doing violence upon her brother was surely not ladylike and a most masculine thing to do. Nevertheless, she felt the desire now, and her cheeks turned red. She took a big breath. "There're some from America who have volunteered to fight on the German side too, Herman. Don't forget about that."

"Those damn Germans are killing innocent women and children. Says so right here."

"Brave men are dying on both sides, I'm sure."

Herman put his nose back in the paper. "I'm eighteen now, able to make my own decisions."

"Herman, you don't know everything."

"You're just a little girl, Liesel. You don't understand things about the world. And war's a man's business."

Liesel felt like crying. Where had the brother who shared all his knowledge with her, who talked to her, who was her friend, gone? What had happened to him? "I'm almost sixteen myself," said Liesel. "Lots of girls get married at my age."

"Well, I don't hear any suitors pounding on the door for you." He stood, gathered the paper, and stomped up the stairs. At the top, he yelled down one last insult. "Unless you count the retard." He didn't know why he'd said it.

21

FOR HOW LONG had Pernilla, Harald Sutter's oldest daughter, looked softly upon Luther Richter? Ages, it seemed. He was quite a few years younger than her, she knew, but she didn't care. He was tall and blond and muscular too. He'd had a deep, man's voice for as long as she could remember. She liked to watch him working in his father's field adjacent to the Sutters'. On the pretense of delivering food or drink to her own brothers in the field, she would walk over to the line fence and holler hello to Luther and his brothers.

On Sundays, Pernilla would sit on the wall of the left-field foul line of the New Germany baseball diamond and shout encouragement to Luther while he played third base or batted. Sometimes when he'd scoop a grounder out of the dirt, she would stick two fingers between her lips and whistle, or she'd push past all the other girls standing near the bleachers sipping on lemonades to hand Luther a beer as he exited the baseball diamond. She didn't care what those other girls thought, those girls who were too proper and stiff to go after what they wanted. Recently, Pernilla had begun to run into Luther down at the boat landing on weekends, drinking beer and talking farming and politics with the other local boys.

Pernilla's body was as long and svelte as a mink's, and she prided herself on not playing games like the other girls. She prided herself on not preaching religion or morals. She didn't care for promises and commitments, though she liked compliments and presents and kind caresses. And she genuinely liked the feeling of a man filling her up. She felt useful and alive, as if her body were a vessel for pure pleasure. She was the only one who could give such pleasure to those boys. Until they married, at least. And they always did. But there were always more boys ready to become men, and Pernilla knew her role and found power in it. The only boy Pernilla had ever wanted more than a romp from was Luther Richter. For one, he was the only boy who was taller than she. She'd seen Luther hoist boulders and fence posts with little effort. She'd seen him tug and pull out a tree stump with nothing but a rope and the bulging muscles of his back. Pernilla herself could tote bales and water pails and full potato sacks the way no other girl and most boys could not.

Pernilla knew that the Germans were bad, that they were cowards who didn't want to fight in the war over in Europe because they were getting rich off it. She didn't know how they were doing that, exactly, but she'd heard her pa meeting with a group called the Watchdogs of Loyalty. Once, the leader of this group, Commissioner Patterson, had come to their farm. He had stood in the middle of the yard squaring off with the old rooster, which flapped its wings and stepped to the right or left depending on which path the commissioner tried to take toward the porch. Finally, the commissioner used his cane to scare back the big red devil and ran to the porch. With the knobbed end of his cane, he rapped on the wood frame of the broken screen door of Pernilla's kitchen. Pernilla unlocked a hook and eye at the top of the door and opened it to let him in.

"That's to keep the little ones out if you were wondering about why I had it locked," she said, nodding to the hook and eye. "I'm Pernilla."

"Ahhh," he said. He stepped into the kitchen with a heavy stomp. The commissioner always walked in a way that announced his coming, treading harder and with more weight than his 145-pound frame would seem to be able to produce. "Couldn't the 'little ones' just reach through the broken screen and unlatch the hook themselves?" He stuck his cane through the ripped screen to make his point.

Pernilla looked at the hook and squeezed her lips together for a second. "They never thought to yet, I guess."

"Lucky for you then," said the commissioner. He removed his hat and handed it to Pernilla. She tossed it on the table.

John Patterson had been given his positions as Commissioner of Public Safety and creator of the Watchdogs of Loyalty by his old friend the governor of Minnesota, whom Patterson had met on an African safari ten years before. Patterson had saved the life of the governor by inadvertently diverting the attention of a rampaging bull elephant; as it was bearing down on the politician, Patterson had accidentally discharged his rifle into the canopy of a tree teetering with screaming, red-assed monkeys. The monkeys commenced such a racket that the elephant forgot its original target, gave up the rundown of the governor, charged head-first into the trunk of monkey-heavy tree, and fell over dead. The governor wiped his brow with a handkerchief, looked at Patterson, and said, "Timely shot." Patterson nodded and said, "It was nothing." He and the governor split the profit from the ivory tusks. The governor had found a position for Patterson at his law firm and then placed Patterson in his own cabinet.

"Could you tell your father that Commissioner Patterson is here to see him?" said Patterson.

Little Sutter children gathered around the screen door, peeking just above the frame to peer inside at the man with their sister. When Pernilla yelled, "Hey, Pa! Come here quick!" most of them scattered.

The commissioner was several inches shorter than Pernilla and had a long dragoon mustache that flared in a great blond bush beneath his nose and then curved around his lips and hung down past his jaw. When he spoke, it wavered in a way that Pernilla couldn't ignore and made her reach to her own face and scratch. He wore odd yellow-brown pants cinched at the knees where the tops of long black boots met them. Pernilla could see her reflection in their shine.

"You going wading for frogs in those rubbers?" Pernilla asked him.

"Ha!" he replied. "Certainly not, young lady. I do not 'wade for frogs.'"

"What you got them rubbers on for then?"

Commissioner Patterson tapped the tip of one boot with his cane. "These boots are made from the finest snakeskin available, not rubber."

Harald Sutter came into the kitchen wiping his greasy hands on one of Pernilla's dishtowels.

"All we got are garter snakes round here, too small to make boots out of," Pernilla said.

"Shut up now and get me some water," Sutter said to his daughter.

She stood near the men while they talked of all the traitors to America living around there and reaping all the benefits of being Americans but not really being Americans at all, just using America to get rich and to give money and tell secrets to the German king. Harald Sutter recited the names of all the New Germany men he knew to be traitors to America.

The commissioner raised his eyebrows. "Who else?" he asked. "I need more names."

"Archie Richter."

146

"You're sure?" the commissioner said.

"As sure as I'm standing here," said Sutter.

"All right," said the commissioner. "This'll do for now."

"And there's the rally they're planning, of course."

"What rally?" asked the commissioner.

"Big peace-type thing with a guy named Townsley coming," said Sutter, "to tell all the boys not to enlist."

Townsley. Patterson hated Townsley, a man elbowing his way into public politics and stirring up all the people without any regard for the old ways of forging friendships among politicians. "A public disregard for the United States of America?" Patterson smoothed his mustache.

"I guess," said Sutter. "We got some big traitors down here, sir. Big ones. You want me to put a stop to it?"

Patterson thought for a bit. If he stopped the rally, he'd surely get some recognition from his colleagues at the capital. But what if he let it happen? What if he let it happen and he attended? What if he attended and put a stop to it then? What if he delivered a speech? Wouldn't the newspapers be there? Wouldn't they report such heroics? Wouldn't his name be known all over the state, and probably the nation? Wouldn't President Wilson hear of it?

The commissioner handed Sutter an envelope and said to keep quiet about the rally. "Do get some boys together for the day, though," he said. "Have plenty of men prepared."

For Sutter, what had started out as a grudge against Richter over land had turned into something bigger. Sutter was entirely sick of the Germans and their pride. They needed a good humbling. "I'll get plenty," he said. "As many as you need."

Pernilla stared and listened until her pa told her to quit sniffing around the men and get to making supper.

Pernilla didn't know where Europe was, only that it was a place where real Americans would soon go to kill the greedy, baby-killing, woman-raping, bloodthirsty Germans who were trying to take over Europe, trying to take what didn't belong to them, same as the Germans here in Minnesota were taking what didn't belong to them. Two of her brothers had boarded a train to go and fight these Germans over in Europe, and she hadn't heard a word from them since. She wondered sometimes if they'd been killed or taken prisoner by the Huns, if they were being fed sauerkraut, the foulest corruption of a vegetable Pernilla could imagine, and those fat red sausages, *landjaegers,* which smelled to her like burned dog hair, both of which seemed to be some great treat to all the Germans she knew. Really, Pernilla didn't worry about her enlisted brothers too much, what with all the work she had to do around the farm now that they were gone and their having been the only real help she'd had in the first place. Pernilla knew that her own pa had lost forty acres to Luther's father a while ago. Her pa hated the Richters, all the Richters, because of it.

But she didn't think much of her pa's farming and she sometimes wondered about his views too. She couldn't remember her pa or the farm being in any better way before Richter started buying up land. She couldn't remember a time when there had been more food or more money. She couldn't remember a time when the Sutters' homestead wasn't in a sad state and in dire need of a heap of straight boards, nails, and wood planks, not ones as crooked as an old man's fingers. And any damn fool could see the difference easy enough between the Sutters' homestead and the Richters' homestead. The Richters had fresh white paint on the house and outbuildings. They had fields clean of weeds, fields thick in the wet low spots as well as the dry high areas, and crops taller than her. The buildings on the Sutters' place had been slapped up with split logs from every class of tree, had never been painted, were hard to keep the weather out of, and were getting ruined from the inside out, every one of them. The house had a porch on the front, but the supports had sunk into the soft soil and it leaned heavy to one side, as though the old rooster who was forever perched on the roof on that side and cackled at every creature that dared come near had weighed it down with its few pounds of fluff. Whenever that rooster swooped down in a great flutter of brown and red feathers to scare the hounds off the porch, it shat and left great long gray streaks that went down the side of the house and onto the ground, as if the house were crying. One day, she'd catch that rooster, twist its neck, and throw it in a pot, but until then, she appreciated the frenzy it stirred in the dogs, keeping them away from the kitchen door and their scents from seeping through. Those hounds too were nothing but a mess of burs and long ears and were good for nothing but dragging already-dead carcasses up into the yard to attract the flies that Pernilla so hated. Not one of the dogs had enough gumption or sense to hunt, catch, or kill anything on its own. They were scavenging hounds only, loping around with rotting meat in their filthy teeth all the day long.

The Sutter boys had broken most windows on the farm's buildings with slingshots and rocks, and one had been broken when they held a contest among themselves to see who was the bravest and could punch a bare fist through glass. Cal won. With delicate webs, the spiders soon filled the empty spaces between the jagged glass remains and the frames. The webs trapped insects large and small, insects that the little Sutter boys plucked and challenged one another to eat. The pigs had chewed off one entire corner of the barn, and their trough was a veritable haven of fat rodents squealing for food as loud as the sows themselves. The Sutters' milking herd, a half a dozen Holsteins skinny as saplings, leaked through the rotted cattle fence in a steady stream all year round. None of their cows was tagged or branded the way the Richters' cows were, and the little Sutter boys spent great parts of their day hunting down the beasts and slapping sticks against their behinds all the way home. The boys often chased home cows filched from other farmers' herds, and Pernilla had long ago stopped fussing when a neighbor came to claim his best milker —her brothers, though not very educated, had a talent for picking the best-producing bovine, once one of Wilhelm Richter's herd. When Liesel had noticed it missing, she told her pa, who had driven up to the Sutters' farm in his wagon and had called to Pernilla from his seat. "You haven't seen my best milker, have you?" He smiled and tried to look friendly.

"What color is it?" asked Pernilla. She pretended she didn't know that her brothers had tied up a new cow in the granary the night before.

Richter laughed. "Black and white, like all the rest of them," he said. A low bellowing came from behind the doors of the granary.

"Nope." Pernilla stared at the granary. "Haven't seen any like that around here."

Richter looked toward the granary too. "Well, if you do," he said to Pernilla. "Giddap, team," he said to his horses. "If you do," he yelled, "be careful with her. She bites."

Pernilla sent Lester on over to the Richters' that evening leading the stolen cow, which nipped at his hind pockets, one of which held a folded note from Pernilla Sutter to Luther Richter that read, *Boys take cow while you at lake with me. Tie up cows better. Love, Pernilla Sutter.* She'd also made Lester rehearse this speech: My sister found this cow eating the onions out of her garden. Is it yours? Would you please do something about keeping your herd out of Perny's garden?

By the time Lester arrived at the Richters' and presented the cow to Liesel, the story sounded like this: Here is your cow. This cow likes onions. This cow ate one of my pockets.

Lester handed over the rope to Liesel. She took it and stroked the cow's long velvety nose. Then Lester revealed a wadded-up note in his fist and presented that to Liesel too. She unfolded the paper. One entire half was gone; the remaining half was soggy.

"Cow teeth," said Lester.

Liesel read what was left. "I think this is for Luther," she said. "I think she and Luther are in love."

"Yep," said Lester.

Liesel pulled the cow back to the barn, slapped her rump until she moseyed in, and then led Lester to the garden. Liesel selected and pulled a few of her tallest onions, shook the soil off the bulbous roots, and told Lester to take them home for his family. He turned around and left through the same field he'd entered when he'd led in the cow, only this time it was he, not the cow, who lollygagged through the rows, chewing bean pods and swatting winged, stinging insects. Liesel watched him until he climbed over the fence to the Sutters' fields and took off at a head-forward sprint toward his house with the onions bopping against his thigh.

The Sutter fields sprouted tenacious patches of thistles, cocklebur, and milkweed, which nobody pulled or bothered about. The only tidy place on the farm was Pernilla's own little garden, where she grew cukes, onions, potatoes, string beans, and dill on one side and strawberries, tomatoes, rhubarb, and melons on the other. She spent much of the late summer canning and freezing. Pernilla had little opportunity for pride except in her garden.

When Lester dumped the onions on Pernilla's kitchen table, she said, "They ain't as big as mine." But she sliced them anyway and threw them in a pot of beef stock for soup.

Another source of satisfaction was her imagined future with Luther, the son of Wilhelm Richter, and the way in which she was sure she had won him.

22

WILHELM RICHTER HAD BEEN preparing for the antiwar rally for weeks. He and Archie, along with the mayor and the city council, had organized this day to unite the citizens of New Germany as well as to show the politicians in St. Paul that German-Americans wouldn't be bullied into fighting a war they didn't want. "Into the wagon, my children," he had said to his boys and daughter that morning.

Liesel Richter had spent all morning washing her hair and pinching her cheeks. She'd never, not once, ventured farther than Spider Lake, and she'd never seen more than ten people in one place. But her papa had demanded that every one of them get ready to go into town for the parade.

"Me?" she had asked then.

"Yes, you," he'd replied. "It is important we all go and support the cause." He'd looked at Herman long and hard.

"You look nice," Herman said to Liesel now.

"Thank you," she said. Since their argument over the war, Herman and Liesel had mostly avoided each other and certainly avoided speaking of anything that might create further tension. Liesel spent more and more time out of the house, taking Otto on walks with her or spending time with Lester. Sometimes it felt like the three of them, she, Lester, and Otto, were a family. She wondered if Lester'd be in town today.

Herman had said he'd not be going, but Wilhelm ordered him into the wagon too.

"I'm eighteen now," said Herman.

"Damn you," said Wilhelm. "If you say that one more time, I'm going to give you the beatings I should have given you as a child. You are not eighteen until I say you are." Wilhelm's voice quivered. He never spoke to his children this way. "Now get in."

Luther followed behind the wagon, thundering in the Richters' new tractor, sending out a holy racket for miles. The wagon and tractor passed the Richters' own grove; Spider Lake; the Sutters' grove, in which cows and pigs foraged for things they sniffed out of dirt; acres and acres of fields; other farm places; and kids walking into town, who covered their eyes and noses when they passed. A dirty cloud rose a mile into the sky from the skip of the horses' hooves, the roll of the wagon, and the grip of the Richters' new tractor. The wind picked up the earth and swirled it into a spinning dust devil that crossed over the road and sped off into a field laid out with cut alfalfa, lifting the grasses into flying, swirling clumps of green.

"Bad omen," said Herman to Liesel. She watched the dust devil until it wore itself out and left a pile of alfalfa on top of a far-off hill.

"Bad omen, I said," Herman said louder.

Liesel nodded at her brother. She couldn't speak. Her tongue felt like a loaf of bread in her mouth, dry, big, and wheaty. The closer to town they got, the worse she felt. Her stomach spun. She saw black spots and could hear only a whooshing noise. Once in town, she managed to ask her papa for a drink of water, which he gave her from his own canteen. She tried to swallow, but her throat wouldn't let it down. She coughed and spit it out. Wilhelm slapped her on the back and said to relax. Then he left his children and was off to look for Archie. Benjamin made a beeline for Mueller's bakery to find Sonnen. Herman turned in the opposite direction, toward the doctor's house, to pick up Betty.

Luther took a flask from his trouser pocket, pulled Liesel aside, and said, "Here, have a drink of this."

"I'll have a sip," said Otto. He jumped up to reach it.

Luther stretched it above his head. "I bet you would, you little shit," said Luther. "But no. You're too little."

On any other day, Liesel would never have considered in a million years drinking what she knew to be in the flask, but today she thought she'd take anything that calmed her nerves. Anything. Luther unscrewed the lid and handed the flask to her. She put it to her lips and tipped it. Oh, what a sweet fire. Her tongue shrank and allowed the liquid to pass. On its way down, it lit up her chest. Luther grabbed the flask back and swilled a big drink.

"Good?" asked Luther.

Liesel brought her hand to her mouth. Her eyes watered.

"She can't talk," said Otto. "Is she going to die?"

"Not likely," said Luther. "Gotta go."

Liesel spotted a place alongside a brick wall in front of one of New Germany's saloons, just across the street from the baseball field. She walked to the wall and pressed her back and palms flat against it, as though for support. She held Otto's hand in hers but soon lost him to a gang of other boys running and pushing their way to the front of the crowd for the best view of the speech and the baseball game.

It felt strange to be even a few miles from home. The town of New Germany was small, but its noise, tall buildings, smells, and people seemed a different world to Liesel. "Come right back here after the game," she called after Otto. Her voice sounded odd to

154

her, and she was embarrassed by its depth. The chirping of the girls around her whirred high and sharp. Even their German sounded clearer than the low and grumbled dialect she and her brothers spoke. These girls spoke German the way Mrs. Lehrer did. Distinctly. Proudly. Liesel figured the difference was in the teaching of it.

A group of men spoke English inside the saloon, loud enough for Liesel to hear them above the clanking of glasses and the scrape of chairs and boots against the floor.

"That goddamn Richter'll get what's comin' to him," said one.

Liesel's skin goose bumped.

"You betcha," said another. "Thinks he's really somethin' with all that land and his new tractor."

Liesel peeked her nose around the corner of the door frame. The long bar was empty except for a few men in the center sitting on stools. Harald Sutter sat near the middle of the bar.

"If I see Richter at the bank negotiating any more loans . . . ," said one man. He trailed off and took a drink from his mug. When he set the glass down, white foam clung to his mustache. "I don't know what I'll do."

"We'll get it back," said Sutter. "All of it."

"Traitors is what they are," said the mustachioed man. He stuck his tongue out and swiped it to each side of his mouth, licking up all the froth. "My pa always said you can't trust a German." The man leaned in toward Sutter's ear and whispered, nodding toward Liesel.

"Damn right," said Sutter. He glanced over his shoulder and caught sight of Liesel. She quick pulled her head back and stepped away from the door. Had she heard that right? Were people after her papa? Why? What would they do to him?

Commissioner Patterson stomped down the walkway toward the saloon. He patted his cane on the ground and hummed a little tune to himself. When he passed the young lady standing along the wall, he tipped his hat to her and said, "Good day."

"Good afternoon," said Liesel quietly. She sidestepped along the wall, and with the commissioner watching her every move, she turned and strode as briskly as she knew how away from there.

"Better run along," the commissioner called after her, "and get a good seat. It's going to be a fine show."

Liesel wiped her sweaty palms on her skirt and quickened her pace even more. She didn't turn around.

Beneath a tall, peaked pillar, a monument that had been erected by the sons and daughters of the men and women who'd died in the Indian Wars fewer than fifty years earlier, Archie Richter stood to deliver the speech that would kick off the anti-war rally, the baseball game, and the parade.

Those people loyal to the Nonpartisan League and the peace movement crowded all around. Wilhelm collected Benjamin, Herman, Luther, and Otto and pushed them front and center. He didn't want them to miss a word. The few who championed the war cause, members of Sutter's Watchdogs of Loyalty, stood in a shady place beneath an oak tree at the back of the square. Commissioner Patterson and Harald Sutter stood in the center of these men, Lester beside Harald, hunched in his overalls.

And though he usually kept his eyes to the ground, Lester this day swung his head back and forth, took in the whole view of so many people and so much excitement. Lester smiled big when he saw Liesel. He waved in a large swinging motion above his head. Liesel pretended not to notice him. She didn't know much about social etiquette, but it seemed to her that he was in violation of most social behaviors. She wasn't sure she wanted to draw attention to herself by acknowledging him.

The crowd hushed when Archie approached the podium, and it was at that moment that Lester yelled, "Hey, Liesel!" across the square. Harald belted Lester on the arm, and Lester stopped waving and put down his hand. Liesel raised her own hand to her midsection and lifted a few fingers to say hello in return. Then she turned her attention to her uncle.

"Hallo, hallo," he said. "Welcome, friends and neighbors. Folks, I'm going to speak in English today, the language of this great country, because I want our non-German company to understand what I have to say."

Most of the crowd turned to look behind themselves toward the Watchdogs. Commissioner Patterson stood with his legs apart and leaning forward on his cane. Harald Sutter was bent to one knee. Archie cleared his throat, which garnered the attention of the audience again. He accepted a glass of lemonade from Frieda, took a drink, and then spoke.

"We stand here today on the eve of a most dangerous conundrum. We are gathered among friends and allies, as well as watchdogs with judgment and self-righteousness in their hearts."

Harald Sutter put a cigarette to his lips, cupped his hand around his mouth, struck a match, and lit it. He took a deep drag, tossed the match to the ground, and tucked the matches into his shirt pocket. The match sparked the dry brown grass. Tiny fireflies of light flashed inches above the match before burning out and dying. Lester bent over it and spat. He rubbed the spittle all around with his finger until his pa kicked his leg and told him to get up.

"Need rain," Sutter said to his companions but loudly enough for the people in the crowd to hear. "These fools should be organizing a rain dance instead of a war protest."

The backs of the men near the rear of the crowd stiffened. They straightened their shoulders so as to cover more space, and a few curved their arms behind their backs and clenched one hand in the other. One man moved his wife forward and slung his arm around her shoulders, offering her some small gesture of protection against Sutter and the Watchdogs. Wilhelm and Benjamin stood shoulder to shoulder behind Herman, Otto, and Luther. When Wilhelm gestured for Liesel to come stand with them, she shook her head no.

Archie lowered his chin for a moment, then raised it again.

"But I believe just as we, as neighbors, can settle our differences peacefully, so can the United States and Germany," he said. "On this day, as we gather here to celebrate our unity, culture, and freedoms, a massive battle rages overseas in the homes and fields and towns of our European family and friends." Archie pointed east to battlefields that were many cities and an ocean away, but as close to home as the fields, hills, and sloughs of New Germany. "We must remember that this war was not instigated by Germany." At this, Archie nodded at Frieda, who brought him a piece of paper. Archie straightened his glasses and unfolded the paper. "Many of you know that Wilhelm and I, like most of you, have family in Germany and fighting with the Germans. Here is a letter from Gunther Richter, our eighteen-year-old cousin." Archie cleared his throat.

Dear Wilhelm and little cousins,

Excuse the poor writing. Dark and wet here.

I wish I had better news to report, but this letter too is fraught with bad news. One lady was trying to get out of the village on the train with her children. The Belgers shot her and then her children. One of the little chaps was suffering from the shot and so he was bashed against the wall and died finally. I swear to you of this.

There is terrible mistreatment of German prisoners. We found one of ours strewn across the road with his eyes cut out. Another whose hands had been removed with an ax and placed in his pockets. If this is the civilization America wants to come fight for, then America is out of her right senses.

Some good news is that Mother and the rest are fine and safe. They were lucky to have money enough to leave the village early. Mother will never forget your kindnesses, cousin.

Root for Germany. She is in the right.

Gunther

The crowd applauded. Wilhelm Richter nodded and put his hands on Otto's shoulders. Harald Sutter kicked at nonexistent rocks. Commissioner Patterson scratched notes on a piece of Sutter's cigarette paper.

"Getting ready for your speech?" Sutter asked him.

"Yes, my man," said the commissioner. "I am indeed."

"Are you gonna mention my name?"

"Not likely." He licked the tip of his pencil and wrote some more. "All right. Got enough here, I think. I'd like to cool off with a drink, boys. Back to the saloon."

"Yep," said Sutter. "I've seen enough a this. Let's get that man a drink." And in a noisy herd of stomping and kicking, they headed back to the saloon.

"Hi, Liesel," said Lester as he and his pa passed her.

"Get movin', you idiot," Sutter said. He winked at Liesel.

Archie waited for the Watchdogs to retire to the saloon before he began again. "Friends and neighbors, how can we send our sons to shoot bullets into their own relatives? Against the very country that bred most of us? Against the country that some of you veterans fought with in the Prussian War? The right thing to do, it seems to me, is not fight. It seems to me that the right thing to do is not allow our sons to be drafted into this war. Today, friends and neighbors, sign your name to the petition we have written asking our American Congress not to draft German-American boys who do not want to fight German boys."

The crowd applauded again.

Herman's face reddened. "Roosevelt says we have no hyphenated Americans here," he said. "Either you are American or you are not."

"Do not start with that nonsense today, Herman," said Wilhelm. "It is not that simple." He herded all four of his boys toward the petition. "Get in line."

"I cannot sign that petition," said Herman.

"You can and you will."

"I'm signing it," said Luther. "I can't waste my good looks fighting in war." He raised one eyebrow.

Wilhelm slapped Luther on the back and gripped him by the scruff of his neck. "You, my son, just might not need a war to get yourself into trouble. That mouth of yours will do just fine, I'm sure."

"Can't help the way God made me," said Luther.

Betty Mathiowetz took the stage to sing a tune popularized by Morton Harvey, "I Didn't Raise My Boy to Be a Soldier." At her ascent, Wilhelm elbowed Herman in the ribs. "Pretty little thing," he said. Herman relaxed his tight lips and brow. He actually smiled. He stared at Betty and thought himself a lucky man.

Liesel couldn't take her eyes off Betty either. Here was a perfect woman, she thought. All that a woman should be. Beautiful. Delicate. Ladylike. She admired her and disliked her at the same time. Liesel tried to imitate Betty's posture. She threw her shoulders back. She tilted her head just a bit.

Betty folded her hands in front of her skirt, took a deep breath, turned, and signaled to the small band in the corner of the stage, who whipped up the tune. She sang:

> Ten million soldiers to the war have gone
> Who may never return again;
> Ten million mothers' hearts must break
> For the ones who died in vain —
> Head bowed down in sorrow, in her lonely years,
> I heard a mother murmur thro' her tears:
>
> "I didn't raise my boy to be a soldier,
> I brought him up to be my pride and joy.
> Who dares to place a musket on his shoulder,
> To shoot some other mother's darling boy?"
> Let nations arbitrate their future trouble,
> It's time to lay the sword and gun away.
> There'd be no war today
> If mothers all would say,
> "I didn't raise my boy to be a soldier."

What victory can cheer a mother's heart,
When she looks at her blighted home?
What victory can bring her back
All she cared to call her own?
Let each mother answer in the years to be,
"Remember that my boy belongs to me."

Archie plucked a white handkerchief from his breast pocket and dabbed his forehead. He turned his face to the blue sky, perhaps wondering when the heat would let up and the rain fall. He laid his hand on Betty's shoulder and said, "Fine, fine. Wasn't that a fine song from our doctor's daughter?"

Betty smiled at him and then waved to the crowd. Herman broke away from his pa and brothers and rushed to the front to help Betty step off the stage. Herman didn't agree with his father about much, but he did agree that Betty Mathiowetz was a good-looking girl, the kind a boy such as himself should marry. But he had things to do before that time.

"Folks," said Archie. "Our boys are going to put on a game for you. Let's head to the baseball diamond and see what they've got. And our ladies have been working their fingers to the bones preparing food and treats for us. Let's go."

Liesel watched Herman and Betty stroll arm in arm toward the diamond. She wondered if anyone would ever hold her that way, walk with her that way, look at her the way Herman looked at Betty. Liesel didn't have much in the way of social skills, but she did know that her blatant staring was strange, and she hoped no one had caught her at it. She stooped her shoulders again and pretended to study the dust on her boot.

Right around then, the Watchdogs of Loyalty were having their pitcher filled for the fifth time that day. Harald Sutter was unusually sweet to his boys Lester and Cal. He got them each a mug and allowed them to drink. When Cal got up to go to the game, his pa wished him luck, said to show them other boys how to play baseball. Harald Sutter had always liked baseball. He'd been a good player himself, once upon a long time ago, before he'd gotten that girl pregnant, his own second cousin, and had had to marry her. He was only seventeen at the time and was just messing around in the hay barn with her. If he had known what those acts would lead to, he'd have wrapped himself in sheep's bladder before pulling up that girl's skirt and poking her, or he would've demanded that she rinse herself out with vinegar after he was done. That first baby, Pernilla, screamed a sacred racket her entire first year of life, nearly driving him to throw a rope over the barn rafters and hang himself. And then there were more and more children. My God, how the children came. You wouldn't have thought a woman could generate so many. And oh, how the wife liked to drink and mouth off. He couldn't slap the filth out of her fast enough before the next abuse came sputtering out of her fat lip. That woman had a dirty mouth, and the first thing she did was teach those kids to talk dirty too.

But here, now, at this table, his life felt fine. For the first time, Harald Sutter felt he was getting the respect every human deserves. He was getting good money for a job done well. He was getting a little bit back in exchange for what he had lost to Richter. It was never easy to lose land, Sutter knew. But to lose land given to you by your own pa was just a crime. To have that land sitting there in Richter's name nearly drove Sutter to retch. But here and now, he could see that all those bad moves made by Richter would come back to get him. It felt good.

"Cal," Harald said, "you have a good game."

"You bet, Pa," said Cal.

"Don't let that Richter boy get on your slider."

"No, Pa. I won't."

Lester got up and said, "I'm going home."

"Yep," said Harald. "You go on home." When the other men

162

asked him what was wrong with his boy, Harald told them, "Nothing. He's as nice a boy as you'll ever meet."

When Liesel Richter spotted Lester Sutter emerge from the saloon, she ran to him. "Where are you going?" she asked. "Are you going home?"

"Home is right," he said.

"I'll walk with you," she said. Maybe it was that little bit of whiskey she'd had or maybe it was the heat getting to her, but she took his hand in her own. "I want to go home too."

They walked that way the miles it took to get to the road that led to both their farms. At the place where he should've turned off to go to his own farm, Lester kept walking. Liesel's hand in his felt so nice. He walked her up the Richters' driveway and to the place behind the barn. There, she removed her hand and let it travel up his arm and to his face, down his neck and farther. He grew hard in her hand, and neither of them voiced any objection as she slid her hand inside his overalls.

23

THE NEW GERMANY BREWMASTERS, wearing gray uniforms with black socks and caps, took the field. Luther ran to third base, pulled a beige sack from inside the thumb of his mitt, and pinched a fingerful of tobacco from it. He shook the strays off the bunch, stretched his bottom lip, and tucked the black mess into the pouch between his lip and gum. He leaned first one way, then the other, limbering those long legs. He tipped his cap at a couple of girls along the foul line. Pernilla Sutter set down the child she'd been carrying, hitched up the hem of her skirt, and tucked it into her waistband.

"Good heavens, Pernilla," said Betty Mathiowetz. "Your drawers are showing." Betty stood dressed in her Sunday best, which meant petticoats, gloves, and a hat in place no matter how heated the day.

"I ain't interested in your man so you don't have to worry," said Pernilla. "It's just so damn hot these days." She picked up the little girl again, took hold of the girl's arm, and waved it up and down at Luther. The girl's fingers flapped like a broken wing.

Luther brought an empty cupped hand to his mouth and pretended to drink. Pernilla barged past Betty and the other girls to the concession stand, where she bought a caramel for the little girl, a beer for herself, and a beer for Luther. In between batters, Luther jogged to the fence where she stood and gulped it. Herman yelled for him to get back to his position. He stood with his hands on his hips when Luther didn't get back in position immediately.

The people of New Germany hadn't intended to have two baseball teams. They hadn't intended for those teams to be separated by nationality, Germans on the New Germany Brewmasters team, coached by Herman Richter, and everyone else on the Spider Lake Nine, wearing pinstriped uniforms with red socks.

A baseball diamond was to southern Minnesota what war was to the countries of Europe: a field of grass and dirt where boys who spoke a common language and wore the same uniform battled against other boys who spoke a different common language and wore a different uniform. As in war, on both sides of the field old men stood behind the boys and called out instructions and demanded stronger effort, truer aim, better strategy. Also as in war, women waited on the periphery for the business of the day to be done so that they could gather up the survivors and cool their tempers or compliment their skills, whatever the outcome demanded.

Luther Richter liked to chug a few beers before his games and liked to nurse a couple more during. But even so, when Luther Richter grabbed the bat and eyed the pitcher, there was no fence long or wide enough that could hold in his blow. The baseball soared as if carried by an unearthly buoyancy, over the infield, outfield, fence, and into the deep rows of the tall, dry corn. Afterward, the boys'd meet up at the boat landing and drink till morning. More than once, Liesel had been wakened by a pounding at the door and had opened it to find her brother slumped over the shoulders of a neighbor boy or two. More often than not, he'd have a black eye or a bloodied nose that needed to be cleaned before she led him out to the barn and sent him on up the ladder to the loft or settled him in the straw beside the cows if the cleaning and swabbing of his wounds hadn't sobered him enough to climb.

Today, Luther Richter batted fourth. There was a man on third ready to score on a hit or a home run. Even a sacrifice fly would have been fine, but everyone knew Luther would never forfeit his own chance to touch the bases for the sake of one measly run. Luther was a glory hound. His swinging stance was loose. He didn't take practice cuts, didn't look to the third-base coach for instructions, didn't raise his hand for time while he shuffled the batter's-box dirt.

When Cal Sutter, the pitcher of the Spider Lake Nine, tossed one up and far outside, the crowd gasped. Cal wasn't the hardest thrower, but years of breaking windows and pitching bales and slugging his brothers had honed his aim. Luther thought the bad pitch was some fluke. When the second one lifted up and out the same way, Luther poked his bat at it and fouled off down the first-base line.

"Better give me something to hit, Cal-girl," called Luther from the batter's box.

The catcher of the Spider Lake Nine stood and stepped to his right, several feet away from the plate. Cal Sutter pitched the ball out.

"Ball two," called the umpire.

Luther Richter pointed his bat toward the mound. "It will be the ball or it will be you, Cal," called Luther. "I mean it."

The catcher threw the ball back to Cal, who caught it in a snap.

"Just get in the box and shut up," said Cal. He turned away from Luther and walked to the back of the mound where he kept a bottle of beer. He tipped the bottle, swallowed all its contents, and then heaved it over the heads of Luther, the catcher, and the umpire. The bottle smashed against the wooden backstop and shattered into jagged shards. A couple of women watching in the stands ducked and screamed. A few men shook their heads. Some laughed. Someone called out to the boys on the baseball diamond, "Just play ball." Cal smiled and nodded as if he'd heard. Luther stepped into the box.

All through Luther's body, charges bubbled and tingled. The urge to hit, to give his nerves and muscles a reason to stretch and breathe and release their tightness, raged. Even his palms and fingers wanted it, felt as though they'd split open if he didn't whack that baseball with every strand of muscle beneath his skin.

Cal went into his wind-up and lobbed the ball high and outside.

"Ball three," called the umpire.

Another went the same way.

On his charge to the mound, all Luther Richter saw was fury. He tossed down the bat and tackled Cal in a flurry of swinging fists and dust. The benches emptied and people poured onto the field. The outfielders and infielders bulled toward the fray. Fans for both teams shouted. Some called encouragement: "Get him." "Knock him out." Others called out for a stop to the nonsense.

"Whoo-hoo," yelled Pernilla Sutter. She raised her fist. "Get him, Luther. Get that bastard." She turned to a group of girls standing near her, Betty Mathiowetz among them. "That's my brother he's getting. He's gonna knock him out, I bet."

Betty, who had at times tried to be kind to this girl, crossed her arms and said, "There's something wrong with you, Pernilla Sutter. You're not right."

Pernilla sniffed and wiped her hand against her nose.

"What do you know about anything, Little Miss Perfect?" she said.

Herman weaved his way through the crowd to his brother. He grabbed Luther beneath the arms and pulled him off the Sutter boy. "Luther!" he said. "Stop. Stop now." Luther fell back into

Herman's arms. The Sutter boy lay on the gravel. Blood poured from his mouth, and his nose was cracked at the bridge, near his right eye socket.

"Jesus, Luther," said Herman.

Cal Sutter lifted his hand to his nose and scrabbled his legs against the hard ground.

"Get him outta here," he said. "Get him away from me. He's crazy. That guy is crazy."

The game went on without Luther and Cal, who were remanded to their respective dugouts. When the game ended and the boys lined up to shake hands, Luther Richter wrapped his arms around Cal Sutter in a hug.

"I didn't mean nothing by it," he said to Cal.

"No hard feelings," said Cal. "But when I see you alone, I'll kick your ass."

"You may try," said Luther.

While the baseball game played itself out, the Watchdogs had the saloon to themselves.

"Well, my boys," said Commissioner Patterson to the Watchdogs, "are we all ready then?"

"We'll follow your lead," said Sutter.

"Yes," Commissioner Patterson said, "you'd be wise to do so. Pour me another lager, would you?" He tapped his cane on the wooden floor.

Sutter poured beer from the pitcher into a mug. Foam spilled over the top and slithered down the side. He wiped the glass clean with his hand then handed it to Patterson.

"Teaching these Germans reminds me of a project I once headed up in my East African railroad-building days," said Patterson. The Watchdogs listened intently, felt honored to associate with so worldly a man. "You know, some of the natives put up quite a fuss at having modernization come to their primitive world."

168

Sutter nodded his head and tried to look obliging. "They shoulda been proud to have you there helping them," said Sutter. He squinted his eyes and tried to look smart.

"Yes," said Commissioner Patterson. He cleared his throat and sighed the same sigh he used to exhale when one of his workmen brought a new complaint from the African porters, guntooters, or construction workers. They were always complaining, it seemed, and didn't understand about progress. "You'd think they'd be appreciative of all the fine machines and goods the railroads brought, but explanations just proved to be a waste of time. In one ear and out the other of all those half-naked chiefs, witch doctors, and whatnot." Patterson thumped his fingers on the knob of his cane in a wave, pinkie to pointer finger, pointer to pinkie.

"You mean they didn't wear no clothes?" asked Sutter. He grinned at this thought and shook his head, enjoying the absurdity. He pictured naked men holding pickaxes and shovels and all the things one would need to build railroad tracks.

"It's our duty then as Christians to just do what's best in the name of progress," said Patterson. He lifted the glass to his lips, brushed his mustache to the sides of the rim, and drank down half the contents. "As we used to say then, 'It won't do to have the monkeys running the circus.'"

"They should wear clothes," added Sutter. "Could get hurt real bad if a stray nail got loose."

Outside, the band that would lead the end-of-the-day parade warmed up. Drummers beat a tune and the rhythm vibrated the wooden floor of the saloon. "Sounds like the parade's started," Patterson said. "You Watchdogs finish up. We better get out there." This moment was to be his shining one. He'd halt this parade and convince these Germans of the error of their thinking, turn them around, get his name in the papers, and head back to the capital with a fat promotion waiting for him, he was sure.

He stood, and each of the Watchdogs swallowed the remainder of his beer and stood to leave too. "Take care of the tab, will you, Sutter?"

Sutter fished in his pockets for money and tossed a number of bills onto the bar.

The Watchdogs spread out among the crowd. Sutter followed Patterson to the middle of Main Street and stood alongside him and crossed his arms. When Richter's tractor came into sight, the two of them would halt the parade and disperse the crowd, send them home with a warning and, hopefully, with a renewed sense of loyalty to America and progress. The other Watchdogs would make sure no Germans tried to intervene.

24

THE TWIN CITY 60-95 tractor was the newest, sleekest model developed and released by the Minneapolis Steel and Machinery Company, and owning one said plenty about one's economic standing. Wilhelm Richter had had his shipped by rail from Minneapolis. On his farm, the tractor would pull a cultivator, planter, and plow. In the New Germany antiwar parade, the tractor would be a symbol of the hearty, productive German people. And Luther, more than Benjamin or Herman, seemed suited to drive it, and seemed best suited to represent German stock too, with his strong body and blond hair. His drinking and brashness worried Wilhelm some, but he knew that boys were spirited creatures and that Luther would soon grow up and be responsible.

"Careful with her now," he said to Luther. "Her clutch is stiff."

"Someone hold my shirt," said Luther. Luther pulled his baseball jersey over his head and handed it to his papa. Wilhelm took it and handed it to Herman. "Hold this," he said.

Herman took the shirt and crumpled it into a small ball. He wanted to shake his papa for creating this big display of disloyalty, for volunteering their tractor for the parade, for encouraging Luther's already enormous ego, for treating him, Herman, like a boy rather than a man. Herman turned and grabbed Betty's hand. "Come on. I'll walk you home."

"We're leaving?" said Betty.

"Yes," said Herman.

"But the parade hasn't even —"

"Never mind that," said Herman. He pulled her along.

Somewhere in Betty's mind, the thought of a marriage proposal danced around. Could this be it? Why else would Herman want so badly to get her alone? She complained no more and walked close to him all the way to her house. Soon she would be an engaged woman! Soon she would have a wedding to plan!

Luther climbed up the front wheels of the metal contraption that was just a bit shorter than he was and walked down the hood of it to the seat. He roared the machine to life and lurched it down Main Street. The spoked wheels whistled when they turned, and the heavy engine carriage grumbled and rattled.

Mothers held back their children as though the front end of the tractor might snap its teeth and eat the youngsters whole. Little girls put their hands over their ears and peeked from behind their mothers' skirts. Little boys reached their arms toward the noise and chased alongside it. German flags and signs protesting the war were taped to the side of the machine and fluttered in the breeze. On both sides of the street stood German immigrants, friends of the Richters and Archie and Frieda, farmers who ran land, farmers who raised cattle and hogs, schoolteachers, the local Catholic priest, girls propping little brothers and sisters on their hips, the brewer and all his employees in coveralls sitting on empty kegs, and the round butcher in a bloody apron. German, every one. Luther lounged in the seat of the machine with one hand guiding the steering wheel and the other wrapped around a bottle of beer. He would at times lift the beer in recognition of someone standing in the crowd. When he passed Herman and Benjamin, he gave a big grin, showing two rows of straight teeth, white as mother's milk, against his tanned skin.

Archie and Frieda had toted large stacks of fliers and handed heaps of them to their sons to pass out to the onlookers. The words translated into English as "Germans Don't Kill Germans" and "Keep Americans Out of a European War." Archie had prepared materials to persuade each person, German or American, against the war.

"Good turnout," said Wilhelm.

"Yes," said Archie. He pointed toward the saloon. Harald Sutter, picking his teeth with a toothpick, stood leaning against the door frame. "Even our friendly Watchdog has abandoned his post at the bar to enjoy the show."

"He didn't hear enough this afternoon, apparently," said Wilhelm.

"We have some men keeping an eye on him," said Archie.

"Well, here they come. To get a better view, maybe?" said Wilhelm.

"We'll see," said Archie.

The early summer day had nary a cloud. New Germany hadn't seen rain for weeks, and the crops drooped with thirst.

Benjamin shoved a piece of carrot cake into his mouth. He waved to his brother passing on the tractor. Sonnen used her sleeve to dab frosting from his chin. Luther raised his bottle to his oldest brother.

"*Ein prosit*," he yelled. "Is she fiery?" The girl's face blossomed into pink, and she tucked herself under Benjamin's arm. Benjamin pulled her close.

From behind the pair, Commissioner Patterson barged through, spreading Benjamin and his girlfriend apart and pushing them against the other parade-goers, then stomping with his light frame out into the street and toward Luther on the tractor. The commissioner raised his cane and his other arm, yelling, "Whoa, whoa, now. Stop this contraption, boy." Harald Sutter followed the commissioner out into the street.

Luther, for his part, paid no attention. He had turned his interest to a gaggle of schoolgirls on the opposite side of the street. He flexed one biceps, then the other, put one hand on the wheel, then the other. The throttle was wide open, and the tractor coughed a cloud of black smoke and a racket of engine noise into the air.

People in the crowd looked at the commissioner, then at one another, everyone wondering what was going on and who was going to do something about whatever it was that was going on.

Patterson walked alongside the tractor, tapping his cane on its fender. "Stop this thing this minute. Come down from there, boy!" he shouted. But still Luther rolled on.

And before anyone had had even a minute to assess the situation and do something about it, the commissioner's cane caught in one of the spoked wheels of the tractor, and, instead of giving up the cane to the tractor, he tried to wrestle it free. As he tugged and panted and commanded, "Whoa, whoa. Stop this blasted contraption," the bottoms of the commissioner's snakeskin boots slid against the smooth gravel of the street and he slipped onto his bottom, legs splayed wide. Luther finally took notice and stamped down on the clutch, which only slowed the tractor to a stagger as it rolled slowly over the right leg of Commissioner John Patterson and stopped there.

The only other time such a high, whinnying wail had escaped the lips of the commissioner was when his rifle had discharged and blown off his toes. It was a noise that rattled the rib bones of every man, woman, and child present at the parade.

"Shit," said Luther. He wrestled the tractor into park and hopped off. Before Luther could lean over the commissioner,

Harald Sutter had shoved him out of the way and wrapped his own arm around the commissioner's neck. He pulled and pulled but couldn't loosen the man from the wheel. More screaming and yowling came up from the commissioner.

Archie, Wilhelm, and Dr. Mathiowetz wound their way toward the mishap. And while Wilhelm held back Harald Sutter, and Dr. Mathiowetz worked to release Commissioner Patterson from beneath the tractor wheel, Archie reassured the crowd, told them to wait, not go, and remain calm.

Harald Sutter was a yelling, flailing mess, uncontrollable by Wilhelm Richter until Luther reached back, clenched his fist, and punched Sutter out cold.

"Luther!" said Wilhelm. "Damn it. Control yourself."

"He was making me nervous," said Luther.

They looked around for other Watchdogs or family to come claim Harald, but all had suddenly assimilated into the crowd or disappeared altogether. So Wilhelm and Luther set Sutter under a tree. When Dr. Mathiowetz finally freed the commissioner from the tractor, he directed Luther to pick the man up, and the two of them carried the crying pile to Mathiowetz's office, just a few blocks away. There, Dr. Mathiowetz injected the commissioner with a heavy dose of morphine, set his leg, and left him asleep on a cot.

At the back door of the Mathiowetzes' house, Herman pushed Betty up against the wall and leaned heavily into her. "Oh, Betty," he said. "I want you so bad."

Betty giggled. She put her little arms around Herman's neck and said, "You do?"

Herman pressed his lips alongside her temple, then her ear, and then down to her neck.

"You're so beautiful," he said.

Betty held still and waited. Herman nuzzled her neck and then reached around and grabbed her backside. He pulled her to him and pressed his groin against her. When he knelt in front of her, Betty thought surely the time had come.

Instead, Herman reached under her skirt and pulled at her drawers.

"What are you doing?" Betty said.

"Relax, baby," he said. He placed his fingers inside the waistband and tugged. He couldn't wait to get inside her. It had been so long since he'd had a woman. Well, he'd had only one before, Pernilla, but that was different. Pernilla hadn't appreciated him, though she had been accommodating. Since he'd started seeing Betty seriously, he'd had to give up the business with Pernilla. Anyway, he hadn't liked that Luther was on Pernilla too and knew that Pernilla was always comparing the two of them. Like everyone else, she had the wrong idea about Luther, thought he was way better than he really was. Herman couldn't wait to have Betty, a real woman, a woman he truly loved. And who truly loved him. Love from a real woman, a respectable woman, was something Luther would never have. Herman nipped at Betty's hipbone.

"Stop it," said Betty.

Herman yanked the underwear down and cupped his palm against Betty's privates. Betty felt good and horrified at the same time.

"Stop it," she said. She beat her fists against Herman's shoulders. He kissed her thigh.

"No, Herman," she whispered. "Stop it. I mean it."

Herman stood and unbuttoned his pants. In that short moment, Betty's disappointment settled upon her. Where was her ring? Where was the proposal? She had no intention of ending up like a Pernilla Sutter. She had other options. There were plenty of other boys in New Germany. Didn't Herman know that? Didn't he care? Did he just want to use her? "We're not doing this."

"Baby," Herman said.

"We're not married!" said Betty. "I'm not doing this until I'm married."

"I thought you loved me," said Herman.

"I thought *you* loved *me,*" said Betty. She pushed past him and went into the house.

The whole episode at the parade took fewer than ten minutes, during which the crowd mumbled, some biting their fingernails or twisting strands of hair or pretending to look for children, and waited until the parade began again. The mayor wondered if the people shouldn't be sent home. Archie said no, they'd worked too hard to organize the thing. The journalists from the state's newspapers took down every detail, scribbling with a ferocity rarely seen at small-town affairs. After a while, the people felt brave enough to chuckle and then bend over with hearty belly laughs at the scene they'd just witnessed. Finally, Luther returned and eased the tractor into gear. The band began playing again, stout men puffing their cheeks into brass tubas and trumpets and pounding on drums big as barrels. A little girl swirled the skirt of her dress to the music. One old man grabbed the hands of a fat old woman and pulled her into a few steps of polka dancing. People around them laughed and clapped. The highlight of the parade was the presence of Charles August Lindbergh, the Nonpartisan League candidate, in the last of a succession of shiny black Tin Lizzies hopping down the street and honking their cartoonish horns. Next to Mr. Lindbergh sat his sixteen-year-old son, Charles Augustus, waving and smiling a small grin at the people on the streets. Years later, all these people would read about Little Lindbergh's nonstop flight across the Atlantic Ocean and remember the boy sitting next to his father on this day, and they would remark, "My, my. Who would have thought?"

Behind the Tin Lizzies, bringing up the end of the parade, came a gaggle of children tossing out hard candies, butterscotches and lemon drops, and riding in a big, black topless 1903 Model A Ford was New Germany mayor August Frische, a former lawyer turned politician and the son of German Turner immigrants, a group of people who had little tolerance for the mighty influence of the church, the military, and, especially, the government. Frische's wife, Helga, sat beside him and peeked out from beneath her thick-brimmed hat. Helga was something of a starlet to the women of New Germany because she ordered her clothing from magazines rather than making them. The women leaned forward to catch sight of Helga's latest purchase, a navy and tan walking dress with a small blue jacket. She twisted a long strand of pearls around her thin fingers. Helga was a beauty, but she was smart too. Many folks speculated that she was really the brains behind Frische's political career. Helga was a dear friend to Frieda. The two met each week in Frieda's home to organize social services for the town of New Germany. A new hospital and women's clinic, staffed by real trained nurses and a physician, Dr. Mathiowetz, stood at the east end of town, thanks to them. The New Germany Turner school boasted full classes at each grade level. Students learned to read in English and German and could run their fingers over the titles of thousands of books in the library, many from the personal collection of Helga Frische, whose elegantly looped signature could be found inside the front covers.

Whoever was responsible for it, the term of August Frische had so far been one of prosperity and growth for the town of New Germany. And if this war ended soon, he'd have a real chance at a Senate seat. And that would mean an open post in the mayor's office.

"Archie," said Wilhelm later, in the newspaper building. "Perhaps you could be the next mayor of New Germany." He lifted his glass of beer as if in a toast.

"Perhaps, Wilhelm," said Archie. Archie admired Wilhelm's

pride and confidence, but he himself had a more nervous disposition.

"Today was a great day to celebrate peace," said Wilhelm. He rested his glass against his forehead. "Even if it was a bit hot and all things did not go exactly as we'd hoped. But we got the petition signed."

"Yes," said Archie. "Even in the best of times and under the best circumstances, some among us will work to pull down what others have worked hard to build. They will see unity and peace and call it conspiracy and dissent."

"You ought to write that down, print it in tomorrow's paper."

"I think I will."

25

THE NEXT MORNING, Frieda Richter was putting together the afternoon edition of the paper when a man in a navy suit opened wide the door of the *Deutsche Chronik*. Its editorial on the crippling of Commissioner Patterson as a metaphor for the state of the nation in general had not been regarded kindly by the legislators at the capital. Two law men from St. Paul stood on either side of the door with their arms crossed over their chests. Another tore the German-language and rally posters from the windows outside the newspaper building and threw wads of the paper onto the ground, letting the wind chase them down the street like scattering chickens. Another slapped glue onto the backs of notices that read: *This newspaper has been declared treasonous. Anyone caught distributing or reading it will be arrested as an agitator!* He smoothed the signs over the glass, left glue streaks dripping down. Frieda Richter looked up calmly from the desk where she worked. She smiled as if she had been expecting him all day.

"*Guten Tag,*" she said.

The man ignored the greeting of Frieda Richter and ignored

her two boys folding newspapers on a table off to her right and asked to see Archibald Richter, the editor of the newspaper. Frieda set aside the articles she'd been editing for print and asked the man whom she should say was asking.

"Ma'am," the man said, "I'm not sure you understand the gravity of my visit." He removed his hat, licked his hand, and slicked his hair to the right. "I am Merriwether Andrew Grossman from the Commission of Public Safety in St. Paul."

"Oh?" said Frieda. "Have you taken over poor Commissioner Patterson's post?"

"I have, and if you don't deliver Mr. Richter to me within five minutes, I will not only have this newspaper shut down, I will have you arrested for obstruction of justice. Do you understand me?"

"My husband?" said Frieda. "Have we done something illegal, Mr. Grossman?"

"I have it from a trustworthy source that your husband read a false testimonial from a German *soldier* to a crowd of citizens, with the intent to create disloyalty to the United States. And the testimonials from German citizens regarding the war that you have been publishing in your paper are not considered . . . very patriotic."

"Testimonials?" said Frieda. "And what does a testimonial from an old German woman or a young soldier gassed almost to death by the Allied Forces have to do with patriotism, Commissioner? We are simply publishing truth as experienced by people in Germany, some of whom are relatives of people here, citizens of this state."

"Mrs. Richter. Your version of the truth is not what we at the capital believe to be the truth."

Frieda slapped her palms on the counter in front of her. Her sons straightened their backs. She leaned forward toward the commissioner. "Mr. Grossman. The world is at war. I can assure you that victims can be found on both sides of the fray."

The commissioner pointed his hat at Frieda. "That is where you are very mistaken, Mrs. Richter. I don't think our fighting boys would agree with you and neither would their mothers. In war, there are victims and victimizers. A German soldier is a victimizer and will be portrayed as such in this country, in this state, and in this newspaper."

Frieda raised her eyebrows. "My God. What nonsense is this? Who champions censorship?" Frieda crossed her arms. "We'll not do it. We will print war testimonials from all sides. Just because you and your cronies find the truth inconvenient, or even horrific, does not mean that the truth should not be told or be written."

"Understand me," the commissioner said. "You will not print horror stories from the perspective of the enemy in this paper. Minnesota citizens do not want to read such unpleasantness. Morale is at stake."

"Morale is fiction. These testimonials are not a matter of readership desire, Mr. Grossman. We all need to read the truth."

Frieda Richter tucked her hands into her apron pocket. She didn't want the commissioner to see them shaking. She faced the man, and then turned her head slightly to her cowering boys and smiled. She'd birthed these two sons only in all her years of marriage. Now she poured all of her passion and knowledge into them. She said in German, "Look, boys, look who has come to New Germany. It's a big man from the government. Do you remember what I told you to do if this happened?"

The boys nodded yes. The little one's hands, nails blue from folding newspapers, trembled. The bigger boy, Hans, pulled his brother's hands below the table.

"Good then," she continued in German. "I want you to go warn your father. Tell him not to come to work and to hide at Wilhelm's place."

"*Nein,* Mama," the bigger boy responded.

"You must trust Mama now," she said. "Take Heinrich's hand and go."

She held the commissioner's stare and then said to him, in English, "My boys will go and get their father. May I offer you some coffee, sir?"

"Yes, Mrs. Richter. That would be very much appreciated. It's been a long journey."

"Go on, boys," Frieda said in English. "Do as I say." The boys scattered out the back door.

"Seem like nice boys, Mrs. Richter," said the commissioner. "May I ask why they are not in school today? Seems to me that school is in session for another week."

Frieda turned her back to the commissioner. "I'll get your coffee," she said.

"You realize it's truancy you're encouraging, Mrs. Richter. A blatant disregard for the compulsory education law. I could have my men pick up those boys."

Frieda turned to the commissioner. "You do that and you will not have their father, will you? Are you a bully to children, Commissioner? These are difficult days, but surely you haven't resorted to bullying children."

"I'm just curious as to why obviously bright children are not in school today."

"They are not in school because you have closed their school, Commissioner. Let's not play games. I haven't the stomach for it."

"Their school was deemed treasonous, Mrs. Richter. There are other schools here for studying, schools that teach in English."

Frieda again turned her back to the man. She poured coffee into a tin mug. "My boys speak English very well, Commissioner. My husband and I merely preferred a school that taught great literature, a school that nurtured the body as well as the mind."

"That school was teaching the language of the traitors. It was encouraging young Americans to have disdain for America."

"It was doing no such thing, Commissioner." Frieda faced the man. "The teachers simply allowed the boys to ask political questions and then simply responded with facts. The boys are free to make up their own minds."

"We have evidence that the schoolteacher was encouraging boys to refuse to fight."

Frieda lifted the tin of sugar. The commissioner shook his head no. "You arrested a good teacher for teaching reconciliation and compromise," she said. "I know of your evidence. *In dieser übringes so äusserst vlatten Welt.* The irreconcilable appears to me quite absurd." Frieda walked toward the man and stretched out the coffee to him.

The commissioner reached out his hand to accept first a napkin, then the mug. "Yes," he said. "The words of one of your great German writers."

"Goethe."

"The English-speaking schools teach literature too, Mrs. Richter. English literature." He sipped his coffee.

"Well, it's a good thing none of those writers are writing in Minnesota." Frieda walked back toward the coffee table. "You'd probably have them arrested for treason too."

"Mind your mouth. It's going to get you into a lot of trouble, Mrs. Richter."

"Perhaps."

Frieda poured herself a cup of coffee, stirred in a bit of sugar, and leaned against the desk. She faced the commissioner and watched him flip page after page of that day's *Deutsche Chronik*, stopping only to get a good long look at the cartoon drawing of Commissioner Patterson under the tractor wheel. *Rolled over by peace!* the caption read. After several minutes, Grossman replaced his hat on his head and turned toward the window. He pulled back the curtain.

"I'm tired of this nonsense, Mrs. Richter. Where is your husband?"

Frieda sipped her coffee. "He's not coming. If you honestly think I'd hand over my husband to you, you are as unwise as the politics that sent you."

"Very well then, Mrs. Richter. I thought perhaps we could do this the easy way, but I see that it is impossible." The commissioner rapped on the window to get the attention of the men standing outside. "Larson. Get in here."

A stout, bearded man burst through the door.

"Arrest her," said the commissioner. "And destroy everything. Good day, Mrs. Richter." The commissioner tipped his hat to her and walked out.

Frieda sat on the bunk in the county jail, holding her head high. Her pants legs were pressed and creased. From her vest, a gold watch chain hung, an anniversary present from her husband. She thought on many things. Her marriage had gone well. She'd raised two good boys. And though she couldn't know it yet, one of them would grow up to be a college professor and the other an editor of a Minnesota newspaper.

Frieda was proud of her own work at the newspaper. She'd come to this country with the intention of doing something worthwhile and felt she had done it. She'd put together a fine newspaper that reported the news from here and abroad and reported it as objectively as possible. She wanted to make her readers think. She wanted her readers to know how the mothers of Germany felt in comparison with the mothers of America. The worst that should have come out of such knowledge was a little more compassion and empathy for fellow human beings and, possibly, hopefully, a stronger distaste for violence, guns, and war. Violence, guns, and war, Frieda decided, were men's creations. And the only way for a woman to destroy what a man had created was for her to infiltrate the man's world and show him the error of his ways.

The only regret Frieda had in this world was her unresolved

relationship with her sister and her sister's daughter. And though Maggie had been dead for years, Frieda thought of her nearly every day. Frieda knew Maggie hadn't been thrilled to marry Wilhelm Richter, but Frieda knew Wilhelm was a good man, a good father, and a good citizen. No woman could ask for more. Wilhelm had loved Maggie and done his best by her. She just never quite got over leaving her Jewish lover behind. It was a circumstance that couldn't be helped. Frieda thought of Maggie's strange daughter, her own niece, Liesel. Frieda often meant to invite the girl to work at the paper or come over to the house for a visit, but she never did. Such a strange child, Liesel. Quiet, but thoughtful, obviously. Never looked anyone in the eye. Always seemed to be hiding. She made Frieda nervous.

Frieda Richter sat in a cell all by herself and wondered how it was that a woman could be jailed for a crime but couldn't vote. She sat there and knew she'd sit for two more weeks obsessing over that. *When I'm released,* she decided, *I will pack up my two boys, kiss Archie goodbye, and take a train to Minneapolis to begin a new campaign.*

26

THE YOUTH OF NEW GERMANY congregated to swap news at Spider Lake, the place they came each weekend. On Friday and Saturday nights, a small fire could be seen glowing in the distance, and young men and women, both towners and farmers, Germans, Norwegians, and Swedes, could be seen sneaking through the woods and creeping along the gravel road to its promise of beer, of conversation, of eventual marriage matches made or carnal lusts satisfied. And although it wasn't a weekend night, the young people of New Germany flocked to the water's edge this late evening with many interesting tales to tell of what they had seen and heard in town the day before.

The Richter house was filled to the brim. Archie and his sons had come that afternoon, and Wilhelm told Liesel to set them up as if they were staying indefinitely. At their first chance, Benjamin, Herman, and Luther had taken off toward the lake. To relax, they said. Liesel didn't mind. She had much to do and didn't need her brothers bothering her.

· · ·

From the Sutters' kitchen window, Pernilla could see the small orange fire near the lake. Her heart did a little jig at the thought of seeing Luther Richter, and so she washed and rinsed the dishes with new fervor. She could throw back beer with as much gulp and gusto as any common brewer. She never missed the chance to sneak away to the boat landing. She would tuck the little ones into bed and tell them to stay put. She'd wash her face and change her dress and lightfoot her way across the fields to the lake.

At twenty-eight years old, she had missed out on the chance to marry and raise a respectable family of her own; instead, since the death of her mother, she'd been put in charge of running the Sutter household and managing her younger brothers and sisters, the ones who remained after her father shipped off two of the boys to Canada to train for war. Other than these nights at the boat landing, Pernilla was never seen without two or three little Sutters trailing behind her. Some said the littlest Sutter was in fact hers, a remnant from one of her weekend frolics, but no one could ever say for sure. Others grumbled that something more sinister was going on in the Sutter house, something that involved Old Man Sutter and his own daughter, but people didn't get involved in family matters. And if Old Man Sutter was siring his own grandchildren with his own child, who could talk sense into a man like that anyway?

The girls of New Germany had no kind word for Pernilla no matter how awful her life might have been. They knew that probably all of their boyfriends had been trained in by Pernilla, and they called her all the names that threatened young women call the woman they are threatened by: *whore, Jezebel, harlot.* They called her other names too. Some were in English and some in their native languages, but Pernilla understood them all and tried not to mind. At these dark parties, she'd just stare at the girls who were frantically chatting and sipping on the same beers hour after hour while she downed one every twenty minutes and drank herself into a sweet place where no mosquito could bother her and all these country boys loved her.

The boys of New Germany and the surrounding area didn't much worry about who had been with Pernilla before. This girl was a chance for them to rut their desires without the nonsense of courting or the shame of rejection or the fear of consequence, far as they could tell. Pernilla hung back in the shadows of the landing, and after an hour or two a boy would declare his need to relieve himself, walk past Pernilla, and disappear into the black of the woods. She would soon follow, grab hold of a tree, and ram her backside into the eager groin of the boy.

If this was his first time, she was kind enough to lie in the leaves, pull the boy on top of her, and guide his body to fit with hers. Usually, two or three strokes completed the transaction. For a while afterward, she would stroke the boy's hair or face, if he wanted. The new ones were her favorites. They were always grateful and leisurely after. They liked to feel up and down her body, a body so different from their own, with soft pools of flesh and hairless skin. In the beginning, they would usually bring her sweets or trinkets. For other boys, weekends with Pernilla were regular encounters, and she could stay standing and face the tree. For the more experienced, Pernilla would first open her mouth and then her body.

Both Benjamin and Herman Richter had been trained in on the girl. Benjamin felt remorseful and ashamed after, and when the mood struck him again he made sure he entered her from behind so that he wouldn't have to feel her breath on his cheek or hear her grunt in his ear. And since he'd started seeing the red-head, he hadn't visited Pernilla at all. Herman, before he'd gotten serious with Betty, had thought he loved Pernilla and brooded when he imagined the other boys she'd been with. He wrote poems about her sad eyes and her long body and recited them to her at the boat landing. She looked at him with an arched brow and asked him if he wanted her to stand or lie down and if he had brought her any candy. Herman said no, he didn't have any candy, but offered to recite more poems for her, and Pernilla said sure and listened. *Ich sehne mich nach dir.* She offered no comment. When the time came for Luther to follow his older brothers to the boat landing on the weekends, Herman worked hard to distract him with much beer and talk. Sharing Pernilla with Benjamin and neighbor boys was one thing, but sharing her with Luther, careless, thoughtless, and probably the best-looking of any man, was too much for Herman. He knew that Luther wouldn't be gentle, would be coarse and vulgar probably. He also feared that Pernilla would take a liking to Luther's swagger, his arrogant jaw, his strong body. He had seen how Pernilla, how all the girls, gathered thick as flies whenever Luther was near. But eventually, Herman decided not to entertain himself with Pernilla Sutter anymore. He decided to totally commit himself to Betty.

Pernilla wiped the plates with a dishtowel and clanged them back into the cupboard. Harald Sutter dipped a comb into a cup of water and slicked his graying blond hair first one way, then another. He opened his mouth, cracked his jaw, then closed it again. Still hurt.

All around, Sutter children climbed, banged, and sat, stuffed as tight in the house as sheaves of wheat in a shock. Cal stood slicing apples and watching his pa and thinking about how they'd both been clobbered by Luther Richter. A little girl, face ravaged with mosquito bites, blond hair long and silkier than circumstances should have allowed, and eyes as bright and wide apart as a horsefly's, sat at Pernilla's feet and sucked on a handful of her dusty skirt hem. Pernilla pushed aside the little girl with a swipe of her bare foot.

"Get on outside or something," she said to the girl. The child fell over and yelped at the gesture. Her brother Lester put down his whittling knife and wood and swooped up his little sister with his long arms.

"There," he said. He rubbed his chin in her hair and took a mouthful of the blond tresses between his teeth.

"You dummy," said Pernilla. "Spit that out and put her down or you'll spoil her and I'll be the one having to tote her around in my arms all day. You can just forget about any supper then. You can just forget it, you slow thing."

She slammed the cupboard door.

"Slow in the head as them turtles you catch. Why don't you get yourself out to the barn where you belong? You bring in the flies with you every time you set foot in this kitchen."

Lester ignored his big sister and rubbed his chin in the little girl's hair again until the girl gurgled and laughed.

"Both of yous shut up," said Harald. "Shut your damn traps."

He sat at the kitchen table and swept an oilcloth up and down the long barrel of his shotgun. "Lester, put down that one and get your boots on," he said. "Cal, you too. We've got something needs doing tonight."

Pernilla wanted to ask to go along, but she knew better. She waved around the room at all her brothers and sisters. "You could gather up a couple more if you need them and take them with you," she said, "wherever you're going. You could take the whole lot of them, you know, and leave me a little peace and quiet for a change."

Harald blew a gust of air out his lips. "So's you can run off to the lake and get to whoring? You think I don't hear about what a daughter of mine is doing?"

He put down the oilcloth and pointed the gun at her.

"You got business here to attend to, and these ones are yours to mind." He swung the barrel all around the room.

He thought for a few seconds and then said, "I'll take the big boys. They'll see what men do and learn to be men tonight, I guess."

Pernilla looked at the boys, heads shaven to the scalp to deter the nesting bugs, skin hugging their ribs, common as any wild dog.

"You call these men?" she asked, then pointed at Lester with his mouthful of little-girl hair. "That one there is a man? Ha. I ain't seen no men around here in a long time. No big strapping men."

She stuck a washcloth in a pan of dirty dishwater and squeezed it out.

"No men like Luther Richter anyway," she added.

Harald pushed back the chair and stood. At shorter than five and a half feet, he didn't have much in terms of size to intimidate his daughter, but his voice could shake the rafters down off any building's frame.

"Whore!" he shouted. The bustle in the Sutter house stopped. Cal swallowed a chunk of apple whole. Pernilla held her breath and turned around slow. The little girl in Lester's arms scratched a mosquito bite on her eyelid, and Lester pushed her hand down away from it. "Shhh," he said to her.

Pernilla kept her face pointed toward the ground, but if Harald Sutter could have seen his daughter's eyes, he'd have been afraid. "If I'm a whore," she whispered, "it's you what made me."

Harald told Lester and Cal to get on outside. They did. And just as the screen door slapped against the frame, he flipped around his gun and swiped the butt of it across the head of his oldest daughter. Cal heard the crack and collapse of his sister. He yelped and took off running toward the barn, where he grabbed a bottle of his pa's whiskey. He took off toward the lake. He didn't want to be next.

Pernilla lay crumpled on the floor. Her eyes rolled back and a swell of blood poured from the corner of her eye. The little girl who just moments ago had been in Lester's arms crawled to her sister. The little girl rested her head with all its corn-silk hair, the hair her older sister washed and brushed and oiled with lard every night, in the crook of Pernilla's neck. She stuck her thumb in her mouth.

Harald Sutter knelt to check that she was breathing. He told some of the other kids to get a cool rag and hold it on her head. Then he left out the front door. "Let's go, Lester," he said.

Harald Sutter and his boy first went to the dark office of Dr. Mathiowetz, where Commissioner Patterson lay reading a book by lamplight. His broken leg, casted in white to his hip, hung from a chain hooked in the ceiling. A neck brace held steady his swollen neck, sprained by Sutter in his efforts to rescue Patterson from beneath the tractor.

"We're here to bust you out," said Sutter to Patterson. Patterson's eyes opened wide, and though his mouth moved, no words came out.

"Get that chair with wheels over here," Sutter said to Lester.

When Pernilla woke, it was dark outside. She touched her jaw and forehead. The little girl next to her stared.

"Is my face broke?" Pernilla asked her.

The girl pulled the fingers from her mouth and nodded yes.

"Boys gone?"

The girl nodded again.

"Pa?"

Again.

"We better get you to bed." She stood and hoisted the girl to her hip. "You're not scared, are you?"

The girl shook her head no.

"That's good. Perny will always keep you safe." The little girl wrapped her arms around Pernilla's neck.

She brushed the girl's hair until the child fell asleep, then she heated water over the stove and pulled her mother's old hand mirror out of the dresser. She studied her face. She took a wash-cloth and dabbed away the blood. Good enough, she decided, and headed out the door and toward the boat landing.

In a quiet place, away from the other people at the lake, Luther stood watching for Pernilla. He was all charged up tonight and couldn't wait to get on her. His eyes were glazed and squinted with drowsy drunkenness.

"What happened to your face?" Luther asked when she got there. He tipped into Pernilla, and she steadied him with her strong arms.

"Got smacked," she said.

Luther accepted this easily. Truth be told, he wasn't that interested in Pernilla's face or the story of how the purple bruising, swelling, and red eye had come to her. He'd had enough black eyes and cuts himself and had delivered enough blows that marks of those sorts didn't concern him much. They faded. They went away. If anything, bruises and swelling marked a man's man, a tough woman. His blood surged as Pernilla unbuttoned his shirt and circled his nipples with her fingertips. They pulled each other deeper into the grove to the darkest place.

Luther entered her. He was the only boy to ever take her breath with his length and girth. She cried out from beneath him, pounded on his back, asked him for more, at which he grew harder and more determined. He gave her a dozen more thrusts before a sudden and great weight settled on him. He collapsed on top of the tired bosom of Pernilla Sutter.

"Done already?" asked Pernilla. She waited for a response but got none. "Luther?"

Later, witnesses would say that she had had a mean look in her eye all night and that she must've poisoned him or somehow strangled him. But there was no evidence of either of those possibilities where Luther lay stretched out, face-down, pants around his ankles, legs between Pernilla's, and his lips turning cold, and where Pernilla lay beneath him with her hands clenched in her blond hair, screaming.

"He's dead!" she yelled. "He died on me." Cal Sutter and his group of friends were the first to find the pair. He saw first the round white bottom of Luther framed by the kicking spider legs of his sister. On one foot she wore a boot. On the other, she did not. Cal bent and heaved Luther off her, onto the soft grass of the grove floor. Pernilla scooted to sitting and held her bodice closed with her hand. Cal placed a hand on the chest of Luther and felt a faint rise and fall.

"He ain't dead," Cal said. He stood and looked down at his sprawled sister. "Straighten yourself up."

She pulled up her drawers and smoothed out her skirt. Cal bent again and grabbed Luther by the shirt. "I oughtta beat the hell out of him." He touched the bridge of his nose. "Help me set him up." Two boys leaned in and pushed Luther up against a tree.

"Jesus," said one boy. "You musta gave him a good one, Pernilla. I want what he got."

"I didn't do nothing to him," said Pernilla. "We were just messing around."

"Serves him right if he would be dead," said Cal. "Look at him now. A little poking knocked him out."

"Looks to me like he didn't even finish." The boy pointed to Luther's groin. "He's still rock hard."

"You wanna finish, Pernilla?"

"Shut up, you bastards." She stood and grabbed her brother's arm.

"Maybe we should get his brothers," said one boy.

"Hell, no," said Pernilla. "Help me get him home."

She and the boys toted Luther across the field, through the grove, and onto the Richters' porch. Cal knocked on the door. No one answered at first.

"Got Luther here," he called. "He's passed out again."

Otto opened the door just a crack, since he'd been warned not to let anyone in, and he pointed the crew toward the barn. The group picked Luther back up and took him to the barn and up the ladder into the hayloft. Pernilla put her ear to Luther's chest and felt the rise and fall.

"He's fine," she said. She kissed his forehead.

Cal leaned over Luther too. He pulled his sister back and then punched Luther in the nose. Luther's head turned into the straw, but he slept on. No bone broke, no cartilage cracked, no wound opened. Luther sneezed but didn't wake. Pernilla pushed her brother back.

"Now we're even," Cal said to the closed lids of the sleeping man. "Let's go."

"I'm staying," said Pernilla. She lifted Luther's limp arm and curled into it. "I'll be home in time to fix your breakfast."

"Pa'll be mad if you're not," said Cal.

"Pull the covers up on the little ones when you get home," she said. "Now leave me be."

Cal and his friend stepped back down the ladder and skulked across the yard.

27

HARALD SUTTER WORRIED himself none over her or the others. They were strong children, if nothing else. He and Lester grappled with the big wooden chair with wheels that held the broken body of Commissioner Patterson and pushed and pulled it across the street to the saloon. Whenever they wheeled over a rock or rut, Lester would say, "Ouch," for the commissioner, who could not speak. The whole town of New Germany seemed asleep. No people lingered on the streets or near the buildings. The windows of the newspaper offices were black. The building that was always alive with lights and movement, through all hours of the day and night, was now subdued and silent. Harald shepherded Lester through the door and lifted his eyebrows at a pair of men, other Watchdogs, already hovering over a pitcher of beer and whispering back and forth.

"Quiet in here tonight," said Sutter to the old German barkeep. The barkeep ignored him and poured himself a shot of schnapps. He sloshed it around in his cheeks before he swallowed. He'd have kicked this group out, but he was afraid the commission would come for him next and shut his business down. These were strange times.

"Paper got shut down today," said one of the Watchdogs. "Folks must be scared to go out."

"German folks, anyway," said Sutter. He pulled out a chair and rammed Commissioner Patterson's wheelchair where it had been. He poured a glass of beer for the commissioner and went to the bar for a straw through which he could drink it. He poured another for himself and sat down. He put his feet up on the table.

"Get them feet off my table," yelled the barkeep. Sutter scraped his boots across the top and dropped them to the floor.

Lester backed into a shadowy crook of the walls. He picked the skin around his fingernails.

"Heard that newspaper woman got arrested," said Sutter, "but her husband got away. I bet I know where he's at." He helped himself to another pour from the pitcher. He took a drink, swallowed, and grimaced. He poured the rest of his glass onto the floor. "I never did like German beer."

The barkeep yelled, "Hey," grabbed a bat from beneath his bar, and made his way around it and toward the Watchdogs' table. Three men stood to confront him. Sutter grabbed the pitcher, flung its contents at the old man. Another Watchdog yanked the bat from him and cracked it once, twice, over his knees. The bartender fell to the floor. He moaned and held his legs close to his round belly. Lester grunted from the corner. "Ow, ow, ow," he repeated.

"Let's get goin'," Sutter said. "We got work to do."

Sutter stopped his team about a quarter mile from the Richters' farm. He left Patterson in the wagon while he, the two men, and Lester felt their way through the grove to the headstone where Wilhelm Richter spent so many hours standing above the body of his dead wife, where Lester Sutter had first seen Liesel. Sutter and the others whispered and plotted until the time was right to bring down the Richters that night and forever after. The Watchdogs waited beneath the long-limbed trees, their branches swaying and creaking and grabbing at their collars. The men waited under the watchful eyes of bats, possums, raccoons, and other night creatures curious about the human intrusion into the animals' nocturnal lair. From all directions, shadowless bodies carrying kerosene, tar, rope, hammers, and guns crept.

Lester nervously leaned on one foot, then the other. The grove that had once felt so familiar to him now seemed haunted. Lester'd been here to watch or meet Liesel many times. He'd been comfortable then. He felt protective of her, like he was watching over her and her family somehow. Now he felt anxious. He didn't like the way these other men held claws and ropes and hammers, the way they pointed at the house, the way they planned for acts that sounded mean and hurtful. Lester didn't like the way they smelled. Lester didn't like leaving his sister lying on the kitchen floor. He especially didn't like leaving that little gold-haired sister sitting next to her. She was probably scared. Patterson was probably scared sitting alone in the back of the wagon. Lester wasn't too bothered by that, though. Even if the man *was* all broken up and couldn't talk. In a way, the man seemed less bad like that. Whole and standing up and talking, that man felt like a very, very bad man to Lester.

"Quit fidgeting," Harald said to Lester, who quit fidgeting.

"I heard he's got Archie hid up in there with him," whispered one of the men. He pointed toward the house.

"I expected as much," said Harald. "That's why tonight's the perfect night. We'll take them both."

Many lights shone in the Richter house. Liesel was up late tending to Wilhelm and Archie, both of whom had been figuring out ways to continue distributing the *Deutsche Chronik,* trying to think of a plan to get Frieda released as well as keep themselves from getting arrested. Otto was up too. He hadn't told anyone about Luther's condition, but seeing his brother that way had energized him somehow. Luther was always having adventures and making life exciting. Otto was at that rocky age where he wasn't old enough to join his brothers for drinking and socializing but was wise enough to know that if he kept still, his pa and Liesel wouldn't send him to bed like a little kid who was too young to hear the goings-on of adults. He didn't want to miss any excitement. Liesel made them a meal of chicken broth with onions. A little fire burned in the stove, and water for tea bubbled on top. She looked out the window into the black night. As she had before on numerous occasions, she felt the turtle catcher's presence nearby, but an ominous weight pressed on her too. Her uncle got up from the table and thanked her for the meal and then excused himself to bed.

Ever since Archie'd shown up, Herman had been more and more restless and belligerent toward Wilhelm. Liesel had been relieved when he decided to join Benjamin and Luther at the lake tonight.

A pounding rattled the door. Before she could respond, a handful of men masked with handkerchiefs around their noses and mouths burst through the door, wielding guns and ropes and other things of sharp metal picked up from workbenches and taken off mantels and pulled out of toolboxes. Liesel put her arms around Otto. Wilhelm braced himself against the table and stood. He placed himself between the men and his children.

"Mr. Sutter." Otto poked his head around Wilhelm's shoulder. "Why are you wearing that mask?"

Harald stepped forward and pointed his knife at Wilhelm's neck. Wilhelm didn't move.

"Where's Archie at?" Harald demanded.

"Sutter, you better get the hell out of my house," Wilhelm said. His voice was hoarse.

"Please," Liesel said. "Leave him alone."

Harald yelled, "Shut up," to her but didn't take his eyes off Wilhelm. "Either you and Archie are coming with us or we'll take all of yous." He looked at Liesel and Otto then nodded at another masked man, who quickly stepped up and grabbed Liesel's elbow. Wilhelm tried to put an arm out to protect his children, but the men simply swatted it out of the way. As much as Otto wanted to react, he could not. Fear held him motionless. But even though his arms and legs could not work now, his mind was already making promises to himself never to let fear hold him again.

"Cowards is what you are," said Wilhelm. "Scaring children is what cowards do."

Archie, still in his working vest and ink-stained shirt, appeared in the kitchen doorway. As if he'd been prepared for such an event, he held a two-by-four in his hand but kept it close against his thigh.

"What's this?" he said to no one in particular. He moved toward the man holding Liesel. "Let go the girl."

"Get back, Archie," said Harald. Another man lifted a hammer and stepped from the huddle toward Archie, who raised the board and yelled, "You let go of that girl. You back off!"

Liesel instinctively folded her hands over her middle, over her secret. *Oh God,* she prayed.

"Then put that board down," said Harald.

"When you let her go," said Archie.

Sutter nodded toward the man, and he released Liesel's arm. Archie dropped the board.

"Now, gentlemen," Archie said. "We are civilized men and can settle this without violence. I'm sure you've heard already, but in case you haven't, my newspaper has already been shut down. You have nothing to worry about."

Harald yelled above Archie's words. "Look around, boys," he said. "Look at this houseful of traitors to America. I don't like traitors. Traitors making thousands off of America but willing to whore her out to Germany."

Sutter tightened his grip on Wilhelm Richter.

"Tonight yous are going to find out how Americans deal with

traitors." He pushed Wilhelm toward the door. "Tie them both up and take them outside," Harald said.

With little trouble, the Watchdogs led the Richter men to the waiting wagons. They tied them up and gagged them. Regardless of the masks, Wilhelm recognized these men. Here was Oleson, whose plow he'd bought last year. Here was Klaviter, whose twenty acres Wilhelm now owned. Here was Peterson, whose farm had gone up for auction two years ago and whom Wilhelm had insulted by buying his cultivator and then complaining that all the bearings were rusted and not well cared for. Here were others Wilhelm hardly remembered but who remembered him very well.

Wilhelm's jaw and chest tightened. He raised his shoulders and shivered, and to Sutter and his men, he looked afraid. Commissioner Patterson sat in his wheelchair, and Lester crouched at his foot, supporting the commissioner's broken leg on his own shoulder. Even in the dark, Wilhelm could see the corner of Commissioner Patterson's mouth turn up in a smirk. He closed his eyes as the wagon rattled on to some wooded place.

When the wagon stopped at a little clearing, the men stripped Wilhelm and Archie naked. They retied them to the wagon wheels. They took the lid off a bucket of pine tar and dipped bristly brushes into the sticky liquid. Earlier, it had been heated to a runny consistency, but now it was simply warm and thick. No matter. It would do. The Watchdogs painted the bodies of Archie and Wilhelm as the Richters writhed and tried to bend to cover their privates. When the brushes ran over chest or leg hair, the hair pulled out, and Archie cried like a girl. The Watchdogs had wanted to use feathers for the final touch, but not enough could be gathered. So instead, they sprinkled straw all over the bodies of Archie and Wilhelm.

"You think you're too good for us," the Watchdogs said.

"You're a land stealer," they said.

"You're a traitor."

"You're a German-lover."

"You're a coward, too afraid to fight for what's right."

"You're selling America to the kaiser."

Because humiliation is the fastest route to rehabilitation, the men unbound the Richters from the wagon wheels, threw them in the back, and drove them on to New Germany, where they worked to tie them up tight to a hitching post outside the newspaper building.

Wilhelm Richter was so tired, he could barely muster a whispered plea, in German, to his dead wife. "Oh, my dear Maggie. Help me. Help me. Take me to where you are."

He wondered about his other boys and only hoped that they wouldn't see their papa in such a state. He knew for sure that Herman would never respect him after such a sight. He knew Luther would rage in, swinging and punching, and probably get the whole family killed. He guessed that Benjamin would try to stay in the shadows and not get involved in the melee. His only comfort came in knowing that Liesel would take care of them all, of her brothers and her cousins. She could take care of it. Wilhelm Richter had one final thought that even in his state made him chuckle: of all his children, his daughter was the most capable. Four sons and Liesel. And she was the one.

He said her name. "Liesel."

And then he succumbed to an encompassing black veil under which he slept and dreamed of acres and acres of green fields and dozens of Richter children and grandchildren growing tan and tall beneath the great sun.

Archie Richter dug his heels into the dirt. When the men picked up his legs, he flipped onto his stomach and scratched into the ground. "*Schweine, schweine,*" he repeated, calling the men pigs. He made bargains and pleaded. He tried for a while to speak calmly but ultimately gave in to kicking and yelling in a high-pitched scream. Archie Richter lost all decorum, but eventually he was secured to the post as well.

Lester heard what Wilhelm said. He too was thinking of Liesel. He dropped the commissioner's leg and ran away from there. He ran toward her on his own two feet.

Harald Sutter wasn't finished with Wilhelm Richter after he'd left him on the steps of the newspaper. He handed Commissioner Patterson off to another Watchdog to be cared for. He steered his wagon toward home, and when he passed Lester walking, he didn't stop to pick him up. Sutter put his team in the barn and crept across the yard, into the grove, and toward the Richter farm. The lights were on in the house, but Harald Sutter was not deterred by that. He stole into Richter's barn and beheld that brand-new tractor. He leaned against her. He rubbed his hands over her smooth metal. He sat in her seat. He smelled her engine. He opened the gas tank and let the fuel stream onto the straw below. He lit a match and waited for it to ignite the straw, then he hightailed it out of there. He was just to the grove when the explosion knocked him to the ground.

He turned around. What a beautiful, glorious sight it was. Harald Sutter was so enthralled by the vision of fire and smoke and flying boards and tractor parts that he hardly noticed his own boy Lester race past him and toward the inferno.

28

THE BLAST BROUGHT Liesel and Otto running from the house toward the barn. Otto, finally thawed from fear, ran barefoot across the yard and into a great hole where a door had once been.

"Luther!" he screamed. "Luther!" Otto put his arm over his eyes and disappeared into the orange and black ogre.

Liesel hitched up her skirt and dashed toward the barn after him.

"No, Otto!" she called. "Stop!" She had been holding that boy across her lap since the men had left with Papa and Archie. Otto's long legs had draped over her and his dirty feet almost reached the floor. He'd rested his head against her bosom; she'd laid her chin on his head. He was getting far too big and too old for such affection, but tonight he'd needed to feel safe and secure.

But Otto didn't listen this time. She lost the shape of him within seconds.

The barn was all ablaze. The tractor had been blown to bits. Chunks of glowing metal lay everywhere. Otto kicked his foot against a scorched fender but kept going deeper. He coughed and squinted his eyes. "Luther," he choked. He reached out his arm in search of the ladder that led to the loft. Fire bits rained all around him.

It was lovely. In the sweetest sleep and dream of her life, Pernilla Sutter lay in a large white bed surrounded by dozens and dozens of tall grandfather clocks ticking and chirping and chiming. The bed linens smelled of freshly peeled oranges. Luther Richter stared down at her from the blue ceiling of the room of clocks. He was floating and eating a piece of cake. Crumbs dropped onto Pernilla's forehead and cheeks. The cake was still hot from baking. She tried to catch the morsels in her mouth. Luther said, "I planted an ocean under our bed." He shook the cake to shower her with crumbs.

Luther, too, was dreaming. Blazing baseballs came at him from all directions. He swung and swung and swung, knocking each and every one out into a yellow pasture.

Claws of fire climbed up the barn walls. The straw beneath Otto's feet was nothing but smoke and hot sparkling cinders. He didn't even feel the burn. The fire roared so loud that Otto could not hear Liesel, who stood at the edge of the fire screaming for him to come out. Otto turned around and around. The smoke was so chalky that his eyes could not be forced to stay open or adjust. Soot heavy as wool soon covered his every inch.

A long black finger of smoke wrapped around him and pulled him deep into the belly of the fiery barn.

Lester didn't have a scream in his body. No noise above a low mumble escaped his lips. Had he shrieked, neither Otto nor Luther would have heard him anyway. Otto was too far into the noisy snarl. Luther couldn't be waked from the stinging smoke lifting from the golden straw and poisoning his body or from the inflamed rafters falling down all around and on top of him. Since

Lester couldn't scream to save Liesel's brothers, he dashed past her and into the barn.

Lester knew two things especially well. He knew fear and he knew love. What he loved most were things that were afraid. For all the years now that he and Liesel had been friends, he had smelled her fear. He didn't know the reason for it, but he knew the fear simmered always. He loved her for it. His heart was so filled with love for Liesel Richter that he couldn't stand to see her afraid.

He had a way of finding hidden things. He could root out grouse from tall grass, turkey from tree groves, and turtles from muddy water. Now he put up his arms, shielded his face, and strode in his humped way into the leaping flames. The roof above him creaked, and the fire barked. He plugged his nose and mouth but had to sip small breaths. Otto lay spread on the floor in smoke as black as the bottom of any lake or pond sludge. Lester found the boy with the toe of his boot. He knelt, threw him over his shoulder, and felt his way toward the door.

The great blast could be felt and seen at the boat landing, just a couple miles away. The Richter brothers Benjamin and Herman had picked their way through the grove of trees and were racing along the old path toward their farm place when they met Harald Sutter, walking to his farm and filling the air with the smell of cigarette smoke and whiskey.

"Better hurry," said Harald Sutter. "Whole place'll burn down."

"Son of a bitch," said Herman. But the boys hastened on.

A beam fell and knocked Lester on his arm and shoulder. He dropped to his knee, but kept hold of Otto with one arm. With his opposite hand, he braced himself against a burned two-by-four, regained his footing, stood, and found the door he'd come through. Outside, under the night sky Lester had always loved so well, he took in the fullest mouthful of air he could manage and coughed out the smoke and muck that had settled in his lungs.

Liesel ran toward them. When he laid Otto at the foot of Liesel, the loft of the barn collapsed and fell to the ground.

Liesel knelt to gather Otto to her breast. Sparks flickered all around her. She rocked him back and forth.

Lester hunched over his knees and coughed again. He watched the sister and brother. He knew what the crash meant. He knew that Luther Richter lay dead in that inferno. Liesel cried out for her brother.

Lester placed his burned hand on her back and patted.

"It's fine," he said. That was the first and only lie he ever told.

When Herman Richter broke away from the thick trees and brush and saw the son of Harald Sutter touching his sister in front of the fire that he knew Sutter had started, he grabbed a thick branch from the ground and ran toward them. Benjamin followed but focused on the fire, looking for a way to enter the flaming barn and save Luther.

"Get away from her!" Herman screamed. "Get the hell away from her!"

Over the roar of the fire, Lester could not hear the warning. He kept his palm on Liesel's back. She continued to rock Otto, whose eyes stayed closed though his chest rose and fell with breathing.

Herman reached the branch back and swung as he came up behind Lester. The branch landed with a thud against Lester's shoulder. He slumped forward and fell over Liesel and Otto. His mouth opened and closed as if to say something, but no words escaped him. Liesel turned toward Herman. "Stop it!" she yelled. She put her only free hand over the heaving body of Lester, who lay on the ground, curled into a protective position, then put his hands over his ears and screamed. That sound from Lester startled Liesel. She jumped back, amazed that such a sound could come from quiet, gentle Lester. She leaned close to him again and stroked his back. "Shhh."

"Shut up!" Herman yelled at Lester. Lester only screamed more definitely. Herman lifted the branch over his head and prepared to belt on Lester again.

"Benjamin!" Liesel screamed toward her other brother, who was hanging in the back and staring at the fire, now and again darting toward it and then falling back, looking for a place to enter. But there was no way in, no way to rescue Luther. He was gone for sure. Benjamin looked at his sister. "Stop him," she said. Her pleading finally touched his sensibilities. "Stop him," she begged. And he moved toward his brother Herman.

Benjamin grabbed the stick from Herman's hands. Herman turned and swung his fist into Benjamin's mouth. The jab hardly fazed him. Benjamin tossed the stick aside and grabbed his brother around the middle. "Be still," he said to him.

Lester Sutter scrambled to his feet and stood up. He ran across the yard and into the grove. Even over the noise of the fire, his howling could be heard.

The wife of the old barkeep of the saloon woke and turned over in the bed. Her husband's place was cold. Worried, she threw on an old housecoat, grabbed a lantern, and determined to go to the saloon and see what kept him. On the way, she passed one of the strangest and saddest sights of her life. There, in front of the German newspaper building, lay two nearly unrecognizable figures. She was afraid to approach them at first. But the one man's crying called her closer. Wilhelm Richter and Archie Richter said nothing.

The woman ran to the house of Dr. Mathiowetz, woke him, and begged for his help. She pulled an afghan from the doctor's couch and said, "Hurry, hurry," as she ran back out the door. The doctor followed. She covered the men while the doctor used a knife to release the ropes. Then she went and found her husband passed out from pain on the saloon floor.

Mathiowetz took the two Richter men to his own home. He woke Betty, and she boiled water and filled their tub with that and strong soap. When there was nothing but a thick stew of straw and pine tar, she emptied it and refilled it with fresh water until the men had cleaned and scraped the mess from their skin and hair. Like her daddy had taught her, she didn't cringe or get upset or ask too many questions. She pretended she saw naked men tarred every day. When Wilhelm Richter sat wrapped in a blanket near the kitchen stove, he asked for a cup of tea. Betty made that too, and gave it to him in a proper teacup with a saucer.

"Herman would be lucky to have a girl like you," Wilhelm said.

Betty smiled at Wilhelm. "You rest now."

Betty'd not spoken to or seen Herman since just before the parade. She'd been thinking about things. She knew the events of yesterday and the events of this evening would probably drive Herman to finally enlist. What she had to do now was determine whether she'd wait for him or not.

In the Sutter house, all the lamps burned. Cal burst through the door and checked on all the little ones as Pernilla had told him to do. Just as he pulled a blanket up over the littlest girl, a great big boom rattled the windows and shook the floorboards. Several of the little boys woke and jumped out of their beds. Cal lifted the little girl out of bed and went to the kitchen. All his brothers did too. They scrambled about in their long white pajamas. They looked out the window. They stood on chairs. They bopped one another over the head for a better view.

"Do you see anything?" asked Cal.

"Nope," said one. "But here comes Pa."

When Harald Sutter thundered through the door and barred it behind him, none of his children asked why.

"Yous all shut up now," he said. "I don't want to hear a word out of yous."

"Did you hear that boom?" Cal said to his pa.

"Get me my bottle," he said. Cal found the brown bottle, shook it, and handed it to his pa. He sat in the rocker near the fire.

"Not much in there," Cal said.

"Keep that door locked," said his pa. "Don't you open it for God or anyone."

All the way home, Lester Sutter practiced saying what he knew he had to say. He tried to open the door to the house, but it wouldn't budge.

"Let me in," he yelled. He beat the door and jostled the knob.

"Get to your barn," his pa yelled.

Cal walked to the door and opened it.

Lester walked into the kitchen, raised his arm, and pointed his finger at his pa. "Pa is a bad man."

"Aren't you smart," said Cal.

"Pa is a bad man. Pa is a bad man," Lester repeated. He rocked back and forth and beat his fists against his thighs.

Harald Sutter slugged his whiskey and let some run down his chin. "You're crazy," he said. "Get out of here." He turned toward his other boys. "Get him the hell outta here."

The boys didn't move.

"Pa made a fire in the barn," Lester yelled.

Cal pressed his little sister's head into his chest and covered her ear with his hand. He looked at all his other brothers standing in their pajamas waiting for Lester to say more. Whose barn? "Whose barn, Lester?" he asked.

"Richter's."

Couldn't be. He had just been in the Richters' barn not that long ago. He'd just laid Luther in there. He'd just left Pernilla in there. Pernilla was in the Richters' barn. He'd left Pernilla with Luther in the Richters' barn. A fire? Who was going to take care of all these kids? Of this little one, especially? Lester must be wrong.

"What?" Cal asked. He paused. He felt the little girl's pulse on his palm or maybe it was his own heart beating. "Pernilla was in the Richter barn."

Harald took another drink and stared at the fire. He looked at Cal. "What did you say?" His eyebrows raised, then lowered. "The hell you say. Shut up."

"Pernilla was in the Richter barn, I said," said Cal. His voice was louder and forceful. He pressed harder against his little sister's ear until she whimpered. Now, Cal wasn't much for sentimentality, but he was smart. He knew who kept this place in a semifunctional mode. He knew who planted and harvested the garden. He knew who brought in the milk from the cows. He knew who fed these little ones, who'd fed *him* and kept him alive after their mother died. In his mind, if there was a single, solitary person worthwhile in the Sutter house, Jesus Ages Christ, it was Pernilla.

"That goddamn whore," said Harald. He took another drink, but it wouldn't go down and simply sat in his mouth, burning it up. Truth be told, Harald Sutter knew exactly what Cal was thinking because he was thinking it too. Rage came up in him. Stupid girl. Always running around when she should've been home.

"She was in there, Pa," said Cal. He put the little girl down. "I saw her myself." The little girl screamed and ran toward the fireplace. "Where's Perny? Perny!" she screamed.

Harald spit the whiskey into the fire. "You quit that noise!" he boomed, although the little girl wouldn't have quit for all the candy in the world. He leaned forward in his rocker and said it again. "Quit screaming!" The girl screamed louder. Her face was red as a rooster's cockscomb. The other boys stood silently.

"Pernilla was in the Richter barn," said Cal again. "You killed Pernilla? Is she dead?"

"Pa started the fire," said Lester.

The little screaming girl picked up the fire poker and threw it at Harald. Her voice pierced the ears of all in the room and darted off the windows and against the walls. Harald ducked, then stood. He fisted his fingers and stepped toward the little girl.

"Don't you dare," said Cal. He picked up a tin bowl and threw it at Harald. Harald deflected the bowl and turned toward Cal. But all the little Sutter boys were faster. Each grabbed whatever object was handy — jars, chairs, pans, lanterns, and spoons. They descended on their pa like a pack of wolverines. "Get him good," panted Cal. He beat and beat his pa across the back with his own fists. It felt so good to feel his hands hammer his pa's spine.

The Sutter children got him good for years of fear and years of beatings. The children beat him for their mother and for Pernilla and for themselves and for the whole world. Lester picked up a cane and lifted it above his head. He held it tight, but then dropped it onto the wooden floor. He backed out of the room and into the dark night toward town, toward the doctor's house. But not for his pa.

Lester's trip to Dr. Mathiowetz didn't make much difference for anyone. Not for Luther. Not for Pernilla, either. Benjamin, Herman, and Liesel tugged pails and pails of water from the well and threw them on the fire, but it had to burn itself out, big as the blaze was. And the only neighbors, German or otherwise, who came to help put it out, even though the devil could be seen from the second a person got free from any tall building or tree, were Dr. Mathiowetz and Betty, who drove Wilhelm Richter and Lester Sutter in their car, and Cal Sutter, who came just a while later, after he'd tucked the little ones back into bed and put a pillow under his pa's head and a blanket over him. He was hurt, in body and pride, but he'd be fine.

It was Lester and Cal who pulled Luther and Pernilla from the barn and rested them side by side near the house. Dr. Mathiowetz checked them closely, but there was no breath or heartbeat to be detected. Wilhelm Richter let out a mighty roar, and the doctor tried to comfort him by saying it was the smoke and not the fire that had gotten the two.

And so here were all these people together, and Liesel did the only thing she knew to do: she made coffee.

"I'm Betty," said Betty to her. "I'm so sorry."

Liesel didn't even look at her. She was thinking hard about how nice it would be if Lester could stay and lie next to her in her little bed. If he could simply hold her. She served him coffee instead, which he drank as normally as the rest. Herman voiced his objection at having Lester Sutter in his house, but Wilhelm told Herman, "Quiet. For God's sake, shut your mouth for once."

"Don't you shame me, old man," said Herman. "It's you who brought this on."

"Herman," said Liesel. "Be quiet."

Betty took a sedative from her daddy's bag and offered it to Herman to help him sleep. He refused it, said he'd stay awake to be sure no more disasters befell them that night.

"I think it's all over, son," said Dr. Mathiowetz. Before he left, he washed, salved, and wrapped Otto's blistered feet and administered a dose of morphine to Wilhelm Richter.

Before the sun stretched its arm across the horizon, the Richter house was empty of visitors, and Wilhelm and his remaining family sat and beheld one another. If they had known what changes were coming, they might have prayed for the sun to stay down.

WHEN NIGHT WRAPS like a woolly coat over Minnesota and buttonhole stars appear, the creature emerges, plodding one tired leg before the other. Wet, heavy mud slides from its bowed back and thick skin. The tiny ear holes heed the lightest pattering of claws, paws, or feet of prey. The lids open once more and a giant yellow moon reflects as an odd pupil in the middle of the turtle's eyeball. The tongue tastes the new cool air. The creature climbs the lake bank slowly, choosing the simplest path, free of weeds and brush. The nostrils waver.

PART *III*

29

Meuse-Argonne, France, September 1918

T HE GNAWING AND SCRATCHING of the rats bothered Herman most. The rats came each night, like wave after wave of muddy water, swarming the ditches and battlefield. They cared nothing for obstructions. Feet, sandbags, machine guns; nothing stopped them. They were the only living things to thrive in that place. Not even the endless days of canned meat and bread and tomato juice that soured his stomach compared to the rats, nor the lice burrowing into his armpits, groin, and scalp, biting his skin and sucking his blood. And Herman had weeks ago stopped jumping at the constant pop of guns and explosions of grenades. Though he hadn't slept more than four straight hours in months, though he had spent his nights wiring barbed fences and collecting the dead under fire from the German soldiers across No Man's Land, it was the rats that plagued him most.

At times, Herman thought, *I will run. I have done my duty for my country and now I will run to Paris and then find my way home.* But he had seen how the MPs had dragged his friend Private Philippe LeRoche back to the camp in handcuffs after he'd gone AWOL. Herman didn't want to suffer the same humiliation after he'd volunteered to come to France to fight the Germans. Running would only prove to his father that he, Herman, had been wrong. And he wouldn't do it. He couldn't. The pride of his father and his father's father and their homeland throbbed in him still, despite his attempts at denial.

The Meuse River had gone gray from soot and mud, and the Argonne Forest had turned from a lush grove to a pincushion of black, broken trunks. The soil was gray, and the tanks, the shells, the guns, the tinned meat, the bread, and the gruel were gray. Cigarette smoke and even the cheap cigarettes, which were the only comfort to the soldiers aside from a few hours of upright, leaning-against-a-dirt-wall sleep and water-stained letters from home, were gray. The bombed-out churches that had once spread royal colors from centuries-old stained glass over gold altars and had rung bells the size of grown men three times a day were silent now and gray, and a dusty gray at that. Villages that used to bustle with bakeries, creameries, flower shops, and schools plump with dark-haired, dark-eyed children now lay ruined, empty, and gray. The rain, that incessant French drizzle sodden with residue, was gray.

Private Philippe LeRoche hovered over the small kerosene lantern in the early hours of the day and told the younger men about the wonders of France, of Paris, of how beautiful she'd been before the occupation, between the Franco-Prussian and this war. The men pulled on cigarettes and leaned in close to listen. What else, what else? demanded the youngest of them. Philippe held their attention while they peeled away the clinging mud from their boots with sticks. The men just back from the night duties usually coursed with too much energy to sleep when they ought.

Philippe's mother, Claudia LeRoche, was the feline-shaped daughter of a French bottle maker from La Rochelle, an old French shipping port. One day in May 1889, Claudia passed her finger under the words of a flyer stuck to her father's shop window. *World Expo,* it said. *Come climb the tallest tower in the world! Come see America's Wild West brought to Paris! Come see Edison's light bulb!* Claudia packed a meager bag with a few dresses, emptied her mother's money jar, and jumped a train for Paris. Her parents found the flyer folded under the milk pitcher. On it Claudia had written, *I've gone to climb the tower and see the American shooters. I'll write soon. Love, Claudia.* Paris, recovering from its latest war, danced with lights and music and industry. Claudia pulled sixty centimes from her purse and pressed them into the palm of a long-mustached man selling tickets to Eiffel's Tower. She climbed and climbed, up to the observation deck, where she saw all of Paris and beyond. As Claudia rested her elbows on the rail, leaned out, and looked at the scene, an American boy came up behind her and grabbed her middle, saying, "Careful, careful." She turned, startled, to face him and was calmed by his green eyes. Though she couldn't understand a word he said, she could tell he was worried she might fall or maybe even jump. He led her back down the stairs and escorted her to *Buffalo Bill's Wild West* show. The boy squeezed her close at every gunshot. For the rest of that week, Claudia held that boy's hand. They created the sort of scene at which long-married people smile. At the end of that week, the boy would pack up and take a boat back to America with his family, but Claudia let herself love this boy, and with him she conceived a son whom she named Philippe, a son whom ten years later she would move to America, to Chicago, where the boy's father had said he was from. Not to look for the father of the child, necessarily, but to bring the child to the homeland of that boy she'd met on Eiffel's Tower, to see again *Buffalo Bill's Wild West* show and hear the excitement of gunshot pops. All Philippe's childhood, Claudia told him stories of the World's Expo. She kissed the lids of his green eyes and told him his father was a famous gun shooter, too famous to name. In this way, Philippe learned to tell stories and also learned all there was to know of romance and love and adventure.

Philippe told the men stories of the French brothels: The chandeliers and exposed petticoats. The red lipstick. The perfume. He told of the Eiffel Tower, how men threw themselves from the top when their women rejected proposals.

"Oh, it's grand, boys," Philippe said. "A man will stand at the top, declare his everlasting love, and then dive headfirst, arms open and wide to the world."

"Like he's flying?" said a young man, a fresh one from Iowa.

A few soldiers laughed, and the Iowa soldier flushed, but Philippe said, "Yes, exactly. Like he's flying."

The boy looked rapt upon Philippe, as if he'd believe every word that ever came from his mouth. All the boys looked to the older men for guidance, for direction, for mothering, nursing.

Lieutenant Herman Richter that morning had scolded Philippe LeRoche, his best friend and the company mapmaker, for his daydreaming and storytelling. Herman brought a tin cup of coffee to Philippe in the dugout of the trench where he worked, protected from the wet that could ruin his maps. They were crucial for strategy, and there never seemed to be enough for the scouts, trench diggers, fence wirers, rations delivery drivers, and higher-ups who needed updated directions daily.

Herman had pushed aside a heavy canvas and ducked through the small frame and into the dugout.

"Here, Philippe," said Herman. He put the coffee on the little desk next to Philippe's head.

Philippe lifted his eyes, which were just two inches from the grid he was marking. "Thanks," he said. "The light in here is bad. I need more light to do my work."

"I'll see what I can do, but you're the one with the connections."

"The French will not have a new supply of lanterns until next week at the earliest."

Herman nodded. "I'll see what I can do," he said again.

Philippe looked back to his map, marked a village with a little star, and began writing a name.

"Philippe," Herman said.

"What? What is it?"

"You're making the men miserable with your stories, filling them full of all that nonsense. Keep your stories to yourself, why don't you?"

"To myself?" said Philippe. "Certainly not. These boys need some cheer, by damn."

"What they need is a good sleep."

"You are the dreamer, Lieutenant. There will be no good sleep here but the dead kind. So, while I am alive, I will give these boys what they need."

"And what's that?" Herman asked.

"Hope. Good stories. A pretty lady to look at."

"And where might you muster up one of those?"

Philippe patted his jacket pocket.

Burlesque pictures were harder to come by than good meat, wine, or cheese, but Philippe had connections with the French army, the soldiers who fought alongside the Americans. It seemed he could get his hands on anything. Herman laughed.

"What did you have to trade to get her?"

"Nothing," said Philippe. He wiggled his bare fingers, blackened from ink. "I drew her."

"Well, let's have a look, then." Herman felt free to be brazen with his lust here. All the boys were. He'd even made up stories about himself and Betty and the things they'd done together. She'd never know.

"No. No free looks for you," said Philippe. "What will you give me for her?"

"How about I won't thump your thick noggin?"

Philippe pretended to think on it, then smiled and pulled the sketch from his pocket and unfolded it. "There she is," he said. "I named her Eloise." He placed the sketch on the desk, and pulled the lantern close. On the page, a nude woman with dark eyes and long fingers lay on a sofa. One arm rested above her head and the other was between her own legs. Her hair fell in tight curls over one breast. The other hung deliciously heavy on the cushion of the sofa. Her nipple was big and dark.

Herman felt an immediate rush of blood. He hated not being able to control his urges. "Seems we're wasting your talents on maps, my friend," he said. "She's a beauty, all right. Could you make me a girl a little thicker?" He pointed to the girl's thighs. "Right here. Give her some meat."

"You damn Americans with your big women," said Philippe. "You rut like heavy oxen."

"My girl back home is little as a moth, for your information," said Herman. "But what about you? You French are no better than skinny gophers. A man should have something to hold on to."

"How old did you say this sister of yours is? Liesel, is it? Could she provide a skinny little French gopher with something to hold on to?" Philippe reached for the picture, but Herman pulled it away.

"Not old enough for you, I'm afraid." Herman didn't look up from the picture. "Besides," he added, "Liesel wouldn't give you a second look. We've warned her against your type."

"I bet you did," said Philippe. He leaned back in his chair and laced his fingers behind his head. "But I can wait. I can wait a long, long time. It is a fact that American women like my type."

"You think so, huh?" said Herman. He lifted his own coffee cup and drank the last drops. He set the cup on the table. "Drink your coffee now, damn you, before I decide to throw you to the Huns."

Philippe reached for and wrapped his hand around the tin cup. "Cold," he said.

"I know it," said Herman. He folded Eloise and slid her into his pocket. He slipped out of the dugout and back into the trench before Philippe could protest.

Herman slumped against a dirt wall. Day after day, the men sat in their trenches, watching the ditches fill, watching water mold their clothes and disease their skin while waiting for orders to attack or defend. Misery was infectious.

This place, to Herman, seemed beyond Earth. He laid his rifle across his lap, pulled a tarp over his head, and listened to the rain splatter. He lifted Eloise from his pocket and set her aside. He pulled a letter from his pocket and held it in his hand, not to read again, but just to hold. He had it memorized already.

May 1918

Dear Brother,

I hope this letter finds you safe and warm. News here is scarce, though we see the telegrams to the mothers of the boys in the 77th daily. Was there a battle? Was it a bloody one? Pa won't say and Benny's been hiding the news from Otto and me. But since we didn't get a telegraph about you, you must be alive. Are you ever scared?

You should know that Pa is not well. There's a sickness here that's spreading quick. If only you could send him a kind note before it is too late.

Benny is doing a fine job managing the place by himself. He's sad a lot of the time and is still quiet. He spends much time with Sonnen Mueller. They've not heard from her brother in a while and everyone is worried about him. Benny took Otto to the baseball game and said the town seemed to be together. Cal Sutter was said to cry on the mound after the game, maybe for his sister, but maybe for Luther. They fought, but they were friends too. Otto said everyone feels bad about what happened to Luther. Even if not everyone likes the war, most people feel bad about the soldiers there, whichever side they're on. Otto likes his schooling. He learns everything in English now. Mrs. Lehrer keeps him busy enough and sends homework for me too. It's nice of her to think of me, don't you think?

225

She sent me a volume of Emily Dickinson poems. "There's a funeral in my brain, marching to and fro." Isn't that a strange line? But don't you feel like there's one in your head sometimes too? I do.

Bye,
Liesel

P.S. My birthday's coming up. Otto said that one of the older girls got a vial of French perfume from her sweetheart in the war. Maybe you could send me some, even if you are just my brother and not a sweetheart?

Herman thought of life back home under the sun where thunderheads turned everything green in spring and white in winter, where the girls always wore floating dresses of pink and yellow and blue on Sunday afternoons at the ballpark, and where Liesel's gold bread cooled on the counter. He imagined Betty with some of the attributes of Eloise in a dress of green standing in a kitchen pulling a warm loaf from an oven in a house Herman would make himself. He imagined three or four little children running around. But his imaginings turned to unhappy memory.

Herman remembered his father, Wilhelm. He wondered if he was dead now. Two months had passed since this letter. He knew of the influenza outbreak in America. Herman remembered his father's red flannel coat, rich with straw, manure, and coffee aromas, hanging on a nail next to the door. Herman remembered his last day at home, how he'd pounded his fist on the kitchen table, how he'd pointed his finger into his papa's chest and warned him not to interfere, not to thwart Herman's plans to enlist in the American army to fight the Germans. He remembered how Wilhelm had slammed his own palms on the table in return, told him that the Americans were intent on killing German men. "Our own family," his father had said. "Your uncle, your cousins Gunther and Augustan, dead by American hands. And you want to be part of that?"

His shame regarding his father's loyalty to Germany and his involvement with the pacification movement made Herman sick. When he'd learned his papa had been tarred and humiliated, he'd said goodbye to his sister and brothers, said goodbye to Betty and promised to marry her when he returned. He'd paid his respects to the dead bodies in the family plot, and confronted Wilhelm. "It is your fault Luther's dead," he'd said. "It's your fault Mother's dead. I'll be back when the war's done. Keep your traitor friends off this farm."

"My own son, a goddamn Judas. Don't you come back here, boy, unless you come back in a German uniform. You are not my son."

"So be it" were the last words he said to his father.

He scanned the room, saw his brothers and sister standing in the corners. He walked to Benjamin and shook his hand. Herman said goodbye to Otto, and he kissed Liesel on the cheek. He didn't even wait until Luther was in the ground. He took the parcel of food Liesel had wrapped for him and began the walk to the train station. He felt a full-grown man doing his duty for his country. Righteousness walked with him, he'd been sure.

On September 25, 1918, these were the thoughts that swarmed Lieutenant Herman Richter and brought to him sleep and dreams.

He woke to a tap on the shoulder. A boy, a private no more than twenty, stood before him, and at his feet, a rat scurried. The rats were on the move. When the German army had been at its most aggressive, the rats had arrived at the American trenches by the millions, as if they were part of the kaiser's line.

The brown rats, big as tomcats, sought tender tissue. The ears, the eyes, the lips. They hunted for the injured as well as the deceased. Swats and screams didn't stop them from sinking their tiny claws and teeth into flesh and tearing away. The more timid black rats preferred extremities and limbs, fingers mostly. They waited until the victim stunk with death.

"Sir," said the private.

"Yes, Private," said Herman.

"I have an order here from General Pershing."

Herman knew the time was right for the French and American troops to push the line and force the Germans back. He had been waiting for the order for weeks. His men too were anxious. The boy handed an envelope to him, which Herman opened and read.

"Tell the sergeants to ready the troops, Private," said Herman. "We attack at daybreak."

"Yes, sir."

The private saluted and Herman waved his hand at the boy. "Go on," he said.

Evening, September 25, 1918

Dear Liesel,

This battle gets on with a mighty bang.

Supply lines are crucial to the German offensive, and so I have prepared my men to push through No Man's Land to secure the rail hub about a mile out and cut off their necessities. My boys are ready and eager. They are a good bunch and many of them are very dear to me, as if they were my little brothers or even sons to look after. If nothing else, they are happy to be getting out of the cramped and wet trenches. We heard the Huns are low on morale and are deserting by the dozens. Should help our effort. I am well but do dearly miss your cooking, little sister. Half this letter will get blacked out by censors, but I feel I must write it down, where I am, what I am doing. I fear if I don't, I'll be lost forever. Just the act of writing it feels like an assurance that I'll be remembered. That I was here.

Send my love to Betty. I love you all.

Herman

30

FOR HERMAN, THE FIRST PUSH of the offense was to acquire fresh water for his troops. The river was full of rotting animals and corpses and couldn't be consumed. Just on the other side of the line sat a little cottage at which Herman hoped to find a well. He had only to flush it of Germans, if there were any, and secure the building.

It'd be easy. He'd let the men rest for the battle. He found Philippe wrapped up in a blanket, looking like a sleeping bat, kicked him gently, and told him to come along.

"Is that an order or a request?" asked Philippe.

"Both, you lazy Frenchie," said Herman.

Through the dark, they walked unharmed all the way to the old house, and as Herman had expected, he found it empty, though tin cans and cigarette butts lay all around. The Germans, it seemed, had been here, possibly using the water source themselves. Herman and Philippe searched the cupboards for food. Finding none, they stepped outside to look for water. Behind the house, an old stone well poked up in a perfect circle under the low boughs of some trees.

"Lovely," said Philippe. He dropped his gun and ran to the well.

"Whoa," said Herman. "Slow down, friend." He slunk along the wall of the house and looked deep into the forest. He saw nothing.

Philippe unwound the pail and threw it down into the well. It landed with a thunk and a splash, and a bad, bad smell wafted from the opening. Something was not right. Philippe leaned over. It was hard to see, but a damned terrible odor smacked him in the face.

"You better bring a lantern," he said to Herman.

Herman hated to attract any attention, but his men needed water. He lit the lantern and tied it to a string. He lowered it into the well.

At first, it looked as if a little pink towel had fallen into the water and was floating on the surface.

"What is it?" asked Philippe.

"Don't know," said Herman. "Get me a long stick."

Philippe did.

Herman reached down with the stick and jabbed at the thing. The cloth sunk and spun and the next thing that emerged from the water was the face of a little girl.

"Oh God," said Philippe. He clapped his crooked arm over his mouth and leaned over with heaving.

"Sons of bitches," said Herman. He swirled around the water, and more bodies emerged. An old woman. A young woman. Another child, a boy this time.

What came over Herman more than pity was anger. He ordered Philippe into the cottage, where they'd wait for the Germans to return. "Are you crazy?" Philippe asked. "I am leaving."

"Into the cottage, I said."

. . .

Philippe hid, belly to the floor. Herman smoked a cigarette. "Let them come," he said.

"Maybe you give me that picture of your sister?" said Philippe. "For luck."

"No," said Herman.

"Then I want Eloise back," said Philippe. "If these are to be my last moments, I want my eyes to see something of beauty."

Herman pulled the only picture he had of his family from his breast pocket and handed it to Philippe. He peered through the window with his binoculars into the dense forest.

Philippe rubbed the photograph for luck. He wished he were in Paris with this girl. He imagined he was. Maybe enjoying a meal. Maybe a plum digestif. He saw Herman duck quickly and then rise again slowly to the window.

"Are they coming?" Philippe asked.

"Three of them, I think," said Herman. "A ways off yet."

"How far off?"

"We'll have to kill them."

"I do not want to kill anyone," said Philippe. "You said we were just coming to get water."

"Plans have changed," said Herman.

"I make maps," said Philippe. "I am an artist."

"So am I," said Herman. "I'm a poet."

"My ass, you are," said Philippe. He waited for some sort of remark from Herman. None came. "Killing is against my credo."

"Take my gun," Herman said. Philippe fisted his hands and drew away. Herman thrust it forward again. "Take it, damn you. Don't you know this is war?"

Philippe hated when men spoke like that. *This is war.* What the fuck did that mean? That was the type of things men said when they didn't have a good reason for their actions. But he tucked the picture of Herman's family into the rim of his helmet and took the rifle.

"Herman," said Philippe. "You cannot be certain these are the men who killed those people."

No response came from Herman.

"How can you even be sure?" said Philippe.

Herman finally pulled the binoculars down and looked at Philippe. In the quietest whisper, he said, "Shut the fuck up. Do you hear me?"

Now Philippe could hear the Germans talking.

"What are they saying?" he asked Herman. Herman rose again to the window and raised the binoculars.

"Never mind," said Herman. The Germans were talking of fishing. "I caught one this big," said one. "Liar," said another. "Fish tales," said the last.

The light of the moon flashed off Herman's lenses. Two of the German soldiers lifted their weapons and pointed them toward the cottage. "Put down your weapon!" they shouted in German. "Come out of the house. Come out of the house with your hands in the air."

Herman tucked a bayonet in the sleeve of his coat. "I will feign surrender," he whispered to Philippe. "You hide and shoot the second man. I will take care of the first."

"What about the third?"

"He's unarmed."

"We'll take him as a prisoner?"

"Yes," said Herman. "Ready?" He didn't wait for a response. He stood up and raised his hands into the air. "Surrender," he mumbled.

The Germans, seeing a man with his arms raised high, assumed he'd said, "I surrender." They rushed him. As they did, Herman could see clearly that the two with rifles were young, maybe seventeen or eighteen years old. The one behind them carried a radio and was older. His mustache was gray. His face was wrinkled. One of the younger said, *Sprechen Deutsch?*

232

Herman nodded. He took a step backward, and then another.

"Halt," said one, following him.

Herman backed up again until the soldier was in the door frame. Herman pushed down the barrel of the boy's rifle, pulled the bayonet from his sleeve, and stabbed the boy in the neck. Philippe leaned out the door and shot the next German boy in the head. The radio man turned to run.

"Shoot him!" screamed Herman.

"He is running," said Philippe.

Herman took the Enfield from Philippe and chased the man. He knocked him down with the butt of his rifle, then picked him up by the collar and demanded that he march. Herman marched the old soldier toward the well.

"Get in the well, German pig," he screamed. "Get in the god-damn well."

The German tried an appeal. "I will help you. I will give you information," he said in German.

Philippe ran to the well too. "Let him be," he said. "Please, Herman."

"You keep an eye out," said Herman. "There are more coming, I'm sure."

Philippe stood motionless.

"Get back to the cottage," said Herman. "That's an order."

Philippe turned his back on Herman and went to the cottage.

After, Philippe told a story of the incident that did not include Herman forcing the old man into the well, that did not include the screams and begging, a story that did not include any of the shots fired into the well to stop the noise. He invented such a grand story of bravery that each of them was awarded a medal and a promotion.

Herman found new zeal for war. In the morning, he charged across the battlefield ahead of his men, shouting, shooting, and stabbing. In an explosion, he was lifted fifteen feet into the air and landed in the middle of the battle, out cold.

When he next opened his eyes, he couldn't remember where he was or why he was lying on the ground. He could lift his head a little, but not a lot. He saw the American trenches about fifty feet from where he lay. Too far. *That's too far away,* he thought. Up in the sky, big black birds soared. And then the earth was shaking beneath him. The French on the offensive drove their tanks forward. Herman was able to move aside enough to keep most of his body from the tracks. He didn't even feel his arm go beneath the grinding metal.

When he woke again, it was dark. His arm lay mangled and useless at his side. He felt with his other hand the sticky blood sopping the left side of his body. He wanted to call for Philippe but couldn't. Rats darted from body to body. *If this is the end of the world,* he thought, *then the rats are the gods of it all.* And again Herman slept. He woke once to an American medic breathing into his face. Herman was unable to speak. The medic saw the look of understanding in his eyes, but said only, "Sorry," and moved on. That was a bad sign, Herman knew. He closed his eyes.

He was being left to die. *I am dying. My heart is pumping. I can hear it in my head, but the blood is flowing onto the ground. Jesus Christ. Look at all the blood. There's a lot of blood.* Herman said, "Hey! Somebody! There's a lot of blood here." He thought he was yelling, but he was only whispering. He heard others moaning. "We've got hurt men out here," Herman said. "I know you hear me."

He was exhausted. *A tank ran over my arm. A goddamn tank! I can't wait to tell Liesel. A tank. She can't even imagine a tank. What do I say? It's a giant machine on tracks? Like a train. Damn, no. Liesel. She's never even seen a train. I'm dying somewhere in France, in goddamn France! And Liesel's never seen a train. Oh Christ, I'm bleeding. I wonder if I'm hit anywhere else. My skin is on fire, I think, but there are no flames. Something sure as hell is burning the shit out of my skin.* He closed his eyes and prepared to die.

Two German soldiers, looking for the injured, picked their way through the bombed holes, the dead bodies, and the barbed wire. They smoked long cigarettes and spoke loudly, even jovially, to each other. Herman awoke. He heard the Germans. They referred to collecting bodies as "picking poppies for the ladies." When they came upon Herman, the short soldier aimed his bayonet at Herman's heart. The tall soldier knelt beside him.

"What have we here?" the tall soldier asked the short. He spoke in German. "Ours or theirs?"

"Theirs," the short one said. "Only he is wearing good German boots. The bastard is a grave robber. Leave him for the rats."

"What kind are you, friend?" the soldier said to Herman. "French? British? A black American? No? A white American? Yes. A fresh white American new to France, I bet."

"Go to hell," Herman said in English.

The German soldier recognized the English word *hell*.

"Yes," the soldier responded in German. "That is where you are." He gestured in the night. "The fire, the devils, the death. You are indeed in Hell."

Herman laughed at this.

"You understand me, American?" asked the tall soldier. "You speak German?"

Herman remained silent. The German soldier pulled bandages from his pack.

"What is your name, American friend?" the German soldier asked him. Herman tried to feign incomprehension, but the soldier wasn't fooled. The soldier recognized the glint of understanding in his eyes, the relaxed forehead of a man who wasn't afraid of something he didn't understand.

The soldier wrapped a coarse bandage around his arm. Herman screamed, then almost blacked out.

"He has fainted like a woman," said the short to the tall.

"Shut your mouth," said the tall. "He has fainted like any of us. Help me now, you coward. He is practically one of ours."

The soldiers took Herman back to their trench, where they dressed his wounds more properly, and then to a gutted church in a small nearby village that served as a medical unit. They roused him with salts.

"We will not hurt you," the tall soldier said to him in German. "We have nothing and want nothing from you."

The German soldier gestured to the other men in the medical center.

"Look at us. We are tired of fighting," said the soldier. "You Americans. You think the Germans fight, fight, fight. What are you doing here, American friend? It is the Americans who like to fight. Germans fight because we must. Americans fight for fun and money. War is good for the economy. Ask Mr. Wilson."

"Richter," said Herman in the German of his father. "Herman Richter. And I don't like to fight."

"Richter?" said the soldier. "R-I-C-H-T-E-R? We have a Richter here too. A good German Richter, fat on sausage and rabbit. Perhaps you are brothers, American friend."

"Are you going to kill me?" coughed Herman. "I'd like to send a letter to my sister before you shoot me." Herman wished they would shoot him. He wished they had left him to die on the field. How could it be that his own medic left him to die, but these men, these Germans, picked him up and gave him treatment? Perhaps he should tell them of all the Germans he'd killed already. They'd not be so friendly then.

"Ha!" said the soldier. "Yes, we eat little children and wax our guns with the fat of old ladies. That is what you think. This is what you have heard. Propaganda, American friend. Do you understand? You are here because of propaganda. I will not shoot you. I do not like to shoot. I do like little sisters, though."

236

"Go to hell," Herman said. He wished to die. It was dishonorable to be taken prisoner. "I'll kill you first chance I get!"

"Rest now, American soldier. I am having fun with you."

"I've killed many of yours, too many to count," he said, struggling to sit.

"I am sure. You still think you are here fighting for a reason. When you realize you are not, you will stop all this nonsense," said the German. Herman lay back. He relaxed a little. The German soldier continued. "I have little sisters too. I have five of them. As many sisters as fingers on one hand. Too many, my papa says. And me, his one son, off to war."

For hours, the soldier told Herman of his family's farm and butcher shop. How his first job was mopping the blood from his father's butcher-shop floor. He spoke of the little river that wound near their farm and how his sisters brought water from there for cooking and washing. He told of his sisters' marriages, the emptying house, his mother's sagging eyes and widening middle, the nieces and nephews that started coming every year or so. The soldier spoke of good beer and *Schmierkuchen*. And all this came to Herman in the old language loved by his father. The language Herman had seldom spoken before now, somewhat out of spite and somewhat out of American loyalty; the language that had betrayed the United States at a time of grievous misdeeds by Germany toward the world. When the German soldier wrote a letter to Liesel for Herman, he startled when Herman gave him the address, New Germany, Minnesota.

"New Germany?" the soldier asked.

"That's right," said Herman.

"We had a boy of yours," he said. "It was a long time ago. He didn't last long."

"Mueller?"

"Yes," he said. "That is right. You knew him?"

"I did."

"You can tell his people that he died bravely," the German soldier said. "Perhaps not. I am sure it is a complicated matter."

"His family will appreciate the news."

Herman slept again. His first sleep in a bed in months. He slept to the sound of the German soldier telling stories of his sisters.

When he woke, the soldier was gone, and Herman looked around himself. The triage was set up in a bombed-out church. He didn't know which village he was in but suspected Argonne since it was the closest to the battlefield where he'd first been picked up by the Germans. All around him lay men and boys in cots. One doctor served the entire hospital. There were no nurses, only enlisted men clumsily attending to the doctor's operations, amputations, and dressings. The screams shook Herman's eardrums. The amputations were the worst, and he knew that his would come soon. Already his arm was blackening with disease. His fingers had swollen to look like rotten sausages. His nails were black and dead. And the slow purple march toward his shoulder would have to be stopped with a knife for the muscle and tendon and a saw for the bone. Sooner rather than later. He remembered farm accidents back home. The threshing machine had ripped a hand from a neighbor one harvest. The man had managed a decent life after, and Herman hoped for the same for himself. He worried about Betty. Would she want a one-armed man? How to do the chores and the milking? How to build tables and chairs and things a woman wants for comfort? How to hold a gun for hunting? How to play catch with a son? How to balance oneself on top of a woman? He knew other ways to do such things, but when he dreamed of Betty, he always saw himself on top of her, looking down into her face, pushing gently but surely into her body, being a man. A woman wanted a full man.

For weeks, he lay in that cot. Thinking, writing, listening to the stories of other men. When they took his arm, he tried to be brave. He bit into the hard canvas around his canteen and, despite himself, asked for morphine. The doctor shot a syringe full into his shoulder.

Morning, December 15, 1918

Dear Liesel,

Some boys here said that a villager's dog gave birth to a litter of six — three puppies and three kippens, half-dog, half-cat creatures. Apparently a big tomcat got after the lady's little white dog. The bitch is nursing the whole lot of them. Genetic scientists have flown in to study the animals, much faster than supplies or replacement troops ever got here.

It's a small war. I met up with some of Dieter Mueller's people. He didn't make it. Getting news to the families of German soldiers in America is quite impossible. Please pass the word to Sonnen and her family and be as gentle as you always are, dear sister.

I think of the barn fire often. So many reminders here of it. Buildings, trucks, tanks, and even people burn all the time the way our barn did with Luther and Pernilla. Everything is on fire here. I fear I'll never get the soot out of my eyes and ears.

It's raining again. My arm's lost. At night they burn the amputated legs and arms and it smells of kerosene and burned leaves. You can't imagine the things I've seen and smelled. I've had much time to lie here and think about the terrible things I've seen and heard. Many bad things I have done. I will only do right things for the rest of my life.

Herman

31

A T 10:55 A.M. ON THE eleventh day of the eleventh month in the year 1918, a German sniper lines up a Canadian soldier in the crosshairs of his long-range peep sight. With a tender flex of his pointer finger against the cool curve of a hunk of trigger metal, the German sniper releases his shot. The bullet soars uninterrupted over fallen buildings weeping dust and brick, through their broken windows, past boy soldiers weighted with wet coats, binoculars, and the rain, past barbed-wire coils and knots, past tanks smoking and off their tracks, and past more of the dead, some whose spilled and dark blood gives their deaths away and some who don't look dead, only pale and wide eyed. The eyes of the Canadian soldier peek inches above his makeshift foxhole. He hadn't wanted to be a soldier, but the farmhouse where he had lived before the war was too packed with children, his mother dead, his sister overwhelmed with responsibility, and his pa angry and spiteful.

"Go and see the world," his pa had said.

This boy of Harald Sutter, this American-born and -raised Canadian soldier, hears again his pa's words as the bullet shatters his forehead, pierces his brain, and explodes the back of his head. Very soon, the cease-fire to end the world war will be declared and the battle will be over. Private Sutter will stay in a muddy ditch for days before the body collectors find him. A telegram will be sent to the Sutter farm, and the littlest Sutter girl will receive it but will not be able to read it. She'll stick it under the flour tin and forget to mention its arrival.

What a wreck the world was. Sutter was one of the many soldiers to die. Sixty thousand Canadians, a hundred and twenty-five thousand Americans, almost half a million Serbs, almost three-quarters of a million Englishmen, more than a million Frenchmen, and almost two million Russian soldiers dead. Three hundred thousand Austrians and three-quarters of a million Germans. Two million from the Ottoman Empire.

And you would think the world would flood with female tears from all the waiting and praying at home for the fighting men and getting only death notices and body bags instead of whole male bodies back from the frontlines. You would think the world would become a flurry of skirts and pretty cakes, but the world is discriminate, and, as if to prevent such a tremendous gender imbalance, disease, famine, and civilian casualties kill at least as many women and their children as the war killed male soldiers.

Soldiers that survived the war hobbled onto boats and trains home. They left arms, eyes, legs, and sanity behind. They left friends and brothers in the ground on the eastern and western fronts. They carried lice and disease in their hair and clothing. The first soldiers home hugged close their mothers and fathers, little brothers and sisters, sweethearts. And by the time all the soldiers had stepped off the boats and trains, relieved to be home at last, an influenza pandemic was boiling in the bodies of city people and country folks.

•   •   •

In Minnesota, Otto Richter, in between a boy and a man, sings a little rhyme in English that he learned at school. "I had a little bird whose name was Enza. I opened up the window and in-flu-enza."

In an upstairs bedroom of the Richter home, Wilhelm Richter clutches a bloodstained handkerchief in one hand and a letter in the other. *Coming home. Herman,* it says.

Wilhelm's body heats with fever but shivers with chills. Since the night his neighbors tarred and feathered him, since the night he lost Luther, he's shrunk into his house and succumbed to every nature of illness that passed through southern Minnesota. When the Spanish flu swept in on a gusty spring morning as he stood at the edge of his fields and admired their breadth, he took in as deep a breath as he could muster. That same week, he received the letter from Herman. The next week, an unyielding cough settled in his lungs. A few days later, he fell into bed. Today, while the oldest son sits at the base of Magdalena Richter's grave, while the worms and beetles eat away at the body of another son lying in a wooden coffin beside his mother's, while his daughter brings lemonade to the neighbor boy butchering a turtle near the silo, while another son sits somewhere in Europe, and while the last boy tosses a ball up into the blue sky and sings a rhyme, Wilhelm Richter's throat fills with phlegm and blood for the final time, and his last breath of air catches in his mouth. In these last moments, he goes back to a time when he felt safe, snuggled between his parents in their bed. He feels the heat and heartbeat of his own mother one more time. He hears the pounding of feet on the stairs, the burst of a bedroom door flung open, and the thud of club against bone. Wilhelm Richter's heart stops.

Benjamin, Liesel, and Otto Richter lay their papa beside their mother beneath the grove of trees on the farm in the little cemetery filled with so many Richters, practically a whole family of them.

• • •

The sky over the ocean was the familiar shade of gray, and the rats that had plagued him on the battlefields of France followed him onto the troopship and darted between the soldiers' boots on the deck. Herman, or what was left of Herman's mind and body, and those men left of his regiment sailed home from France in May of 1919 aboard the USS *Radnor*. Once he got his last remaining man onto the ship, he wrapped a coarse blanket around his body and sat on the deck looking over the rail and out at the rocky water. Philippe LeRoche brought him soup and coffee. Herman was silent most of the time but seemed receptive to Philippe's talking. And Philippe talked and talked of things he had seen and things he knew and many things that he didn't have the slightest inkling about. He just talked as the waves lapped and passed by the freighter taking half-bodied and half-skinned and shell-shocked soldiers back to their homes.

"When I am an old man," Philippe said, "I will forget all about this war business. But for now, I cannot forget it. Can you?" Philippe offered Herman a drag on his cigarette.

Herman, quiet but awake on a deck chair, just stared.

"Maybe time will soften my thoughts on a few things," said Philippe. "I saw a paper from back home that made it seem like it was all Germans and bad guys we were killing and made it seem like we were saving the world or something, but we know better than they do, no? Saving it from what, is what I would like to know."

Herman stared on.

"I think about those men in the house that night. About the well," said Philippe.

Herman blinked but said nothing.

"I cannot get it out of my head. I am not sure," Philippe went on.

"Stop it," said Herman. "We did what had to be done and that's the end of it."

"That is the end of it?" said Philippe. He puffed on the smallest bit of cigarette, then walked to the rail and threw it over the edge. "There's no end to it, I do not think."

Herman pulled a letter out from beneath his gray blanket and handed it to Philippe. "Don't you ever stop talking?" Herman said.

"What is this?" Philippe unfolded it. "Ohhh. Another letter from the little sister." Philippe smiled and read. "Yes," he said. "This Liesel is my dream girl. I am going to come with you to Minnesota and marry her, you know."

Herman scoffed, then smiled. But not an easy smile. It was a darker thing.

"But first I want to see everything," said Philippe. "Then I will come and visit your little farm."

"I will watch for you."

32

B Y JUNE OF 1919, Herman had bound bales with twine and
stacked them waist-high all around the Richter house. He
had sawed wood and fashioned new shutters for the windows,
and he checked and rechecked that they were closed and secure each night before the family went to bed. He bought locks
from the general store and screwed seven of them into the door,
and the whole family endured the repetition Herman conducted
each night, locking and relocking them over and over again. He
bought gallons of oil for the lamps and kept them burning all
hours of the day. He hoarded food in his room. He inspected
Otto's feet, between his toes, and demanded that Liesel make
more socks so that he'd have a new pair each day. All over the
kitchen and on the clothesline, pairs of gray socks hung, dripping, drying.

When Herman insisted that Benjamin and Otto help him dig
up Luther to be sure he was dead, Liesel had objected, but Herman could not be deterred. "You don't know!" he screamed. "You
do not know."

Herman inspected what was left of Luther's lips. Half was

burned to the skull, but the other half was curled back, revealing teeth that were still white and whole. Luther had always had straight, white teeth. Herman looked into the blank eye sockets. Could humans live without eyeballs? Yes! They could. He'd seen it. Herman stepped back and observed his brother whole, the black, stiff bones contorted as if he were racked with pain. But Herman had to be sure. After all, he'd seen men who'd looked dead and weren't. He'd seen men with most of their faces gone who still breathed. He'd seen men emaciated to skeletons whose hearts still pounded as surely as the Earth turned round. *You never knew.* You could never really know if a person was alive or dead unless you looked close. If Herman had learned anything in Europe, it was that you had to be sure, absolutely sure. You had to put your own hand to his chest. You had to put your own ear to his nose. Herman pressed his palm onto Luther's chest and ash lifted. He pressed his ear to what was left of Luther's nose. Nothing.

Still Herman was not convinced. He hitched up the horse team, urged them to town, and pulled in front of Betty's house. He took her by the hand, yanked her out of the house, and planted her in the seat next to his. All the way to the Richter farm he told her nothing. When he led her to Luther, he had to say only, "Please be sure," for her to understand. Poor Betty. She obliged Herman, this man she loved. She went to the corpse and tested all the vitals for Herman to see. "He's gone," she said.

He was dead. Really dead. "Fine," said Herman. He's gone.

"What about Papa?" he said to Betty.

"My father was there at the end, Herman," she said. "He checked. Your papa is dead."

Satisfied, Herman reburied Luther next to their parents and pulled rocks from the fields and jammed them into the earth over all of their graves so that their spirits could not roam about. Herman rode the horse and wagon to Betty's home. Once in front of her house, he laid his head in her lap and reached up to touch her breast. She slapped his hand away and shamed him with lowered eyebrows. She said nothing to him when she climbed out of the wagon. He sat up and urged the horses on.

But now it was she who could not sleep. All night she hated herself for pushing him away when it had been obvious that he needed her. In the morning, she packed her things in a simple trunk, asked her father for a ride, and arrived at the Richter farm.

Betty waltzed up to the Richter kitchen door, put her face against the screen, saw a solid young woman standing at the kitchen counter, and said, "Hey there."

Liesel set down the potato she'd been peeling and turned toward the door. The only visitor she ever expected was Lester.

"Well, hi to you too," said Betty. "Remember me? Betty? Betty Mathiowetz."

"Oh," said Liesel. She thought about the night she'd seen Betty here, in her own kitchen. She remembered how Betty had tended to her pa in his shameful state. How she tried to tend to Herman now, in his state. She wrinkled her brow.

"I'm here to see Herman," said Betty.

"Haven't seen him," said Liesel. This was a lie. Herman was out scouring the fields for signs of buried bombs.

Betty set her trunk on the porch. She tucked a bundle under her arm, opened the screen door, and stepped up into the kitchen. "Well," said Betty, although not to Liesel in particular. "He needs me."

"Come in," said Liesel. She stood many inches taller than the waif girl and many pounds fuller. Betty wore a swirling skirt and a lace blouse pinched at the neck by a black ribbon. She tugged white gloves off hands as delicate as small doves. Long black lashes and perfectly arched brows framed her black eyes. The girl stared back at Liesel.

"I'm in, dear," said Betty. "You are a silly goose." Betty pushed the bundle of loaves into Liesel's middle. Liesel put her arms around it. "Herman told me you're the one who manages all these boys," Betty said. She studied the tidy kitchen. "I'm here to help you now. When Herman and I get married, we'll be like sisters."

Liesel slid the bundle onto the kitchen table. She straightened her apron, then tucked a few stray hairs back behind her ear, and finally hid her big, dirty hands in her pockets. "Oh, I manage fine, really," she said. "I don't need any help."

"Well, help is what you're gonna get," said Betty. "It's ridiculous the way they've got you cooped up here every day. How you ever supposed to meet a fella of your own?"

"I haven't thought about it."

"Well, you ought to! Herman says the only person you ever court with is that Sutter neighbor with the weird ways."

Liesel picked up another potato and began peeling again.

"Lester," Liesel said. She paused for a moment, then added, "This life is good enough anyway. I like taking care of my brothers."

"Don't be silly," Betty said. "A girl's got to have a fella. You can't expect to live here all your life. Time's marchin', Liesel. Herman and I are gonna raise a family in this house. Didn't he tell you?"

"No," said Liesel. "No. He didn't mention it."

Liesel looked away from Betty, closed her eyes, held her breath, and willed the girl to leave.

Potato peelings flew in a fury from the end of Liesel's knife. Betty pretended to wipe something off her sleeve.

"I've got to get food on the table," said Liesel.

"Oh," said Betty. She peeked over Liesel's shoulder. "What are we havin'?"

Betty asked for a slicing knife. Liesel surrendered one to her, and Betty began slicing the bread into neat rows.

Betty Mathiowetz moved herself into the Richter household that day. When Herman came in from the fields, he dragged Betty's trunk into the kitchen and then tugged it up the stairs to his own room. After supper that night, Betty followed him to his room, where she opened up her body, and he drove himself into her again and again. She accepted him for as long as he could hold out. She resolved to do this until he was better.

But even then, Herman Richter fought sleep. All night, he heard the scratching of rats on the floor of the house and turned over chairs and tables trying to find the little villains. He sat on the porch and wrote poems filled with all the things he'd seen in Europe.

> When the safest place,
> a hole in the ground,
> fills with water cold as granite,
> this will be war. When corpses creak,
> rodents feed on live flesh,
> poison leaks from toenails and ears,
> you will know why there is no sleep here.

And when he couldn't arrange his thoughts any further, he went back to bed and roused Betty. She wrapped her arms around him and settled him between her legs. For a few hours, then, he was still and quiet, asleep and sound. But then it was she who lay wide awake, wondering about this man she loved, about what memories troubled him, about what reasons kept him from getting past all that, about what kept him from making her a proper woman.

Eventually, though, Betty accepted that there'd be no wedding, and she accepted the scandal it'd surely stir in town. She stood stoically by as Benjamin committed himself legally and religiously to Sonnenschein Mueller late that summer in a proper Catholic wedding, the type she'd wanted for herself. Benjamin had proposed to Sonnen using his mother's cameo, and when Betty saw it, she had the briefest pang that it hadn't come to her instead. But she shrugged off that jealousy and hugged Sonnen until the cameo pressed an imprint into her forehead. She didn't even complain when Father Anton refused her Communion at the ceremony. She crossed herself, dipped aside, and hoped no one else had noticed, though of course people had. Her own father, for one; he pulled Father Anton aside after the Mass and said the church'd not be seeing one more dime from him. Betty happily helped Sonnen move her things into Benjamin's room. She happily helped Sonnen acclimate to life in the Richter household even as Liesel ducked away and hid from a responsibility that should have been hers. Betty stuffed her sleeve into her mouth each minute the nausea settled upon her. Betty was pregnant. Unmarried as a girl could be, she was living in sin and pregnant as a rabbit.

Liesel hadn't attended Benjamin's wedding but had diligently cleaned and prepared Benjamin's room to make Sonnen feel at home. She washed the bedding and opened the windows and picked a bouquet of peonies and arranged them in a vase. She was happy for Benjamin. Of course she was. Sonnen Mueller was a nice girl. But there'd been so much change in the past year. Who were these women who'd all of a sudden come into her family's life? What was she supposed to do? What had happened to her role in the family? Sonnen could cook and bake. Betty had taken charge of Herman. Otto was growing too big to need her. Now what? Liesel busied herself around the house and farm, trying her damnedest to make herself indispensable. Her greatest relief came each morning when Sonnen, who'd decided to keep working, walked to her family's bakery in town and Betty went with her to have coffee with Dr. Mathiowetz at his office. Then, for a few hours each day, Liesel'd have peace in the house again. It was almost like the old days.

After supper, Herman and Betty excused themselves for an evening walk. Betty's father had told her that exercise and fresh air would do Herman some good. Sonnen filled a pipe for Benjamin and sat on his lap while he smoked it and spread out his papa's paperwork. What investments and money Wilhelm had left behind had taken much sorting through by Benjamin. Wilhelm had left a mess. Once the war was over, the German factories had closed, and Wilhelm's interests in them had plainly tanked. Benjamin spent great portions of his day with the banker in town, figuring out how to pay off his papa's debts without losing the entire farm. He tried not to bother his brothers and sister with the business, but they could see Benjamin's stress. And he had to deny them money for extras only once for them to understand that there was no money. The financial belt had been tightened in a way the Richter family had never experienced before.

Liesel collected the plates and set Otto to work on vocabulary words at the table. After the dishes, she went to toss the potato peelings. It was that time in early evening when the sky seems to breathe. When she spotted her brother and Betty kissing near the well, she knelt into the shadow of the barn and was quiet.

Herman rubbed Betty's arm with his own, slid her blouse over her arms, and exposed her tiny breasts. Betty kissed Herman's neck and massaged his groin. Herman dropped his pants and lifted Betty's skirt.

"Herman," Betty said, "I'm not ready yet. Slow down. Kiss me a little. Go slowly."

"Are you turning shy on me?" Herman said. His voice was still sometimes hoarse from the poison gases that had hung in a green mist for days in the wet French air, never entirely dissipating.

"You know better than that," Betty said. "But you want it to feel nice for me too, don't ya?"

"All right," he said. "I'm just a little hot tonight. But I know what you like."

"Be serious now," said Betty. She took his face in her hands. "We've got to talk about some things." She pressed his hand to her belly.

"What's that supposed to mean?" he said.

"A baby, Herman."

He jerked away from her. "No," he said.

Betty grabbed his hand and pressed it again to her belly.

"Herman," said Betty. "We are having a baby."

He shook his head, as if that could undo it. "Fatherhood is not for me."

"Not for you?" said Betty. "It's too late for that." Betty wished she hadn't told him. It wasn't too late. She *could* undo it. She knew about things like that, and she knew her good father would help her if she wanted. Her father. She had shamed him in town and among his friends. And he'd stood by her with no ill judgment.

Herman looked hard at this girl he loved. He was overcome with a sense of repulsion. She was trying to trap him. This was an ambush.

"You're not fooling me," he said to her.

"What are you talking about?" Somewhere inside him was a good man. But how patient did she have to be? This man was her only choice. She was ruined for others. "What other choice do you have? You can't keep your face buried in your big ideas and strange behavior all the time. You can't raise a family on that. We need our own place, Herman. It's time to do the right thing."

Herman was quiet for a long while. "The right thing," he said finally. Herman took Betty and pulled her close. A baby. What was he going to do with a baby? He threw that thought away and centered on the only act that brought him any peace these days. He wanted her. He wanted her always. She wasn't disgusted by him. She didn't mind that he was only half a man, no better than a three-legged dog.

Betty lay back on the platform of the well, and Herman pushed aside her arms. He pinched and pecked at her breasts until she giggled.

"Come on now," she said. "Be serious."

"I just love these little moths," he said.

"Never mind them," she said. She pushed down on his head.

252

He moved down her waist to between her legs. She lifted her knees and raked her hands in his hair.

Liesel studied them. Betty didn't seem to mind Herman's left stump. She had caressed and kissed the thing tenderly, as if it didn't matter at all that Herman was missing an arm, that only a shirtsleeve dangled where a limb should be. Herman didn't seem bothered that Betty's chest was as smooth as a boy's, that no womanly flesh and weight filled her breasts.

Liesel watched Herman mount Betty then. She watched them move together until Betty threw back her head and her brother groaned into the twilight. Liesel sat until the pair straightened their clothes and strolled back into the house, Herman's arm folded over Betty's shoulders. Protecting each other, helping each other.

Philippe LeRoche, who'd promised to come and find Herman, did so in early fall with nothing but a tramp bag hanging over his shoulder. He'd worked the railroad for a bit. He'd slept sitting up again, ate little and only when time allowed, and spent most of his days in the company of dirty men. His life was no longer in daily danger, but this life wasn't much different than wartime existence. Seeing the sights fly by the window of the train had been nice. He'd seen mountains, waterfalls, grazing cattle, and cranberry bogs. But he was tired of always moving. He wanted things to stay still. He had it all worked out in his mind: he'd help Herman and his brothers with the harvest, he'd woo and marry Liesel Richter, he'd learn to be a farmer like his friend Herman, he'd spawn a pack of kids, and he'd live a quiet civilian existence.

What Philippe found at the Richter farm was a place in decay. The fields were overgrown with weeds. A big black hole where the barn had once stood growled from the middle of the farm place. The fences leaned left and right. The house needed painting. Philippe wondered if he was in the right place. Until he saw her.

Liesel flipped white sheets over the clothesline and secured them with pins. When she saw the man standing in the yard, she spit a mouthful of clothespins onto the ground.

"Hallo?" she said. She looked behind her and to the grove where Lester often waited. He wasn't there. And she was glad. It was hard to explain Lester. She loved him but was embarrassed by him, too. These contradictions made her ashamed. Who was *she* to be ashamed of anyone?

Philippe walked to her. He set his bag on the ground and reached out his hands as if trying to coax a feral cat.

"Liesel," he said.

Liesel tucked her hair behind her ears. "Yes?" she said.

Philippe rushed her and embraced her. "I know you," Philippe said.

Herman snapped to life again. He hugged his friend, and Philippe pretended to dance with Herman's empty sleeve. For the first time in a long time, Betty and Liesel had a reason to laugh. Betty said she'd move her things out of Herman's room and into Liesel's room so that Philippe would have a place to stay.

"I must not separate two kids in love," he said to Betty.

"No," said Herman. "It's no problem. We're happy to have you. And you and I have shared close quarters before, my friend."

"So we have," said Philippe. "But I wouldn't mind one bit being the one to move into my girl Liesel's room." He laughed and winked.

Herman's eyes slit. Philippe was joking, of course, but that panicky sense of protecting his family overcame him again. What was he up to? Herman tried to shake it off. Why shouldn't Philippe court Liesel? Because. Because he was getting too close. Because if he was here, *always* here, then Herman would never be allowed to forget the bad times in Europe. He'd never be able to put the night at the well behind him and leave it in the past where it was meant to stay. No. It would never do to have Philippe court

Liesel. It was silly anyway. Liesel was a just a simple, naive country girl. Philippe's intentions with women weren't noble, not like Herman's. He misused women. Liesel was Herman's responsibility. He had to protect her.

"Get in the house, Liesel," he said. "Make us some coffee."

Late into the nights, the family sat up talking. Herman and Philippe told stories of each other's bravery during the war. On the first night, after everyone else had gone to bed, Philippe offered to help Liesel clean the dishes.

"Sit with me a bit," he said to her. He pulled out a chair and then sat himself in the one next to it.

"Maybe just a while longer," Liesel said.

He plopped his feet up onto her lap. She swept them off and smoothed her apron.

"My friend Herman is not so well, is he?" said Philippe.

"He's fine," said Liesel. Philippe smiled as if to say, *So be it.* He stared at her until she looked away.

"You have beautiful eyes, Liesel," said Philippe. "My mother had such eyes."

"Don't say such things," whispered Liesel. Outside, the moon shone bright. Always on the rise of the moon, she thought of Lester. He and the nighttime light were inevitably joined for her. On nights like this, Lester always came. And usually, she couldn't wait to go out and meet him. But tonight, other desires kept her in the house.

"I am going to marry you," Philippe said.

Liesel told Philippe she needed fresh air. "Good night," she said. He said he understood and went to Herman's room. She walked outside and picked her way through the dark. There, in the usual place, Lester had left a carcass for cooking. She picked it up and silently thanked him for the gift. She was happy he hadn't waited for him, though. She didn't want to see him.

Liesel thought hard. She had a chance, but first she had to fix herself. How hard could it be? She'd simply go to town, tell Dr. Mathiowetz, and have him help her. He was a good man. He'd passed no judgment on his daughter in her condition. He was understanding of Herman. He'd be understanding and kind to her. It'd be easy. She went back to the house and lay next to Betty to sleep.

The next morning, after Benjamin and Sonnen had left for town, Liesel went into their room and helped herself to Sonnen's things: she dabbed her fingers into Sonnen's face cream and spread it over her cheeks, she used Sonnen's red lipstick on her mouth. When Betty caught Liesel primping, she didn't tease but instead offered to do her hair. Liesel sat at the little vanity and held up her mother's old hand mirror while Betty brushed her thick hair, twisted it into a knot, and secured it.

"Beautiful," said Betty.

"Thank you," said Liesel.

"You like him, don't you?" said Betty.

"I don't know," said Liesel.

"You do," said Betty. "It's wonderful." Betty spit into her hand and tamed a few flyaways on Liesel's head.

"I'm having a baby, you know," said Betty.

"I know," said Liesel. "That's wonderful too."

"Herman doesn't think so," said Betty.

Liesel turned and took Betty's hand. "He'll come around."

All that day, Liesel allowed herself to smile at Philippe. She sat next to Philippe that night at supper. And afterward, the men began their stories again. This time, though, the thoughts and memories that Herman generally kept to himself or wrote in his poems came out. He told the family of the horrors he'd seen. And he didn't stop when Sonnen excused herself from the table and Benjamin followed or when Betty brought a napkin to her mouth and coughed politely into it. He didn't stop when Liesel gave him a warning look and pointed to Otto.

Herman told the tale of lying on that battlefield, waiting for help and feeling death come over him. He told his family about the American medic who finally did come. He told them how the medic looked him over, said, "Sorry," and left him to die.

"He didn't think I'd make it," said Herman. "When he left me, the heaviest loneliness of my life came over me. You can't imagine."

Liesel could imagine. But she didn't say so. She tried to picture her brother lying all alone, dying, being passed over by a doctor. A doctor.

"Doctors are only human too," said Herman. Doctors are only human. No one said a word until Liesel stood up and told Otto it was time for bed.

"When I'm a doctor, I'll help everyone," said Otto. "I wouldn't have left you there."

"Of course you wouldn't have," said Liesel. "Come along now. Time for bed."

At last Herman and Philippe were all alone. Philippe looked at Herman, stared at him, until Herman asked, "What?"

"How has it been for you?" asked Philippe. "Really, I mean."

"Fine," said Herman. He scratched his stump. "It's nice to be home."

"You have a nice family."

Herman nodded. He leaned toward Philippe. It was an aggressive act. "What's on your mind? I can see something's on your mind that you want to get off it."

"Do not upset yourself," said Philippe. "I am only wondering how you came out of it all."

"Fine, I said."

Philippe stood and went to the cupboards. "I think about that night at the house on many days." He opened a cupboard and pulled a tin cup from it. He turned to see if Herman was still listening. He was. "What we did was not right." Philippe took the coffeepot and poured himself a full cup.

Herman smirked. "Did you come all the way here just to give me that? Don't give me that shit. We did what needed to be done."

Philippe took a sip. He could see in Herman's face that he was used to having his word be final. Philippe thought about these words of Herman's. They sounded right, but they were not right. "Those words can come out, but they do not become true by saying them."

Herman stood. "Not another word." He took the stairs two and three at a time. Philippe finished his coffee.

As Liesel lay in her bed that night, she listened to the soft breathing of Betty. She thought about how fragile a life was. And how resilient it was. Herman's story had bothered her. She had to think. Could she trust Dr. Mathiowetz or not? She had to think.

Early the next morning, as she dressed in the dark, she felt she was being watched. She knew she was. She turned toward the door. It was open just the slightest crack, but she could see nothing. She pulled her camisole over her head. Her breasts lifted and fell and swung momentarily in the moonlight. She heard a sigh from behind the door. She looked to Betty, who still slept deep. Liesel touched her own breast. She rubbed her thumb over the nipple.

Philippe watched her. He knew she knew he was there. Her breasts were so beautiful. As he imagined touching them, he grabbed hold of himself and stroked. He braced himself with his other hand on the door frame. His breathing came rapidly. *Show me,* he said to himself. *Show me.*

When Herman stepped into the hall, he saw his friend peering through the opening of his sister's bedroom door. He grabbed

258

Luther's old baseball bat and stormed toward him. The crack that followed echoed in the hall for the rest of the house's years. Herman dragged Philippe out of the house and threw his bag out after him. He watched from the window while Philippe grabbed his bag and trudged down the driveway. Herman locked all of the locks. He checked and rechecked them, checked and rechecked them.

Liesel's breasts overwhelmed Philippe. Her eyes haunted him. He dreamed of them. He saw them in the clouds and in his morning coffee. For the rest of his life, Philippe would draw Liesel Richter's black eyes on the faces of many women. When Philippe died, an old man with no family but many friends, they'd open a trunk and dump thousands and thousands of sketches of naked females onto the floor. All would have the look of Liesel Richter.

THE CREATURE RUMMAGES through the grass and foxtails near the Richter graves. He settles into the foliage. This has always been its waiting place. The night is very black now. A figure emerges from the house, holding a shawl at her neck. She pokes a lantern out in front of her face and then hangs it from a nail on the porch. She leans against a support and crosses her arms. For a long while she waits like that. She waits like that until called inside.

PART *IV*

33

New Germany, Minnesota, 1920

I N T H E T I M E just after the big war, Benjamin, Herman, and Otto Richter led their neighbor Lester Sutter to the edge of Spider Lake. They watched him drown through the sights of their rifles. They drove him in with the barrels of their guns and stood guard among the cattails. They watched him drown through the sights of their rifles. While the rocks they'd stuffed and stitched into Lester's pockets pulled him into the heavy embrace of lake weeds, they watched him drown through the sights of their rifles. The water filled his boots, soaked his overalls, and the stones in his pockets sank him. They watched him drown. The three brothers leaned the rifles against their legs and waited for Lester's head to stop breaking the surface and gasping for air. Through the sights of their rifles, the three brothers watched Lester Sutter drown.

Two miles away, Liesel Richter took a paring knife from the counter, left the stew simmering on the stove, and walked to the place behind the silo where Lester had butchered the turtles she got from him every month, to the place where she'd brought him lemonade or fresh bread, to the place where she'd listened to his rambling and practiced her flirting. She carried the paring knife to the place she had romanced a retarded man known county-wide for his lunacy and his skills trapping snappers.

Many memories saturated her where she knelt. A snapper head hummed with activity: beetles crawled in and out of its eyes, maggots vibrated in its jaws; the sun had drawn all moisture from its leathery skin. For a long while after the turtle catcher had severed the heads from the snappers, their jaws continued to crack and bite. Even now, deep through the sockets, the creature's brain was alive with movement. Liesel focused past the empty portholes and into the well of the turtle's mind. In the most desperate moment of her life, she called out for her long-dead mother.

"Mama! Mama! Where are you? Damn you, Mama."

She pulled taut the growth from between her hips and cut the thing from her body once and for all. She tossed it aside, fell back into the weeds, watched a cicada break from the soil and take flight, then lifted her eyes to the high, sighing sun.

Through the sights of their rifles, three men watched him drown.

After they left, after much time had passed since one gasp of breath had crossed the man's cracked lips, and after millions and millions of pounds of water had pressed down and tried to crush his life with its weight, Lester Sutter opened his blue eyes in that black place, expanded his lungs, and found himself alive.

He opened his blue eyes in that black place, expanded his lungs, and found himself alive.

266

34

IT WAS BETTY WHO found Liesel lying behind the silo.
When Liesel heard Betty call her name, she turned over, her
back bent toward the sky, and tucked up tight and face-down in
the wet grass, lively with insects displaced from their feeding and
breeding by her presence. Betty walked toward the gray swarm
hazing the space and broke into a sprint when she saw Liesel. She
knelt beside her, placed her hand on Liesel's back, and tried to
make sense of the scene. Blood. A knife. A horde of turtle heads.
A measure of severed skin.

"My God, Liesel. What have you done?"

She lifted Liesel's head into her lap.

"Liesel." She slapped her pale cheek. "Can you hear me?"

Liesel moaned. Betty turned her over, lifted the bloody dress,
and saw the wound.

"What is this?" she asked. "You've got to wake up. Stay awake
and talk to me."

"Do not look at me," whispered Liesel. She pushed Betty.
"Please go away."

Betty patted Liesel's head. "I'm not going anywhere. I can help you. Tell me what happened."

Liesel's lips swelled, and she sobbed. She shook her head.

"It's okay," said Betty. "Was there a baby?"

"No, no," she cried. "Not a baby."

"What then? Let me look, Liesel."

"No! Do not look at me!"

"Where's Herman?" Betty asked. She looked around the farm. "We've got to get some help."

Liesel grasped Betty's ankle. "No," she said. "Not my brothers. Please. Not them. Not them. Keep them away from me, for God's sake."

Betty held her closer. "All right now. It's all right. I'm not going to let them see you. I'm here to help you. Let me help you."

Her tiny body struggling under the weight, Betty lugged Liesel Richter to the house. She settled Liesel in the back bedroom. She scratched a note — *Stay out* — and pinned it to the outside of the door for the boys to see. And then she went to work repairing the mess Liesel had made of herself. Betty was a doctor's daughter, and she put aside propriety to wash the wound with water and soap, inspect it gently, and bandage it. No stitching would have helped, and the scar would be hidden anyway. As she mended the wound, she understood Liesel's condition. And though Betty tried to swallow the dirty, sickening bile that crept from her stomach to her teeth, she was sick in the chamber pot. Betty wiped her mouth with the back of her wrist. She closed her eyes and apologized. Betty promised herself never to hurt Liesel Richter again. She composed herself, straightened the wrinkles out of her skirt, and snapped a clean washcloth.

"Liesel," she said. She dipped the washcloth into the basin and wrung it out. Pink-tinged water ran down. "It doesn't matter."

Liesel stared out the window and then lobbed her arm over her eyes. Betty dabbed at the wound again.

"It's okay, now," said Betty.

Liesel's crying shook the bed.

"It didn't mean anything," Betty said. She spread ointment over the wound. Liesel moaned. "You're beautiful, Liesel. Beautiful."

"If I die, don't let my brothers see."

"No one's going to know. Not ever."

All the while Betty cared for her, Liesel cried. The crying felt so good. Liesel cried for herself. Liesel cried for Lester. And she cried because she had let him die. Betty spooned whiskey and laudanum into Liesel's mouth. Finally, when Liesel was patched and bandaged, Betty pulled the cover up over Liesel's shoulders and told her to sleep. Though it was summer and sultry in the back bedroom, Liesel complained of cold. Betty piled on four blankets to cover her. Still Liesel shivered from shock. Betty climbed in and wrapped her skinny arms around Liesel. She held the trembling girl. Liesel could not be warmed or calmed. Finally, Betty closed the curtains and removed her blouse, her skirt, and all her underthings. She climbed into the bed and snuggled close to Liesel. Her thin frame pressed against Liesel's naked back. Her belly, where Herman's child grew, burned hot. She draped an arm and a leg over Liesel's body. "There," she said. "All warm now."

Liesel stiffened.

"It's all right," said Betty. "You're freezing."

Liesel's body softened. The sun was setting and yellow glow warmed the room.

"Quiet now, dear," she said. "I'm here for you."

"I'm a monster."

"Shhh," Betty soothed. She rubbed Liesel's arm.

"They've killed him."

"Killed who? You're half delirious."

Liesel stopped crying. She turned over and faced Betty nose to nose. Her wide tan face was red and wet, and the blacks of her eyes were big as coins.

"I have killed Lester," she said. "I have."

Betty pulled a fisted bunch of blanket up around Liesel's

mouth. "You haven't killed anyone," she said. "You wouldn't hurt anyone. Sleep now. I'm here for you, dear. I'll keep you safe."

When the breaths of Liesel finally came heavier, Betty closed her eyes and slept too.

For months Liesel lay in that bed, curled over her healing wound and facing the window. Summer relaxed into fall, and fall folded under the weight of the most onerous winter to form over the north in years. Otto scratched away the frost from the outside of Liesel's bedroom window and looked through to check on his sister every day. Only when he was sure her chest rose and fell with air would he leave that place. True to his word, he never mentioned what he and his brothers had done to Lester Sutter. Not to Benjamin, not to Herman. And Betty never asked.

Some nights, Liesel lay awake and watched outside until she was sure Lester's breath steamed the window, was sure he was calling her name, was sure she could see his eyes staring in at her.

On a day when the winter sky cast down an ice storm on the Richter house, when the air grew so cold that even the watery tissue deep inside the trees froze, expanded, and then splintered young oaks, Betty opened Liesel's bedroom door, knelt beside the bed, and said, "It's time to get up now."

Liesel sighed and sat up.

"I've heated water," said Betty. "You need a bath."

She didn't resist when Betty inspected her. "This looks fine," Betty said.

For months, Betty had worked hard. Building the baby and caring for the boys the way Liesel had always done. Every day she checked on Liesel. Sometimes she would pull up the chair and tell her about her day. Betty would go on about the disaster she'd made of some meal, or how she'd starched Herman's shirt too stiff and how he now had a rash the size of a wild animal on his back.

She would bring soap and water and clean Liesel's cut, and never would Liesel say a word to Betty. And so Betty worked harder and harder to tell Liesel more risqué or funnier tidbits to get her to at least blink or respond in some way. Betty told Liesel about Benjamin and Sonnen, and how you'd never know it to talk to her in the daytime, but the girl could cuss up a storm when the bedsprings got to creaking, and Betty had had no idea that Benjamin had so much stamina. Still Liesel would not talk.

"God, I swear I'm going crazy in this house," said Betty. She set the bowl on the bedside table. "Last night I swore I saw the strangest-looking creature lurking around where the old barn used to be. Moving as slow as molasses in winter." She stretched her arm out shoulder high. "It was about the size of a bear, I swear. You don't think there could be bears this far south, do you? Herman said no, couldn't be. He said maybe a coon was out scroungin' in the snow for all them turtle heads lyin' around. Hungry enough to eat them, he said. Didn't look like a bear, though. It didn't have a stitch of fur that I could see."

"I will wash myself today," Liesel said. She took the bowl and towel and turned her back on Betty.

35

LIESEL WALKED TO the kitchen, tied an apron around her waist, and pounded flour, water, and yeast into bread dough. After setting it aside to rise, she opened and closed cupboards and the icebox. Betty stood to the side and out of her way.

"Do we have an ounce of meat in this house that's proper for cooking?" Liesel asked. Betty told her that no, they hadn't had meat in quite some time.

"You would think that one of the men in this house would make himself useful," said Liesel.

"Can I help?" Betty asked.

"I doubt it," said Liesel. And she went back to work.

That evening, the family emerged from their various chores and sat down to their first decent meal since Lester Sutter's demise. They talked of regular things, as if Liesel hadn't been holed up in her room for all that time, as if Lester Sutter weren't dead, as if Betty didn't know Liesel's secret.

"Good stew," said Otto. He shoveled spoonful after spoonful

of the pumpkin, squash, onion, and potato meal into his mouth. He had been the one to help Betty gather the vegetables from the garden before the hard frost. He had been the one to help her haul them into the cellar and stack them in small piles.

"Looks like we should have enough for winter," Betty had said, though she really had no idea what it took to feed this family.

Otto had followed Betty into the cellar time and again to stand with her before the vegetables as she selected a few for dinner, as she tried to figure out how to peel them, cut them, and prepare them.

Once Otto had suggested that she could ask Liesel how to fix the vegetables, but Betty had snapped at him and said, "You stay away from that bedroom door, Otto," so he had.

"Yes," said Herman now about the stew. "It is good stew."

"Be better if there were meat in it," said Liesel.

The next day, Otto took down his rifle and snuffed a rabbit out of the brush, which he shot and delivered to Liesel.

She grabbed the gift by the hind legs and said, "Thank you, Otto." She cried all the while she skinned, gutted, and braised the animal.

When Sonnen saw her sister-in-law crying over a rabbit, she decided she'd had enough. What was going on with these people? She'd had it with her husband's family. She told Benjamin she'd not sleep with him one more time until they moved out of that house and off that farm. It was evil, wicked. The air was foul. The people were crazy and dangerous. Benjamin sold ten acres and bought a house in town just a few blocks from the Muellers' bakery. Sonnen took Otto with her. He needed to be around normal people, she said. Liesel couldn't argue.

So many secrets go down with the dead. But sometimes coincidence, accident, or perhaps a greater design brings them back to the living. Take the course of Benjamin Richter's life after his mother's death, for instance. Magdalena died and was buried on the edge of the oak grove, and Benjamin spent hours and hours chipping her name into the boulder that Luther had hoisted from the wagon, but Benjamin didn't know that Wilhelm Richter wasn't his real father, or that his real, biological father lived and breathed in Germany and was a Jew, or that years later, when another war rose out of the smolder of World War I and required a scapegoat, the Germans would accuse the Jews and Benjamin's entire natural Jewish family in Germany would be rounded up and killed. Not one would survive. Not Benjamin's father, who in his last moments in the chamber, as the gas filled his lungs, would feel standing next to him the familiar form of the woman he'd loved years before, who at one time had held his child in her womb, the only child he ever sired.

His son, Benjamin Richter, would find a red-haired German girl, a real breeder, and give to her the very cameo that Benjamin's natural father had given to his mother before she'd left southern Germany, the cameo Magdalena had requested she be buried with but that Benjamin had unhooked from his mother's collar the minute before the family's picture was taken and the casket was closed forever because he couldn't stand to think about spending the rest of his life without some tangible memory of his mother. When he'd presented that cameo to his fiancée, he didn't know that she would treasure it and pass it on as a family heirloom. He had no inkling that it would eventually land in the hands of a jeweler who was a descendant of his and that it would be traced back to Germany and to the family for whom it was originally made. An exhaustive trace of the family line would be carried out by one of Benjamin's brood, a woman such as each family gets: one who, after her children have graduated and moved on, spends an inordinate amount of time digging in old newspapers, death certificates, marriage certificates, and the like, putting together the family tree. Eventually, her search would lead to the most exciting day of her life. The day she'd get to announce something interesting, amazing, scandalous even, to the entire family. "I'm not saying for certain," she would say. "But I just don't see how it could be any other way." After much coaxing and eye-rolling by her family, she would finally blurt out: "Benjamin Richter, firstborn of Magdalena Richter, probably was not the natural son of Wilhelm Richter. It just doesn't add up." She'd take a deep breath and add, "I'm not even sure we're really Catholics."

Further investigation would suggest Benjamin's true heritage and reveal that Magdalena's secret and Benjamin's existence had kept alive the only strain of that long-ago Jewish family from Germany.

Of Benjamin's eleven children, all would reproduce. In that line came many farmers, many farmers' wives, a Catholic priest, a nun who started and ran a children's hospital specializing in the care of those with polio, a woman who cooked for President Harry Truman during the time the United States was making its first moves toward recognizing the state of Israel, and a journalist who worked as a photographer during the Korean War. During the age of McCarthyism, one of Benjamin's brood would be blacklisted for her poetry and plays.

With her son Benjamin, Magdalena Richter did well by the world.

Otto, Magdalena's last child, the one who had taken her last breath, apprenticed himself to Dr. Mathiowetz in town. The good doctor's eyesight was going, and his memory was not so reliable anymore. When Otto was just sixteen years old, Benjamin and Sonnen's little boy Melvin tripped over the dog and thrashed about on the floor clutching his throat. Otto picked him up. The boy could not breathe. Otto tried opening the boy's mouth, but it was locked. Otto grabbed a spoon and bashed through the child's teeth and pulled back his tongue. The boy cried and had to live the rest of his life with a mouthful of fake teeth, but he was alive because of Otto's quick thinking. In New Germany, Otto became famous for nagging parents about inoculations, and it was joked that he never sat down because he kept syringes in his pocket in case he happened upon a child who needed a vaccine.

36

BETTY AND LIESEL, on task to weed and plant new flowers, found a gutted turtle in a burlap sack at the foot of
Wilhelm and Magdalena's grave at the edge of the Richter property. Liesel remembered a great many things in the moment it
took Betty to register interest in the bag. More than eight months'
pregnant now with Herman's baby and always curious as a calf,
Betty exclaimed, "Now, I wonder what's got them flies all in a
tizzy." She bent to see.

"Leave it," Liesel said. Her heart thumped at the sight of the
plain brown bag, the red stain seeping through the bottom of it,
the awkward way it rested against the marker of her parents'
headstone. She remembered a time when as a girl she'd first come
to see a bundle in this place and how it had come to be there. She
remembered the bloody gifts the turtle catcher had left for her
after she'd prepared and fed to her papa and brothers that first
turtle stew. She had met the turtle catcher in the grove and at
the marker and behind the barn so many times after. Liesel had
taught the turtle catcher to spell and to talk and to kiss and to
look a person in the eye when talking and to find pleasure in the

touch of another human being and to share hopes — like being whole, being wise, being healthy, being in love. Liesel remembered holding the turtle catcher in the curl of her fingers. She remembered shame. She remembered letting his life sift through the gaps in her grasp. She remembered a knife and a cut, rain and insects and the all-seeing sun. She remembered guilt. She remembered doing wrong.

Memory at its most pervasive invades a person's body with every rise and fall of lungs. Liesel's lungs on most days rose and fell in a steady rhythm. She never forgot. At the sight of the bag, her lungs and the memories linked to them rose and fell like the quick flutter of cicadas.

"Leave it, my foot." Betty bowed over her enormous belly, untied the string of the bag, and peeked inside. "Some kind of carcass," she said, and held her nose.

"It's a turtle," said Liesel. She helped Betty stand. She shielded her eyes from the sun and looked around the grove. The sun reached through the trees in a thousand warm fingers that clutched at Liesel's clothes, heated them and warmed her body below. Her scar, a thing that had healed into nothing more than a small pink ridge, burned hot, and Liesel put her hand over it. "It's a gift."

"A gift?" said Betty. "For who, for what?"

"For me, I think," said Liesel. "I'm not sure for what. Stay here." She left Betty standing at the graves and walked into the lighted gaps between the trees. Beyond the grove shone Spider Lake, and it was the lake that sent the shards of sunlight reflecting into the Richter grove. The lake shone as the sun did. The lake shone as the moon did. The lake was light, and Liesel wanted to bask in it completely and let it overtake her as she had once let the turtle catcher do.

Betty closed the top of the bag and tied it tight. She stared at Liesel meandering through the yellow shoots beaming between the trees.

"Liesel," she said. "Get back here. Don't you leave me alone for one second until this baby comes. You promised."

Liesel looked at her, the enormousness of Betty's belly, the ridiculous way it extended from her little body, like it might topple her.

"I won't leave you," said Liesel. She paused for a minute before turning her back on the lake and the lights and walking toward her sister-in-law. "I'll be right there. Don't move."

"I just can't imagine having this baby without you. I just couldn't. I need you, Liesel."

"You'd be fine with or without me. You are tougher than you think."

"Don't say that. I'm a nervous wreck these days."

Liesel put her arm around Betty's shoulders. "Lean on me, now."

Betty rested her head against Liesel's shoulder and as soon as she did, the tears and sobs came.

"Good God," Betty said. "What's wrong with me?"

Liesel pulled her even closer, and whispered, "Shhh, shhh," into her hair. "Everything will be all right." Would it? Liesel didn't know. She understood Betty's emotion. To be unmarried in this time, to be pregnant, to be in love with a man whose mind could not be trusted. She considered, for the briefest time, asking Betty if she wanted to discuss it. Maybe she'd feel better. Maybe they'd both feel better. No. To name these fears and troubles would give them power.

Betty pulled a handkerchief from her apron pocket and blew her nose. She sighed. "Maybe it will." Betty took a deep breath and blew out. "Well," she said, "times being tight as they are, I say we take this carcass and cook it up."

Liesel bent and gathered the sack. She hoisted it over her shoulder and took Betty by the arm. "Come on then," she said. "We'd better get this meat home and in a pot before it goes bad." The women began the walk back to the farmhouse.

"I trust you," said Betty. "I trust you with everything, with my life even."

Liesel didn't know what to say. Betty often said things out loud that Liesel herself would never say. But while Betty's words might have been embarrassing at times, they usually made Liesel feel better. She took a stronger hold of Betty's arm and helped her waddle over the lawn and up the stairs into the house.

Herman got up from the table and rushed to open the door for his sister and Betty. It had taken him a while to notice, but Betty had stopped speaking to him days ago. He tried to remember why, but times, words, and memories were not straight in his mind these days. He held the door with his foot and reached for Betty's arm.

"Here," he said. "Let me help you."

Betty pulled her elbow in closer to her ribs and didn't meet his glance.

"Betty, don't be that way," said Herman.

"Just leave her be, Herman," said Liesel.

He nodded but still tried to catch Betty's eye. As she passed him in the doorway, he said, "Baby. Please." But Betty kept walking past and went on through the kitchen and to the bedroom where Magdalena Richter had spent weeks awaiting the birth of her own babies. Betty closed the door softly. Herman walked toward the same door.

"Don't bother her now, Herman," said Liesel.

"I can't take it," he said. "She's crazy."

Liesel tossed the bag onto the counter, this gift from some familiar unknown. This was surely a sign that strange times were coming, that perhaps an end had been sighted, perhaps her own end had been designed for the near future. If not now, when would she have another chance to speak with Herman, to help him? "Betty's not crazy," she said.

"She's making me crazy." He beat at his chest with his fist.

"No," said Liesel. She remained calm and resolute in order to say what needed to be said. "Betty's keeping you from crazy, but now you've nearly driven her to madness."

"You damn woman," he said. "You don't know anything. You don't know the things I've seen."

"Herman," said Liesel. "What else? You have told us many things about the war. Many things."

"But you don't know how bad it can be. There's so much more to it."

"Tell me then."

"I can't."

She studied her brother. The brother who was sensitive and smart and liked reading and writing and stories, but who couldn't calm the demons. His left sleeve drooped limp from his shoulder down. His face hadn't been shaved in days. Dark circles hung under his eyes. He put his hand on his hip.

"Listen to me now," said Liesel, "and I will tell you what is right."

He screamed at her: "I know what's right!"

She waited for the fury to leave his face. "No," she said. "You don't."

He turned away from her. "I've always tried to do what's right."

"I know that. But you need to accept that sometimes other people may know better."

With that, he stomped out of the kitchen and into the yard.

37

BETTY'S FATHER HAD DELIVERED many babies. Now, though, he was too old for such things. So when a warm rush of fluid spilled down Betty's legs and onto the floor of the kitchen where she and Liesel stood washing and drying the breakfast dishes, she asked the boys to leave the house and asked Liesel to help her to bed. When no pains came after four hours, Liesel told Betty to get up, and the two went for a walk around the yard.

"Walking will get this baby moving," said Liesel.

"I hope you're right."

And she was. Betty walked for only an hour before cramps came fast and hard. In the short periods between the contractions, Liesel dragged her back toward the house, up the porch, and into the bedroom.

"I'm not gettin' in that bed," Betty said. "I don't wanna lie down. I wanna sit."

"Fine, fine," said Liesel. "Whatever you want."

She led Betty to the corner rocking chair and helped her into it. She removed all Betty's clothes and folded them. She laid them on the bed. She wrapped her in a blanket and pulled a pillow from the bed. She placed it behind Betty's back.

"How is that?" she asked.

Betty gripped the sides of the chair and hung her head to her breast. "Oh, Liesel. Oh God, it hurts so bad."

Liesel put her hands on Betty's back and rubbed.

"Harder, Liesel."

She worked her hands all over Betty's back, kneading the muscles and encouraging the blood flow. With each contraction, Liesel pressed more deeply and vigorously. For just under an hour, the two women labored together in the bedroom that had birthed every Richter child and had snuffed the life out of their parents. And then, at a quarter past three in the afternoon, Betty let go a cry that startled Liesel into motion. She moved to the front of Betty, lifted the blanket, and tried to spread Betty's knees.

"No. Stop. It hurts."

"I know, Betty. Try to relax." Liesel eased apart Betty's knees and saw the baby's crown there.

"Oh, she's right here. She's ready." Liesel wedged her fingers between Betty and the baby's head.

"No. I can't do this. I'm not strong enough."

"No choice. Push her out now."

Betty sucked in a deep breath and on the exhale pushed the baby down. The tiny head came out, eyes closed and lips blue and pursed.

"One more, Betty. Give me one more push."

Betty pushed again, and the shoulders, chest, stomach, and legs of the little creature landed in the soft hands of Liesel, who lifted the baby onto her mother's chest. Betty lay back in the rocker and held on to the child while Liesel pried open her little mouth, swept a finger along its inside, and then popped the baby on the backside. A loud cry ballooned on the air.

"Listen," cried Betty. "Listen to my baby."

"She's wonderful."

"A girl?" said Betty.

"Yes," said Liesel. "A girl."

Liesel found Herman sitting in the Richter cemetery, staring toward where the barn used to be, where now only the lonely silo stood.

"Come see your child," she said.

"Is everything all right?" he asked.

"She's perfect. And Betty's fine."

"A daughter then?"

"Yes. You have a daughter."

Herman stood and Liesel wrapped him up in her embrace. He stood stiff as a tree limb for a few seconds and then began to pant and cry. He held his sister tight and bawled. He soaked her shoulder with his tears. When his legs gave way, Liesel held him up until he finished. He took a deep breath and spread his arm out wide as if to accept grace from the air. Then he faced Liesel.

"I killed a man over there," he said. "I killed many men, but this one was different. I simply killed him in a bad way. I didn't know anything about him. He may not have done anything wrong in the world. He may have had a family. I threw him in a well and shot him too. I did that." In the few seconds it took Herman to confess this, his back straightened and his shoulders lifted. His eyes opened up to the world again.

Liesel had no idea what to say. Finally, she told him to go to Betty, and he did.

38

For several more years, Liesel lived in the Richter farmhouse with Herman and Betty and their family. After the birth of Pearl, Herman settled into a state closer to peace. He still worried about his family's safety. He still checked the locks and had trouble sleeping. But he stopped forever arguing about what was or wasn't right. Sometimes there was just no answer to that question.

In the months after his daughter's birth, he dug his hands into the work of the farm. He made ready the fields and planted them. He built a new barn and stocked it with milking cows. He woke each morning to their braying. Although the Richter farm never returned to the prosperity it had reached under the guidance of Wilhelm, Herman breathed a modicum of greenery and health back into it.

Each evening, he tucked the covers up beneath Pearl's armpits and told stories of Indian maidens, water nymphs, and battle heroes until her lids closed over her pretty eyes, the same truth-conjuring eyes as his Betty, who four more times would grow big with Herman's babies. In quiet corners on winter evenings, he could be found sitting with a pencil and paper, writing, writing, writing and weaving his thoughts into poems and stories. Years after her parents' deaths, Pearl would find these papers in her daddy's trunk and pull them to her breast.

The winter came hard and cold in 1933. On a bitter winter evening, Liesel slung a shawl over her shoulders and flung open the front door.

"Betty, I am going for a walk."

Betty said nothing for a while, then whispered, "Goodbye, Liesel."

"Goodbye then," said Liesel. She looked at her friend and smiled.

Five inches of clear ice covered Spider Lake. Thin light snow dusted the surface, the air so cold that each individual flake kept to itself, didn't melt into the others, and made, instead of a thick blanket, a lacy curtain over the lake's glass. Crossed and crooked tracks of small birds and animals emerging from their winter hiding places to forage for food ran here and there along the vast surface. Other than wind, nothing moved. Other than Liesel's boots crushing the snow and a moan lamenting from the ice, nature was silent. It seemed to her that the world was on the verge of something new. She felt as if she were moving toward heat. She could feel heat.

For years, she had avoided this place. She'd stood on the edge of the Richter property and looked through the grove and over the fields and toward Spider Lake, but had never ventured near the water. She couldn't ever let her brain settle on Lester Sutter for more than a second or two. If she did, the guilt paralyzed her. The longing paralyzed her. What had changed today, she had no mortal idea. A force stronger than her drew her toward that lake, and in the exact center of it, she stopped.

She knelt and swept away the snow. She lay back on the frozen water and closed her eyes. She rested her bare hands over her lower stomach. They tingled with frost. And beneath them, the old scar burned iron hot. She thought of all the things she would never do. She would never marry, never have children. Benjamin was gone and had his own family. Herman and Betty and their children filled the house. Otto lived in town, practicing to be a doctor. Luther was dead. Mother was dead. Papa was dead. Lester was dead. All the people who had once needed her were gone.

She waited five minutes. She waited ten.

Liesel, Liesel, she heard. A dull, faraway call. Perhaps only a sudden whip of the wind swirling between her ear and the ice. Perhaps her imagination, perhaps an odd winter bird cooing for a wintry mate to cover with his wing and tuck close to his heart, perhaps a memory of her mother calling for her pa across the yard to come in for supper.

Liesel, Liesel, she heard again. This time her name was clear. It growled in her chest and vibrated in her throat. She opened her eyes and turned her head left and right. But there was no one. She lay still on the ice again and waited.

The tender collision of water and cold air is not silent, but you have to listen close to hear each tiny air particle tickle each tiny water particle until they crystallize, stretch, unite, and firm. The ice, then, is that ineffable state between one thing and another, between black and white, between life and death. Only the truest of things can live there, only the things that transcend logic.

Liesel closed her eyes and listened.

At first, she attributed the warmth against her back to her own growing tolerance of the cold. But the temperature rose so that she was brought back to the night Lester Sutter had pulled Otto from the fire and laid him at her feet. Liesel was brought back to the moment Lester had put his palm on her back. And when at last she was sure she felt the heat of his palm against her back, a palm as familiar to her now as it had been the last time she'd felt it, when Liesel was sure her time for waiting was through, she turned over to face the ice. She thought this must be what the surface of the moon was like.

A great wind picked up. Ice chips and snowflakes blew. She swept them away with a gentle brush of her hand and cleared the rime. And there, encased in five inches of ice and facing high into heaven, stared the blue, blue eyes of Lester Sutter.

There he was. His irises bright as crystal. His bald head. His round nose and pink lips. His body creature-like.

He blinked.

Liesel sat up and gasped. A moment passed in which she took control of her breathing and her fear.

Phantoms of spirits lost near or in the lake gathered as a fine mist in the air above it. Here an old Indian man, there an infant baby in the arms of a young mother. At the edge of the trees sat Magdalena Richter, belly still big with her first baby. Near her stood the boy Wilhelm at the feet of his parents. Crouching under some snowy boughs of pine was Luther, bare-chested and in his baseball pants. Pernilla Sutter stood behind him. She placed her hands on his shoulders and kneaded them.

Liesel had never had to be afraid of Lester, she knew. She leaned forward and close to the ice until her nose touched the cold; the ice enlivened every molecule in her body.

"All these cold years," she whispered. "I have wasted." Her moist breath fogged the ice then chilled into a crazy medley of lines and stars brilliant as any cosmos in the universe, brilliant as any night sky bursting with the streaking northern lights and constellations so common on Minnesota nights. Liesel scratched the ice away with the nail of her thumb. And with the eyes of God and the witness of all the dead watching and urging her forward, Liesel Richter pressed her lips onto the surface of the lake and kissed her lover hello.

ACKNOWLEDGMENTS

Thanks to Terry Davis for the first edits on the short story, the Tamarack Foundation for funding, *Minnesota Monthly* for publishing, Jeff Johnson for quality production and promoting, and Scott Simon for judging the short-story contest that put this book on the road to publication.

Thanks to Roger Sheffer for edits on the novel and for being a dear friend and literary ally, and to Rick Robbins and all the teachers and creative writing people at Minnesota State University and in Mankato for fostering an atmosphere stimulating, challenging, and friendly to artists. Thanks to Kate T., Jane R., and Anjali S. at Houghton Mifflin. Thanks to Faye Bender.

Thanks to Isabella, Mitchell, Phillip, Violette, and Archibald. Thanks to Nate. Esoteric and abundant blessings upon each of your heads, my loves.